JACOB'S
Star

SHARK'S EDGE: BOOK TEN

VICTORIA BLUE

JACOB'S
Star

SHARK'S EDGE: BOOK TEN

VICTORIA BLUE

WATERHOUSE PRESS

For David, the love of my life and the brightest star in my sky.

Eternally my guidon, I know you'll always show me the way home.

CHAPTER ONE

PIA

Nine years ago, I stood in my off-campus apartment's cramped bathroom and gave myself a pep talk.

This situation will get better.

Hell, the only way that situation *could* have gotten was better.

I stepped into the equally crowded bedroom of the first place I'd called my own and took a minute to appreciate what I'd accomplished.

Like my psychological stability, my love for the little apartment fluctuated back and forth. I didn't even mind my inconsiderate upstairs neighbors. It didn't seem to matter how many culinary gestures of good will I'd left on their door mat. They still played their bass-heavy music right through the posted study hours—and half the common-sense sleeping hours, too.

After just one complaint to my overindulgent big brother, a brand-new pair of noise-canceling AirPods had arrived to make the last year of my co-ed life a touch easier.

The same way my pep talk had cleared the negativity from my head and heart, the typical Bay-area fog outside gave way to a clear azure sky.

And as the man I had fallen in love with and lazed with on

the single lounge chair we managed to squeeze onto my small balcony stared into my eyes, I made him a hundred promises . . . knowing all the while I wouldn't keep a single one.

Many months after that simple gift arrived from my brother, another gift arrived. The word *simple* fell from my lexicon around that same time and never returned. But so many other words were added in its place.

Mama. Diapers. Colic. Teething. Unconditional love.

"Cass?" His deep voice brought me back to the present day.

Vela tilted her inquisitive face up while slipping her small hand into mine for reassurance. "Mama, why does he keep calling you that? If he's my father, how does he not know your name?"

"Hey, little lady," Elijah said. *Bless his heart for interrupting.* "Why don't you come with Uncle Grant and me? There's something super cool upstairs I bet you haven't seen yet." Elijah held his hand out in proposition, but my daughter wanted nothing to do with his exit plan.

This child was too smart for her own good. Too nosy, too. So much of it was my fault. She was raised surrounded by adults, making her more comfortable around people my age than hers.

I bent at the waist so my torso was parallel to the ground and I was eye to eye with the little ruler of my heart. I lowered my voice so she understood this information was just between us, even though our setting offered no privacy.

"Vela, no one said this man is your father. Please don't get your hopes up thinking that about someone who randomly appeared in your uncle's office today, okay? We talked about this after that incident at school with Mr. Hogan. Remember?"

She balled her small fists by her sides and insisted, "That was different." She had her jaws clenched in frustration.

Oh, this girl was a Shark, through and through.

Nodding, I agreed. "It was, you're right. But this scenario will end the same way." I could feel the fissure in my heart spread a little farther. Every time my child ached to know her father, this particular thorn in my battered heart pierced a bit deeper.

I stood to my full height, and Vela followed me with her assessing gaze.

"What?" I asked, still trying to keep our conversation between the two of us.

"I don't unnerstan what you mean."

"Under-stand," I pronounced in two syllables. There were still a few holdover words she had trouble with, and this one hung her up every time. "Babe, can you go with your uncles so I can get this meeting handled and we can get out of Uncle Sebastian's thinning hair?"

She folded her arms across her chest and looked up at me. Oh, great. Here we go. I knew this pose all too well, and it never ended well. Especially in public, and especially if I was determined to make my point.

"Vela, don't defy me in front of your uncles," I started, but she cut me off with her two cents.

"And my father." She dipped her chin and raised a brow in challenge.

My God, where was the girl getting this sassy bullshit from?

"That's enough. Now you can wait for me out at Craig's desk. Gather your things."

"Mama, noooo," my daughter whined. From teenager to toddler in the blink of an eye.

"Vela Shark, now!" I'd raised my voice, which was rare. I could count on one hand the number of times I had done so in as many years. Not because she was that overindulged, but because she never tested me this way.

Sebastian's desk phone rang just while the commotion was ramping up, and he shot me a fast glare. I instantly passed it on to my child, who had the good sense to still immediately. She had been around these offices since she cut her first tooth, and if there was one thing she knew as law, Uncle Bas required complete silence when he took phone calls.

Only catching the tail end of his conversation as I supervised Vela shove her belongings into her backpack, I didn't pick up on who the caller was.

"I'll let her know. Yeah, not a moment too soon, judging by the look on my sister's face. Yeah, right?" Bas chuckled as he hung up the phone and stood from his desk chair.

I might be seeing things, but the faint grin stayed in place as he rounded the front of his desk, and I thought again how miraculous the changes in my brother were since Abbigail and Kaisan blessed his life.

"Wren's on her way up. Her appointment wrapped early."

"Thank you," I said and turned to face everyone else seated at the conference table. "I'll just get this young lady on her way, and we can get down to business. I'm so sorry for all the delays today."

Grant and Elijah were already striding across the expansive office to say their goodbyes, which included big hugs and squealing tickles and multiple promises to visit or stop by Elijah's to swim or Grant's to play with the new puppy he and Rio were fostering on a trial to adopt as a companion dog in training. Then, finally, my daughter was in the capable hands of my assistant, Wren.

When I finally sat down at the large table in my brother's office suite, I felt like I'd run an emotional marathon. Until I locked gazes with the man across the sleek surface and felt like I barreled into a brick wall. Air squeezed from my lungs and left my throat constricting in panicked gasps that I tried to camouflage by slowly sucking down lungsful through my nose.

I felt my brother's watchful eyes on me from his place at the head of the table. If I didn't stop acting like I was so rattled, he would be on me the moment everyone dispersed from the meeting. I'd be lucky if he waited that long.

"Pia, I know this is the first time you and Mr. Cole have been in the same room together, so, not meaning to put either of you on the spot here, but how have things been going between the two of you?"

"What is that supposed to mean?" I whipped my stare in Sebastian's direction so aggressively, I was surprised I didn't give myself whiplash. Of course, the physical and verbal reaction was so out of line, everyone cautiously tracked their gazes from me, to Bas, to Jack—or Jacob, or whatever the hell he was calling himself—and then around to each other.

"Pardon me," I said with a strange laugh. "I think that showdown with the little ruler of my heart has me off my game. She's growing up way too fast." I shook my head and looked down at papers I mindlessly moved from one spot to another, hoping it threw them off my scent.

"Shark pride, sister. Don't forget it," Bas said and leaned over and gave my hand a squeeze.

I looked into his kind blue eyes and saw the love behind his gesture. It was a testament to how wrapped up in his own life the man was at this point.

Vela was the spitting image of her biological father. The

fact that the pieces hadn't clicked into place yet for Sebastian and that Jacob Cole was still sitting upright and participating in the meeting and not needing dental records to have his body identified down at the city morgue said as much about my former lover's good fortune as it did my brother's disjointed concentration.

The other two men, who were as emotionally close as brothers, eyed me cautiously from across the table. There was a lot of tension building in the room, and judging by their pointed glances between Jack—or *Jacob*—and me, it seemed they were sure this wasn't the first time we'd met.

"Okay, since we got a slow start, I'm sure no one will mind moving things along," Sebastian said. "Pia, can you bring the group up to speed with where you and your team are at?"

"Sure. Thank you. So, everyone should have a design portfolio in front of them with everything you see up here on my board. This way you can feel the fabrics, see the paint colors we've selected in different lighting, and sit with the combinations until our next meeting. If you feel strongly about anything you see in your portfolio, I've included all my contact information as well as my assistant's and my team lead's. One of us should be able to answer your question within an hour or two of receiving the message. At least, that is our goal."

I finally focused on the individual faces around the table, even though I'd been staring at them while speaking. When I first began my presentation, I was still so shaken up, I felt like I'd been asked to sing the national anthem at Dodger's Stadium.

Grant spoke up first. His boyish charm always won a smile from my lips, no matter my mood or the setting. We'd seen so many hard times in our lives, and he always made sure I had a smile on my face, even when I didn't feel much like smiling. Now, the expression was offered to him so freely, especially knowing it would be returned in kind.

"Will you also be designing the retail spaces?" our tall friend asked.

Elijah gave him a playful side-eye. "Gee, Twombley, why would you be interested in that fact, hmmm?" He rested his chin on his fist and stared at his best friend as though he was going to be transfixed by his answer.

Everyone in the know gave an affable chuckle, but it didn't diminish the light of excitement in Grant's eyes. That Rio was one lucky lady to have captured the adoration of this man. From what I could tell, she knew it too.

I turned to my brother at the head of the table. "Have you decided that yet? I haven't formally submitted a bid package, but I'd love—"

Bas held up his massive hand to stop me. "Pia, be serious. The contract is yours if you want it."

"Excellent!" I clapped my hands together and held my palms pressed tightly as though praying beneath my chin. And then I made direct eye contact with the architect for the first time since the meeting started.

"I'll have someone from my team contact you to get started on the first level as well, then."

"You don't want to do the design yourself?" my brother asked, genuine confusion twisting his features. "I don't understand."

"*Oh shit,*" one of his two besties spoke-coughed into his fist.

The whole table turned to look.

It must have been Grant, and he must have known he was

about to get his ass chewed if he hung around too much longer, because the man stood so abruptly from his chair, it was more like watching a rocket launch than a person stand. When you tower over everyone else at six and a half feet tall, though, standing suddenly caught a lot of attention.

"I really hate to bolt, but I need to do a walk-through onsite with our liaison in"—he took a quick look at his watch—"shit, twenty-five minutes. We have some exciting sign-offs today, people, so wish me luck."

He gathered his things, and Elijah quickly excused himself as well, taking the opportunity to catch a lift to the jobsite to deal with a few security hires.

My brother's dream was really coming to fruition, and it was because we all had our part in the effort and took it seriously. Bas said when it came time for the ribbon-cutting ceremony, he wouldn't be doing the honors with one giant pair of scissors but that we'd all line up with regular-sized scissors because so many people had a hand in making this building a reality. Yes, he had the dream and the finances to bankroll the operation, but so many people had put their talent, blood, sweat, and tears into making it really happen.

More and more, I found myself looking at Sebastian and marveling at the metamorphosis he had undergone in the past two years. Gone was the selfish prick who once only showed this kindhearted, generous, doting side of himself to Vela and me—and to Grant and Elijah, to an extent.

In that egomaniac's place, the world was starting to see the man I'd known my entire life. This was the man who cared for me from the time I was three years old and our mother died while delivering Caleb, our baby brother. Tragically, he joined her in heaven soon after. Because, as Bas explained to me then—and it was still as good of an explanation as any—a baby that new and that small needed to be with his mama more than anyone else. Only she knew how to care for him best. Even God knew that was the truth.

One night, our father had heard Sebastian telling me that story while he tucked me in, and he lost his temper. My brother walked with a limp for a month. He also didn't think I saw the way he held his side when Grant tried to make him laugh. We were so young, and our father was a heartbroken, alcoholic monster.

When I dig deep into my memories now, I'm pretty sure he was a heavy drinker before our mother and brother passed. But after that happened, all bets were off. Sebastian did what he could to hold life together for us until he found him dead one morning before we left for school. We got on the bus like any other day, and when we came home that night, he was gone. I never saw him again.

I never had the courage to ask my brother what happened to his body. To this day, I still didn't know the details.

And honestly, I didn't want to.

CHAPTER TWO

"Pia?" Shark called her name a second time, and she finally snapped her head in his direction.

"What?" she barked and then immediately followed with a contrite, "Sorry."

He tilted his head marginally, as if the slight angle shift would give him enough perspective to recognize what had her so off her game.

"I asked if you wanted to go over anything else or if you were ready to wrap this up?" the boss asked.

"I think that's it for me unless there are any questions?"

"Jacob. Floor's all yours, young man." Sebastian swept his upturned palm out in front of him as if presenting the grand prize on a game show stage.

Ooooh, if he only knew just how closely I had my eye on the prize. And once upon a time, my lips, and hands, my tongue, and . . .

Shit. I gave my head a little shake to clear those particular thoughts until she and I could find somewhere to be alone. I already knew she needed a healthy reminder of how good we used to be together. While the ice queen thing was a hot bit, it could only last so long.

"Believe it or not, I don't have anything new today." I gave

Sebastian a crooked grin, and he slapped his hand dramatically over his heart. "I know, I know. If you want to talk among yourselves, I can probably come up with something from in here." I started flipping through Cassie's—or Pia's, as she was apparently going by now—meticulous portfolio.

"That won't be necessary," she quietly seethed and tried to snatch the bound presentation from my grasp.

Keeping my voice at a volume just for her, I said, "Excuse me, Miss *Shark*." Not only did I sneer her last name, but I dropped my tone to a register I'd never used around Sebastian before. In my periphery, I saw his eyes widen to double their normal size before he caught himself and turned away to give us some privacy.

Okay, I thought my volume was for her ears only. Nosy big brother heard everything—it would do me good to remember that one.

But if nothing else, there was a code of respect among dominant males, and with the timbre of that one comment, I just flashed my membership card. The move had the desired effect on the woman too.

The very same woman who used to be *my* woman. Mine. And where had she been hiding all these years? I'd looked everywhere for her. I'd gone so far as to hire a damn private detective to look for her. Then I laughed. It started as a huff but turned into a legitimate laugh. For four goddamn years, she told me her name was Cassie Stapleton. What the hell was that about?

"You okay, man?" Shark came to stand by the table again, blue eyes roaming over me with a hundred questions.

"Yeah, sorry. Just reading a text from a schoolmate. Hey, I'm going to cut out if you think we're done. Message me when you want to smack some balls, though, yes?"

"Absolutely, my friend. Maybe Pia would like to join us?"

"I'm busy," she clipped, never looking up from her phone. "Sebastian, a word when you're through arranging your recreational activities?"

"Ohhh, ouch," I said and grimaced comically. It was good to see she still had the same spitfire temper. "Talk to you soon, Shark," I said, and then I loaded up my belongings and left the room.

And damn how I wished I could have been a fly on that wall to listen in on the conversation between brother and sister right now.

I heard footsteps behind me just as I pulled back from calling the elevator for the second time. Must be busy down below in the hallowed halls of Shark Enterprises today. There had to be days Sebastian's view from his floor-to-ceiling windows made it seem like he worked among the gods atop Mt. Olympus. Maybe that was the whole point of the design of floor-to-ceiling windows in the first place.

The elevator doors slid open, and a lithe flash of lightning slipped into the car ahead of me and angrily slapped the Lobby button.

Well, well, well.

I stepped in close behind her just to get a greedy sniff of her perfume. Still the same scent she wore years ago, and I had to command my body to heel and my mind to focus.

"Don't . . ." she seethed in an almost inaudible hiss.

Christ, was she capable of any other modulation of her voice anymore?

Compelled to lower my own voice, as though we were joined by twenty-eight other passengers and not just the one dust bunny in the far corner, I whispered, "Don't *what*, exactly?"

Okay, maybe that last part came out more like a growl, but she was already pissing me off and making me hard at the exact same time. I hadn't seen an inch of her creamy skin or tasted her perfect mouth, but I already felt like madness was setting in.

"There isn't a square inch of privacy in this entire building, and you're a bigger fool than I gave you credit for if you think there is." Pia busied herself with something in her handbag while issuing the advice wrapped in an insult.

The doors slid open, and she just about took off at a gallop in the sexiest fucking high heels I'd seen since I'd been in Spain.

Barcelona was home to some of the most beautiful women I'd ever laid eyes on. No question. Just not *the* most beautiful. At nearly a sprint, I took off across the lobby behind her, so fucking scared that if I let her out of my sight again, it would be the same as before.

Never to be seen again.

Never to be heard from again.

Nine years. Nine fucking years I looked for Cassiopeia Shark. Ha! The joke was on me. She was in my hometown the whole time. How did the saying go? *Hiding in plain sight?* First order of business when I got back to the hotel would be a phone call to that good-for-nothing private investigator I'd kept on her case for far too long and demand my money back. The dipshit couldn't find the Hollywood sign on a clear day, apparently.

"Cass! Wait!" I finally shouted when we cleared the building.

She stopped before getting into a waiting town car and

spun to face me. Of course she was chauffeured around town like royalty. She'd always been my queen when we were together.

Shamefully, I was panting a bit when I caught up to her. Shit, time to hit the gym for real. Now that I had a reason to drop the six pounds I'd put on since I moved into my hotel room, it wouldn't be such a fight every morning.

"Make it quick. We're double-parked. And unless this is about the Edge, I have nothing to say to you, Jacob. Is that your actual name?" She asked the question with a haughty laugh, and wasn't that just rich?

"Pardon me, lady? Pia? Cassiopeia? Is that *your* real name?"

"Ms. Shark?" her driver said. "Will we be dropping Mr. Cole somewhere?" He had the balls to give me a head-to-toe scan before looking back to her for her decision.

"That won't be necessary, Joel. He can find his own way. I'm sure Bas needs you back here for quitting time."

My heart stuttered for a few seconds because she gave the man the first genuine smile I'd seen since rediscovering her existence this afternoon.

She was as breathtaking as I remembered. Every dream I'd had, every fantasy I'd conjured, and every single memory I'd played and replayed drew her in perfect detail. The woman who had stolen my heart nine years ago hadn't changed a bit. She was just buried so deep under years of anger, bitterness, and hurt, it seemed she'd forgotten how to catch the stars the way we used to.

"Can I call you?" I ducked my head in the open door as she slid across the back seat.

"I don't think that's a good idea," she murmured but wouldn't meet my gaze.

"Cass, look at me," I said in the register that worked upstairs.

She looked up, and a small part of me wished she hadn't. There was so much anguish in her blue stare, I wanted to dive into that back seat with her and hold her in my arms and make her explain to me where the past nine years had gone.

"Stop calling me that, for one thing, and for another, I'm seeing someone. So what do you know, Jacob? You're a day late and a dollar short. Please, Joel, let's go, or I'm going to be late for Vela's piano lesson."

"Yes, Ms. Shark."

She shifted her body to face the window while her driver all but manhandled me back to the curb. I didn't miss the tears she swiped off her cheeks, though, before he slammed the door, encasing her safely inside.

After checking my phone, I decided it was close enough to quitting time. I didn't feel like going back to my room, though, and now that I knew she lived in this town, I had the urge to find something more permanent than a damn extended-stay hotel. Maybe I'd pick her brother's brain about some good places to begin my search. He might even have a Realtor he could recommend.

While I walked and relaxed enough to let other thoughts flow in and out of my mind, I came to an abrupt halt in the middle of the sidewalk. Los Angeles wasn't like other major cities for so many reasons. Even though the weather was close to perfect more days than not, foot traffic wasn't nearly as heavy as other equally populated places. I only caught a few comments and dirty looks for being so thoughtless when I'd come to such a sudden stop before moving off to the side to let others pass by.

That little girl was my child. She looked exactly like me, for one thing. Anyone with two eyes could see the resemblance. Hell, even the child made a comment before her mother made her quiet down with a stern look and private conversation.

Could that even be possible? Could Pia have been pregnant before she graduated? We needed to talk, immediately. I decided not to rejoin the pedestrian flow and ducked into the first eating establishment I could find.

It was a little café type place that had plenty of open seating and even a booth toward the back of the dining area that would offer some privacy. A young waitress came by quickly to take my order, and I told her someone was joining me and needed more time while digging through my bag for the portfolio Pia had handed out at the meeting. She said her contact information was in there somewhere. I prayed her phone number was part of that.

She answered on the second ring. "Hello?"

"Hey. It's Jacob. Yes, that's my real name," I added before she could make another smart remark about it. "I need you to meet me at this place called"—I scrambled for the menu beneath her portfolio and flipped it to the front to find the name of the establishment—"Margarette's Pie Stop. Now. Have the driver turn around and bring you back. I'll text you the address."

"I know where it is." She sighed. "Vela—umm, my daughter—loves the apple hand pies."

Our daughter.

"Mr. Cole, I'm not having Joel turn around to bring me there. Not now."

"He has to come back this way to pick up your brother anyway. You said it yourself."

"Yes, but I have a child to pick up from her caregiver. I can't just flit about town, or the globe, for that matter, at will."

Ouch. Okay. Well, that jab was uncalled for. It wasn't like she ever gave me the courtesy of knowing I had a child. But we'd get to all of that when we spoke in person. She had nine years of single-parenting bitterness stored up to unleash on me. I could understand it, to a point. But I wasn't sure I'd sit idly by while she hit me with zinger after zinger based on something I had no part in the decision about.

"Bring her with you, then," I offered. "She seems charming."

"It's not that easy, Jacob." She sighed, and I could picture the eye roll that went with it. It was also starting to piss me off the way she had been saying my name like that, in two broken syllables, *Jaaay-cub*, each more bitter on her tongue than the time she said them before.

"She has piano tonight. Then homework right after."

"Can't her nanny—or caregiver, or whatever you called her—take her to piano and work on homework until you get home?" I asked with absolutely no clue how parents juggled work and their children's schedules.

"That's not the way I do things," Pia leveled.

"One time won't hurt, Pia. She's what? Eight? Nine? Deviating from her rigid schedule one time isn't going to delay her brain development. I'd say this conversation is important. I'd say it's nine years overdue, come to think of it. Wouldn't you?"

I waited in the deafening silence, gripping my phone so hard I thought I would crush the thing into dust and shards of glass.

Finally, I spoke again, and to make sure she was listening,

I dropped my tone. "I know she's mine."

"Don't be ridiculous," she scoffed.

"Okay, I'll see you when you get here."

I didn't wait for her to reply. I just pressed End to disconnect the call and sat back with a smug grin on my face. She'd show up. I knew she would. She might take her sweet time getting here, but she'd show.

CHAPTER THREE

PIA

"Joel, can you pull over when you have an opportunity. I'm so sorry."

"Of course, Ms. Shark."

What was I thinking? I was going to have to have these conversations with him eventually. I was going to have at least half of these conversations with everyone else eventually too. Yes, he was Vela's father. Yes, I chose to let him walk out of my life and take the opportunity of his young career instead of being tied down to a young twenty-one-year-old, freshly graduated college student who foolishly got herself knocked up.

Yes. I did all those things.

At the time, I thought I was doing the right thing. More often than not, I continued to hold on to that opinion. Yes, there were a ton of hard times when I wished I had a co-parent to share the workload with. But my brother and even Grant and Elijah stepped in as often as they could to give me a break. If I didn't have those three men in my life, I would be much more bitter than I was.

The privacy screen slid down, and Joel turned in his seat to face me. His kind eyes met mine, and he patiently waited for my next instructions. When he saw I was wrestling with more indecision than he'd probably ever seen me struggle with, he offered, "Do we have a new destination?"

I gave him an apologetic look from the back seat. "I'm so sorry."

"Young lady, this is what I get paid for. Don't you apologize again. Tell me where you'd like to go, and I will take you there with a smile on my face."

He wasn't trying to ease my conscience, either. He truly enjoyed his job. I mean, he'd have to in order to remain in my brother's employ for as long as he had.

"Thank you. Looks like I have an unexpected meeting at Margarette's. I'll send a cherry hand pie with Bas in the morning as a treat. Sound good?"

He grinned and held both hands over his left breast. "A woman after my own heart." As he faced forward and reengaged his seat belt, he said, "I know another little lady who's going to be happy you stopped by that place too."

We met gazes in the rearview mirror and matched smiles. Joel knew a lot of Vela's favorite places from driving us around and her endless chatting.

"Yes, as long as I bring her something, she'll be happy with me. I'm afraid I'm not her favorite adult at the moment." I sighed. Thinking about scolding her earlier made me instantly sad. Maybe I'd try to phone her before going into this fiasco with Jacob.

Since I needed to speak with Wren about my change of plans anyway, I quickly dialed my assistant to check in.

"Hey, Mama Shark, how's traffic?" Wren asked, and I could picture the smile on her face just by the tone of her voice.

"There are days I think you're trying to lose your job, but then I think, who else will put up with you?" I teased back.

I loved this young lady as if she were my own. She'd started with me right out of high school and, because her home life wasn't the best, had always been more than eager to spend time with Vela and me. After she turned twenty-one, I offered to pay for a reasonable apartment for her and even suggested she move into the small guest house on my property—as long as she agreed to continue working for me. Lucky for me, she chose to live on my property, and our relationship continued to grow stronger ever since.

"I hope it's not too much of an imposition, Wren, but I had to turn back for a meeting near SE. I'm hoping it won't go too long. I'm going to forward some homework addendums from Mrs. Wong to your email. I didn't have a chance to look at what subject they're for."

"Don't worry about it. I'll handle it. We'll get busy after piano."

"Is that my mama?" I heard my daughter ask in the background, and Wren answered affirmatively.

"I don't want to speak to her," Vela said. "I'm pissed off at her."

"Vela! Language, young lady," Wren corrected. "Where on earth would you have picked something like that up from?"

I couldn't add a single syllable. My jaw was on the floor of the car for so many reasons. I didn't know where to begin recovering my composure.

"My uncles say things like that all the time, and no one yells at them," she said in a sassy, defensive comeback.

Oh, my child was stacking up the transgressions faster than her little eight-year-old self could do the time for. If this was what it meant to be nine, we could just turn back now and cancel her upcoming birthday altogether.

"Yes, but your uncles are grown men. Ladies don't speak that way. It's trashy talk."

"I've heard Mama swear before," Vela argued in the background as my assistant came back on the line. "When she's really mad."

"I think I better go handle this with one hundred percent attention. We'll see you when you get home."

"Thanks, Wren. You're a lifesaver," I professed. "As always."

"As long as I'm the pineapple flavor."

"Yes, darling. Always the pineapple. Bye."

I was deeply considering day drinking by the time we pulled up in front of the little café. When I stepped out of the car, I scanned the storefronts up and down the street. I was pretty sure there was a bar not too far from here, and after hearing my daughter say she didn't want to speak to me for the first time in her entire life, I was ready to throw back a few shots. There was an unmovable lump in my throat and a pain in my chest that seemed to be directly related to it. Neither were feelings I cared for very much.

"Would you like me to wait?" Joel shook me from my thoughts, and I realized that it was the second or third time someone had to call me back to reality since seeing Jacob this afternoon.

Time to take the bull by the horns and regain control of my own damn sanity.

"No, that won't be necessary. I'm not sure how long this is going to take. I can Uber from here. Thank you so much, Joel." I gave the man a genuine smile and took a fortifying breath before wrapping my hand around the heavy worn brass handle of Margarette's and going inside.

CHAPTER FOUR

JACOB

From the time the car pulled up out front, I watched her. She said she knew the little café where we were meeting, so my curiosity grew as she stood back for a few minutes and looked up and down the street like she was lost.

Finally, she came inside and searched the small dining room and quickly found me in the back corner. I gave her a wave and instantly felt like a dipshit about it. There were five other people in the place, if that. Why the hell did I just wave? She was making me act like a schoolboy meeting my first crush.

Though, my feelings for this woman ran way deeper than a crush, and I was much more mature than a schoolboy. I'd done a lot of growing up in the years we'd been apart, and there were desires raging through my blood that made me feel more like an animal than a man while I watched her walk across this cramped restaurant. If I got my hands on her now, I'd be concerned for her safety.

"All right, I'm here. What did you want to talk about?" Pia asked, not making a motion to sit down.

"Let me help you get settled," I said, jumping to my feet to slide her handbag down her slim shoulder and then pull out the chair for her. Shockingly, she didn't protest my assistance, so once she was seated, I shimmied her closer to the wooden table and went back to my own seat.

"Do you want some coffee? I've been eyeing the milkshake that guy over there has for the past ten minutes. Trying to decide if it's worth the extra fifteen minutes on the treadmill tomorrow." I smiled and motioned to the dairy dessert guzzler with my chin, and Pia followed my gesture.

"I don't know." She forced the faintest laugh. "I've had the milkshake here. I think they use actual cream instead of milk. It may be a full hour extra added to the cardio routine. I for one can't spare the time or the calories."

"You need to loosen up a bit, Cass . . . iopeia. Live a little." This new name thing was definitely going to take some getting used to.

"What did you want to talk about?" she asked again, but thankfully, the waitress showed up to see if we were ready to order.

"We'll have the milkshakes. Chocolate for the lady." I gave her a quick wink but kept talking so she couldn't cancel the order. "Strawberry for me, please." I plucked the menu from Pia's hand and handed both to the waitress. I didn't miss the dirty look she was giving me after my bold move.

"Thank you," she said quietly to the waitress, who also noticed the death stare. "Oh . . ." She held up her finger to signal the server back before she got too far. "Can I also get one cherry and one apple hand pie to go, please? Thank you."

"Of course. Be back in no time," the young girl said and headed off toward the counter to put our order in at the service window.

"What if I'd become lactose intolerant since you've last seen me?"

"Have you?" I replied.

"No. But that's not the point," she bit back.

"What is your point, then? Because I know you didn't stop loving chocolate. There's no way that happened." I threw in a laugh, even though it was forced like a golf ball through a drinking straw. The fact that she was going to make this so difficult—every single point a new argument of its own—was already pissing me off. We could easily settle right back into the place we left off and work out the details as we went. A love like ours didn't just disappear.

Even if she had...

"My point is, we aren't the same people we were back then. So much has happened. So many life-changing events. You can't just waltz back in here and act like you're going to pick up where we left off when we were foolish kids in college." She leaned back in her seat and crossed her arms over her chest. Did she think she just issued the final decree?

I narrowed my eyes until they were useless slits. "Do you really think that's what I'm trying to do?"

"Isn't it?"

"No. In fact"—I leaned halfway across the table to keep our conversation private—"I'm neither a fool, nor a kid. You're right, Pia Shark. So much has changed since we saw each other last."

The waitress came back with our milkshakes, forcing me to sit back in my seat properly so she could access our tabletop.

"Okay, here we go. World-famous milkshakes. Chocolate for the lady—my favorite too." She had a genuine, kind smile for Pia as she set her drink in front of her. "Strawberry for the gentleman. I'll bring your hand pies with the check when you're ready to go. I know the tables can get pretty crowded with all the extra stuff on top."

"Thank you," Pia said quietly.

"Wow, this looks great. Thanks!" I said like I had a pulse. One of us at the table had to appear to be among the living, and clearly my date wasn't making a run for the flag.

Pia took a sip from her straw, hollowing her cheeks in the most adorable way as she tried to suck the thick goodness through the thing. All the while, I couldn't take my eyes off her.

"You're staring," she said matter-of-factly.

"You look good, Star. No, you look better than good," I told her honestly and watched her instantly bristle. "You're more beautiful than the last time I saw you."

"Don't—"

"Don't what? Don't be polite? Don't be kind? Don't speak the truth? I realize almost nine years have passed, but you can't possibly have changed that much. You don't even smile anymore, and it's breaking my heart to watch. What happened, Cass?"

"Stop calling me that!" she shouted, and the three diners left in the place turned to look at us.

I just raised a brow, waiting for her to continue. If she wanted to chew me out with a three-person audience, the floor was hers.

"I just don't understand..."

But instead of inquiring more about my ambiguous statement, she let the silence hang between us.

In danger of a serious brain freeze, I had to push the milkshake aside. Damn, that thing was good, though. When I looked up, I caught Pia studying every move I made.

"Why did you come back here?" I asked, meaning the diner, if she was planning on being this closed off.

But she led our conversation in a different direction.

"I grew up here. It made the most sense for me to come back to Los Angeles, where my brother was. Especially knowing I was probably going to need help with…" She paused there, catching herself, probably before bringing up our child. "Well, knowing I would need a job after graduating." She pushed her drink aside, not even finishing half. "Listen, Jake, I know today was probably a big shock." She dug around in her purse and pulled out her wallet.

When she produced cash and looked at the check the waitress had snuck onto the edge of the table while we were talking, I slammed my hand down on top of the small slip of paper, and our glassware hopped about half an inch to the right.

"Yes, it was a shock, but don't you dare blow this or me off with some sort of platitude about not needing my help. Or that you'll let me see her on school breaks or some bullshit like that. If she is my child—which, judging by her age and physical appearance, she is—you won't be dictating how I spend time making up for the nine goddamned years you just robbed me of!" My temper was flaring, and I took a steadying breath to try to calm down a bit.

"Keep your voice down," she hissed, looking around. "I don't need to be in the damn rags by the morning."

"So, you're more worried about the"—I took an overdramatized visual sweep around the café—"one person posing a threat of overhearing our conversation, because that dude"—I pointed to a young college-aged guy a few tables over—"has had earbuds in and hasn't looked up from his phone since he sat down two hours ago. But you have more concern about who might overhear us than you do about coming up with a logical reason to stop me from getting to know the child you didn't—what, Pia?—think I was good enough to be a father to? Because I wasn't from the same shark-infested waters you were from? Did you think you'd pass her off as someone else's? How many men has the girl called *Daddy* in her short life so far?"

"You are so out of line right now, Mr. Cole. I'd strongly advise you quit while you're ahead," she said with that haughty fucking attitude that made me want to take her over my knee and go at her ass until she begged for my forgiveness.

"That's the funny thing, though. Don't you see? I'm not ahead here. I'm nine fucking years behind!" No doubt, everyone in the place, including the kitchen staff, could hear me now.

I stood up, fished my wallet out of my back pocket, and swooped the check off the table before she could grab it. Marching up to the register, I mumbled angry recriminations as I went. I couldn't remember the last time I was so pissed.

Once outside, she scrolled through her phone to find a ride.

"I'm heading west a few blocks. Want to share a ride?" I asked, still angry but also still a gentleman.

But the woman was never one to forgive easily or quickly. Well, hey! At least there was something about her I still recognized.

"Are you taking some sort of mood-altering street drug?" She tilted her head to one side the way one of Sebastian's friends Elijah did routinely.

"Pardon me?"

"Do you really think I would confine myself inside a car with you after the way you just spoke to me?"

"Who the fuck died and made you the queen?" I turned the judgmental tone on her. "Where is this haughty attitude coming from? It really doesn't suit you, Cassiopeia. I sure as hell hope you don't behave this way around my daughter. I'm going to have to undo a lot of damage if you have." And before the words finished crossing my lips, I knew I'd struck a nerve.

"Damage? Are you fucking serious?" She charged at me, covering the six feet that separated us in less than three strides. Quite an accomplishment in those incredible shoes and the curve-hugging dress she was wearing.

Instinctually, I backed up as she charged forward until I thumped into the brick wall storefront of Margarette's.

Pia was in my face with her threatening index finger in the next beat. "Don't you ever question my parenting or having that child's wellbeing at the forefront of every single decision I've made for the past nine years. Ever! Unless you want to spit your balls out in little pea-sized pieces." She stepped so close to issue the final part of her threat, her heaving breasts rubbed against my ribcage with every inhale and exhale she indulged in.

And it was downright heavenly.

Through clenched teeth, Pia seethed, "Because I will ram those suckers so far up your ass, they'll have no other exit option but your stupid, motherfucking mouth." She backed off and straightened to her full height, which wasn't more than five and a half feet to my six.

Uncontrollably, a grin broke out across my entire face, which only seemed to fuel her rage more, because the moment her dial-a-ride app signaled her car had arrived, she dashed to the curb and dove headfirst into a sensible hybrid.

If the driver could've been persuaded to pull a Ken Block maneuver to slam the door shut with the car's forward momentum alone, I'm sure his newest fare would've paid any amount to make it happen.

The same grin stayed planted on my face while I watched the dim taillights disappear in the distance. As I enjoyed the early evening cool-down and walked a few blocks toward my hotel, that damn smile held.

I missed her. I'd missed her so damn much when I first took the internship overseas. It was the hardest decision I'd ever made in my life. Still, to this day, it hurt my heart when I remembered those first few weeks when I got to Spain. There was so much there I wanted to share with her, but over time, she withdrew.

I would've had no problem with the long-distance relationship. None. But as days between phone calls grew into weeks, and then no returned calls at all, I had to face the fact that she'd moved on. I'd known that possibility existed, but I believed we were above it.

Of course, now I knew the reason for the communication drop-off. My beautiful star was struggling with motherhood. Alone. And for her to have gone through all of that herself made me feel even worse. But she had made that decision and given me no say in the matter.

How could I... No, *why should I* feel guilty about something I wasn't even aware of?

The only part in all this mess that I did feel true guilt about was that the child didn't have a mother and father for the first eight years of her life. But I guess that wasn't completely true either, because I knew Shark had played stand-in as often as possible. He'd talked about it off-handedly because he cherished his niece and worshiped his sister.

Oh, shit.

Sebastian Shark was going to have me executed in a back alley on the east side of town by one of his old neighborhood cronies he kept on the payroll for situations just like this. A problem needed to be handled, but he couldn't get his hands dirty. Yeah, I was in deep shit and should probably hire a bodyguard.

I already knew after finding Elijah's girlfriend that morning at the Edge jobsite that these guys were tangled up with some really bad people. People who didn't fuck around if they had a score to settle. People I wanted nothing to do with. And now that I knew I had skin in the game, people I didn't want my daughter or the mother of my child tangled up with either.

Christ. I could just imagine broaching that kind of topic with her.

On my pathway up ahead, I saw a lively looking place. There were a few neon signs flashing in the early dusk, and suddenly a few beers sounded really good. As I approached, the crowd spilling out onto the patio along the sidewalk got louder and louder, and I had second thoughts. Maybe I'd be better with the IPAs in my minifridge back in the room.

"If it isn't Jacob Cole," rumbled a deep voice.

I searched through what I could now see was an entire sea of faces to locate Grant Twombley and Elijah Banks. If Sebastian was with them, I wasn't stopping. My mind was already made up on that one.

Grant's tall frame made him easiest to spot in the crowd as they were pushing their way to one of the pub tables out on the patio. There was a waist-high wrought-iron fence around the patio, so if I wanted to join them, it was either up and over the thing or elbow my way through the massive crowd inside to come out through the proper doors.

"Hey, guys. How's it going?"

"Not bad, not bad," Grant answered with his usual affability as he stretched out a long arm for a fist-bump. Elijah waved from his new perch, his other hand tilting back a cold one.

"Come around and join us, brother," Elijah offered then covered his mouth to stifle a belch. "Sorry, boys, couldn't be helped. I don't think I've tasted a beer that good in a month."

"Some days are like that." I nodded. And if this wasn't one of those days, I didn't think I'd ever have one. "Is it just the two of you? I don't want to intrude . . ."

"Well, it was supposed to be boys' night, but Bas had to go home. Abbigail wasn't feeling well, and the little dude is teething," Grant answered, assuming I meant the third of their typical trio.

If they'd acted odd about my question, I'd already planned on playing it that I meant their ladies. Twombley's data dump gave me the information I was really after without having to look suspicious about it.

Up until this afternoon, Sebastian and I had been getting along great. And hell, who knew? Maybe I was overestimating his reaction to the bomb that would explode in my carefully plotted world when he found out I was the father of his niece. His sister was the one who needed to explain the whole thing to him, as far as I was concerned.

After she explained the whole thing to me.

When I refocused on the two guys in front of me, they were both quietly observing me like a museum exhibit.

"What's up?" I gave them a crooked grin but could already tell I was a made man. There was no way I was getting out alive. I could feel it in the way they were looking at me.

They had already worked out the details, and for all I knew, these two refined gentlemen were the thugs from the east side of town Shark kept on retainer. It could very well be what kept their friendship so tight.

"Calm down, Cole, before you piss yourself," Elijah said before looking at Grant and grinning. He raised his chin and said to his buddy, "Still got it."

"Shut the fuck up." Grant laughed and took a long drink from his beer.

"Are you joining us or what?" Elijah asked.

"Yeah, I've got to make my way through that throng, though, to get there." I pointed out the route I'd have to take. "I was hoping it would thin out a bit while I stood here."

"Fuck that." Grant motioned with his beer. "Step over the fence."

"Fine." I looked around for any bar staff and hopped over the fence in one easy move.

When the server came by, Elijah ordered another round, and we settled into some back-and-forth about the office.

Once our beers arrived and I'd had at least half mine down, Grant finally lit the fuse.

"So, congratulations! It's a girl."

"Right? That was one hell of a way to find out." I tried to laugh, but the sound got stuck somewhere in my throat.

"Yeah, no offense, bud, but I kind of wish I had that on video today," Elijah added.

"You're a cruel man, you know that?" I said, easing up a little. "You wouldn't think it just by looking at you, but it's right there. Right under the surface."

"Nah, everyone knows he's an asshole."

"Careful, now," Elijah warned.

"That only works with Haaaann, or are you forgetting?" Grant's blue eyes flickered with mischief as they caught the reflection of the bar's outdoor neon signage.

"Like your bullshit only works with Blaaaazze, I'm afraid," Elijah shot back through a languid grin.

These two were a trip to be around. You could tell they'd known each other their entire lives by the easy ribbing they gave each other about nothing and everything. It made me miss my own brothers terribly.

"Let's be serious for a minute, though. She never told you?"

I shook my head and met their watchful stares one by one before saying, "Never."

"You have to understand, we've known that woman our entire lives. Just like we've known each other and Sebastian. Pia has always been part of the equation. Bas and Pia were a package deal. That's why he worked so hard to keep them out of the system. He wouldn't be separated from her."

"Yeah, I've heard his story a bunch of times. Even read about it before I came back to LA to work for the guy. I had no idea his sister was the same as the one and only love of my life."

"Real shit, dude?" Grant asked in doubt of my declaration.

"To this day. I don't think I'm capable of loving another. And believe me, there were so many lonely nights, especially after she ghosted me, that I wanted to be able to fall in love again . . ." I just shook my head as I trailed off.

"So what happens now?" Grant asked.

"You mean, if he survives the beat-down when Bas finds out?" Elijah chuckled into his beer.

Grant rubbed his chin thoughtfully. "True. There's that hurdle."

"How fair is that, though?" I defended with a good amount of ire.

"Explain," the two sitting opposite me said at the exact same time.

I darted my gaze back and forth between them, wondering suddenly if this whole thing was a damn setup. Did one of them just step on the other's line delivery?

"What's going on here?" I asked suspiciously.

"It's a stupid thing we all say," Grant clarified. "Just explain what you meant, and don't start acting all woo-woo *X-Files* on us."

With his face screwed up, Elijah gave him a sideways stare. "Woo-woo *X-Files*?"

"Shut up."

I laughed into my bottle before tipping the thing back and draining it.

Grant held up his hand to signal our waitress to bring another round. This dude was super handy to have at the table because with a reach as long as his, I was sure the bartender at the front of the establishment saw his hail.

"Finish your damn thought, Cole."

"I don't even remember what I was saying." With both hands, I squeezed the top of my head, trying to relieve some of the day's pressure.

"You were saying something wasn't fair, and I think it was with regard to Sebastian flipping his ever-loving mind when he finally puts all these pieces together." Banks refreshed my memory while not missing another chance to let me know just how pissed the big guy was going to be about all of this.

I leaned back to let the server set our fresh beers in front of us while supplying, "Or the two of you do it for him?"

"Or that," he muttered.

"I don't think he should take it out on me when I had nothing to do with the secret being kept. Do you honestly think I'm the kind of man who would father a child and then shirk my responsibilities? I get that you don't know me the way you know each other, but if she throws me to the wolves like that to protect herself? Also not fair."

Elijah spoke with reason then. "I hear you, man. This whole situation is fucked up. It always has been. Having to watch her struggle to raise that little girl by herself? Only taking help from any of us when we either forced her to or she literally had no other choice? It's been very frustrating."

Grant nodded along in agreement and then added, "Yeah, Cassiopeia is a Shark through and through. Always has been."

"That's another thing!" I shouted, only realizing how much volume my voice had gained when patrons at several of the nearby tables turned to look at us.

"What are you looking at?" Elijah growled, and most went back to their own conversations. One or two women became more interested.

"Sorry," I apologized. "Sorry. But she never told me her real name. In four years. Why all the secrecy?"

They both stared at me like I was an idiot missing the big reason.

"Now that you know who her brother is, why do you think? The woman wanted some privacy from the press and from people trying to get in good with her big brother."

Frustrated, I said, "But we were in love."

They both tilted their heads, one to the left, the other to the right, and it was like watching a rehearsed routine.

"It's like a portal to nineteen fifty-five opened up and spit you out, Jacob Cole."

"I'm not sure what that's supposed to mean, but I'm ready to change the subject. What's new with you guys?"

CHAPTER FIVE

PIA

Fighting every urge to tell the driver to head west to the water, I confirmed my home address and tried to recover from the conversation I'd just had with Jack.

Or Jacob.

For fuck's sake, this whole thing was ridiculous. From dancing around remembered names and trying to forget old feelings that came right back to the surface regardless of how successfully I thought I'd banished them. How? How with seeing him just one time did it all change?

Years. It had been years without him in my life, and I was fine with that. I was totally fine. And yes, I'd finally started dating again, but I certainly wasn't in the market for a permanent man in my life now, either.

But no. One look from him at that meeting this afternoon, one statement in that deep, sexy voice he used to bathe me in to have his way with my body, and here I sat in the back of a freaking Uber, rethinking every detail of the life plan I had laid out for us.

And by *us* I meant my daughter and me.

I didn't need a man to swoop in and fix my world. There wasn't a thing wrong with it. In fact, it, unlike this day, had been going right along as planned. And that plan was perfectly fine before he showed back up.

I was very young when I graduated from the University of California, San Francisco. I had done so much studying and overachieving through high school, by the time I was ready to move on with my life at a university, I already had enough credits to start with my second year. In the end, it meant a very young, scared, and accidentally pregnant twenty-one-year-old woman had walked across the commencement stage, smiled for the cameras of her loved ones in attendance, and then ran to the nearest restroom to hurl my guts out.

Luckily, I blamed that day on nerves and my screwed-up health in general. I was the lucky winner of the type 1 diabetes lottery and quickly found out another thing I'd been naïve about. Getting pregnant and carrying a child to term could be dangerous, if not deadly, for the unborn infant *and* me if I didn't step up and take responsibility for what was going on inside my body.

It wasn't long before I had to come clean with my brother, who in true Sebastian Shark style launched a manhunt for the *person responsible for ruining my life,* as he so coldly labeled my pregnancy for the first five months.

I'd infuriated him by refusing to provide a single detail about the father of my child and, for the first time, was thrilled he had left the country. Not that an ocean would've stopped Bas from tracking the man down, but by the time I was hospitalized the first time during my pregnancy and the doctors warned whatever stress I was under needed to lighten up or I'd be right back there again, he saw what his version of support was doing to my unborn child and me.

I slipped my key into the lock of the front door and quietly went inside. Sometimes I could sneak in and find Vela reading to Wren or sitting at her piano, practicing with a deep scowl of concentration. Both activities always melted my heart the moment my ears were treated to the sound, so the extra caution entering the house was worth it.

"Hello." My amazing young friend smiled up from whatever she was stirring on the stove. "I didn't think you'd be back so soon."

"Hi. Yeah, it was just a quick meeting." I set my bags down on one of the kitchen chairs and looked around. "Where's Vela?"

"In the tub." Wren raised a brow. "She said she wanted some alone time."

"Is that right?" I couldn't help but smile because the girl was truly growing up too fast, and at the same time had a habit of repeating things she'd heard the adults around her say with no actual idea of their meaning.

"I'll peek in on her when I get changed. Hopefully, she's not giving herself a haircut again." I kicked my heels off and scooped them up with my fingers as I headed down the hall toward my daughter's bedroom.

"Hi, Star," I called into her bathroom. "How was your afternoon, sweetheart?"

There was some sloshing before she answered. "Mama? That you?"

"Sure is. I'm just going to get my pajamas on. Then I can dry you off if you'd like?"

"I can do it myself," she called from behind the closed door. "Is dinner ready?"

"Almost, I think. Hungry?"

"Mm-hmm."

"Hang up your towel, please."

"'Kaaaay."

Laughing to myself, knowing I'd be in that bathroom picking up the towel later, I went into my own closet to strip away the day. The thought of a hot bath sounded so good, but after the altercation I had with Vela at SE earlier, I wanted to spend some time with her before she went to bed.

I wasn't fond of her having dinner so late, but sometimes a homemade meal just couldn't be accomplished sooner. I learned a long time ago to let go of the little stuff and do the best I could, where I could. Even with a full-time helper with her, it was hard to keep her on the perfect schedule.

"Pia?"

"Yeah?" I poked my head out of my walk-in closet to find Wren at my bedroom door. "Come in. What's up?"

"I heard your phone chiming," Wren said, thrusting my handbag toward me. "Not sure if you were expecting anyone still this evening."

"Thank you. Vela should be done but said she wanted to dry herself off. But also mentioned she was hungry. Can you tap on the door again on your way past and tell her it's time to get out?"

"Already done. She's getting her pj's on. Are you hungry? Do you want me to set a place for you?"

"No, I ate, but I'm going to come sit with her while she eats. I hate the way things went today at SE. I can't shake it and feel like I need to get some cuddles or something."

"All right, see you in a couple minutes, then."

Digging through my purse, I fished out my phone and unlocked the screen to see who was trying to reach me. A new text message was waiting from a number I didn't recognize.

I appreciate you meeting me this evening.
I wasn't kidding when I said you really
look good.

> *Sorry, who is this?*

The father of your child. Add me to your
contacts, Star. You're going to be hearing
from me a lot.

> *Jacob, don't do this. We aren't going to be*
> *rekindling any sort of relationship.*

You know I don't give up easily.
Remember how we met in the first place?

Damn this man. What kind of question was that? Of course I remembered how we met. I remembered everything about our time together in vivid detail. Detail I tried to banish from my memory so many times I drove myself mad with the effort.

Now, nearly ten years later, when I'd finally given myself permission to live a little, date again without guilting myself until I was all but sick over it, he materialized out of thin air.

I refused to think about it tonight anymore. I'd vowed to spend time with Vela, and that was what I planned on doing. So I pulled on my comfiest pajama set and robe and shuffled back to the kitchen, where she was kneeling on one of the stools at the island, as she often did. It nearly gave me a heart attack ever since she'd fallen from that exact position and hit her chin on the granite counter on the way down, biting through her lip in the process.

Lord, the blood and the wailing, which in turn just caused more bleeding. Between Wren and I, we couldn't console the girl. Thank God my brother was in town when it happened. One fast swoop in from Uncle Bas and his on-call doctor.

The man had her laughing and stitched up while my assistant and I cleaned up the kitchen and all sanguine traces, and by the next day, she was kneeling on the damn stool again, not having learned a single lesson from the incident. I'd had the counter stools replaced with a different style that had backs that circled nearly three quarters around the entire seat and threatened to have a lap belt installed on one if she kept kneeling on hers. That had worked for about a week, and well, here we were.

"Please sit on your bottom, my love. Remember when you fell?"

"Mammmma," she said, exhausted with me already, "that was eight hundred years ago." She rolled her eyes for good measure in case I didn't pick up on her feelings for me by tone alone.

"Did you just roll your eyes at me, Vela Shark?" I asked, and Wren shuffled out of the room to give us some privacy.

"You so overdamatic all the time, though," she said and shoveled some dinner into her mouth with her fork.

"It's over-dra-matic," I corrected.

After swallowing she repronounced, "Overdramatic."

"Better."

"I'm not a baby. I'm not gonna fall."

"Going to fall," I corrected.

"Mooooom," Vela dragged out.

"Do you want to sound like a Neanderthal, or do you want to sound like a proper, educated young lady?"

She scrunched up her little face. "What's a nee...a knee...a what?"

I laughed. "Never mind. How else will you learn the proper way to say words if you're not taught?"

"I know, but you just sound like a nag. Uncle Bas is right."

"Uncle Bas said I'm a nag? Is that so? Hmmm."

"Oh, now he's in trouble. I know dat sound." An evil little grin spread across her lips as she shoveled the last bite of her dinner in.

"*That* sound," I corrected.

"Mooooom!" She whined again, and I grinned.

"And you're right, he is in trouble. Lots and lots of trouble."

I waited to be sure she was finished chewing before engaging her in more conversation, or I'd be wearing her dinner. "What do you think of Uncle Elijah and Auntie Hannah expecting a baby? It's so exciting, isn't it?"

"Yes! I hope so very much they have a girl. Since K is going to have another brother, I really want a girl this time."

"How do you know Aunt Abbi is having another boy? What makes you say that?"

She tapped her temple and narrowed her eyes. "I just have a feeling."

"Have you now? Interesting. Are you done?" I motioned to her empty supper dish. "Do you want seconds?"

"No, I'm so full," Vela answered and comically rubbed her tummy. "Thank you, though. Do I have to go to bed?"

"I'd like to spend some time with you if you would like to?" I offered hopefully.

"Yay! What do you want to do? Play a game? Watch TV?"

"You pick tonight. I'm all yours."

Well, that was all she needed to hear, and she was off like a shot. "I have a new game in my room. Do you want to see?"

"I would love that. Let me put your dishes in the dishwasher really quick."

But of course, Wren reappeared the way she always did and snatched them right from my hands so I could spend some precious time with my daughter.

Vela and I sat in the middle of the floor on her big sunflower area rug as my brilliant little star explained the rules of her board game to me, and we set off on a fiercely competitive round of the game. We were Sharks, after all, and there was no sense playing a game if you weren't playing to win.

"You know how I correct your words all the time?" I asked between rolls of the bright-pink dice.

"Yes," she answered. "Oh, I almost got the bad queen there! So close!" She threw herself onto her back with relief.

"That was a close call!" I agreed when she sat up and then got serious as I took my turn. "It's just part of my job as your mama, that's all. I'm not trying to act like I know everything. Goodness knows I make tons of mistakes every day."

"You make mistakes?" She looked up so fast, as though I'd just told her Santa was stopping by to play the winner.

"Heck yeah, I do. Look at what happened today at Uncle Bas's office. When I scolded you. That was a mistake." I held up my hand so she would let me finish. "The part that was the mistake was losing my temper in front of everyone. I definitely didn't appreciate all the attitude you were giving me, but there were a lot of confusing things going on for both of us. I should not have taken it out on you. But here's how I'm going to fix it."

I waited for her to realize the silence that settled over the room meant I was waiting for her attention.

When she met my eyes with her innocent, guileless, blue ones, I told my daughter, "I'm sorry, Vela. I'm sorry I lost my temper today. If I embarrassed you at all, I apologize for that as well. Please forgive me. I love you more than the entire world, and sometimes I don't get it right. But I do the best I know how."

Vela patted my hand with her much smaller one. "It's okay, Mama. Here, it's still your turn." She put the pink dice in my palm, and we finished our game.

While she might have beaten me in the board game that I honestly never really saw the actual objective of, my heart felt like I won the night. When I tucked her in bed, she hugged me a little tighter and a little longer than usual and told me she loved me three times before I turned out the light and her night light clicked on.

Stars projected onto her ceiling like they had every night since the day I brought her home from the hospital, and a peace settled over my world.

Wren was putting the last of the dishes away when I came back out into the kitchen and went straight for the bottle of wine in the refrigerator.

"Join me?" I lifted a brow and the bottle, and her grin was the only answer I needed. I pulled two glasses down from the cabinet and brought the wine into the family room, and we both fell into the sofa. I poured us both a healthy amount and then plunked the bottle onto the coffee table and sank back into the cushion.

"One of those days?" the young girl asked.

"My God, if you only knew."

"Does this have anything to do with Vela's latest daddy sighting?"

"What?" When I looked at my friend, she was hiding her grin—or trying to—behind her glass.

"What did she tell you? My God that child is going to give

me gray hair before I'm due." I downed half the wine in my goblet after saying that.

"Well, she made it very clear this was not the same situation as with Mr. Hogan at school, so I wasn't even to mention that," Wren said, and we both burst out laughing.

When we finally calmed down, I asked again, "Seriously, though, unless you feel like you'd be betraying her confidence—because I want her to have someone other than me she knows she can have private conversations with—I'd love to know more about this."

"She asked me on the drive home if I noticed that man in Sebastian's office that wasn't one of her uncles, and I told her I only got a quick look at the faces in the room. But she kept pressing the issue with 'the one my mommy was staring at, the one my mommy was being mean to, the one that looks like me. *Just* like me.'"

"Christ, the girl is too smart sometimes, Wren," I said softly.

"She's your daughter. What did you think would happen? She'd have a lukewarm IQ, Pia? You are constantly engaging her on top of her natural ability. It only makes sense. Not to mention, she has more adults around her than anything else."

"You know, it's funny you mention that. I've been thinking about that a lot lately, too. Maybe she needs to have more playdates or something? Do you think you can try to sniff some of her friends out?"

"I thought Mr. Shark said no?"

"Goddammit."

"What?"

"I forgot. How, I'm not sure. I guess I want a normal life for my child and let it slip my mind." I playfully smacked my forehead with the heel of my hand. "I'll make it a point to check in with the guys and see where all that"—I waved my hand through the air in front of myself—"is currently. What the threat level is, realistically."

"Just let me know," Wren said. "So is Jacob Cole her father?"

I almost choked on the wine I just sipped. "Jesus. A little warning, girl. You know, when you're going in for the kill like that?"

"Is that a yes?" she persisted. When had the Sharkness of this household rubbed off on her too?

I bugged my eyes at her but wasn't sure she'd relent.

"I just know you. You're not always forthcoming with the uncomfortable stuff. This is the closest we've come to finding out." She shrugged and took a gulp from her glass instead of a sip.

"We?"

"Well, at this point, I'm in the same boat as Vela—not knowing, you know? Well, I guess it's not just us. It's everyone. You have us all at a disadvantage."

My assistant held up her hands as though surrendering and ducked her head into her shoulders sheepishly. "I'm sorry. I know that's your prerogative. Your personal life and all. But I have to admit, I Googled Jacob Cole when we got home. There is an uncanny and undeniable resemblance to our queen. The child wasn't joking."

My friend said all of that with barely a breath between sentences, as if giving me an opportunity to object would be giving me a chance to tell her to mind her own business.

I sat forward and set what was left of my wine on the coffee table then buried my face in my palms. Sitting like that for long moments, I contemplated how good it would finally feel to just talk about this with someone. It was going to all come out soon enough anyway, if Jacob demanded a paternity test, like I suspected he would.

On a heavy sigh, I sank back into the sofa once more and gave Wren my truth. "Yes. Yes, he is Vela's father." I stared at her for an eternity, but she stayed silent.

Now the cat had her tongue? Just three minutes earlier she had a string theory so long it could circle the globe. But now that I admitted she was right, she couldn't do me a solid and turn off the damn Klieg lights?

Finally, I succumbed to the pressure to fill the room's deafening silence.

"He and I were college sweethearts. I haven't seen him since the day we graduated. Actually, he didn't walk with our class, so technically, I hadn't seen him for two weeks *before* graduation. He was offered a rare opportunity to study with a prestigious architectural firm in Spain, so he left about two weeks before our commencement. I probably conceived my daughter the last night we saw each other. I never let him know it happened because he would've been on the first flight back to the States and given up everything. I didn't want to be that girl, you know? I didn't want to be the reason he gave up his dreams."

I drained my wine before I had the courage to meet her gaze again.

"Couldn't you have gone with him?" she asked quietly.

"With my type 1 and my brother? I just didn't foresee it going down that way. So I kept the secret as long as I could. I was so young, Wren. So young. And scared. By the time I could even think clearly, it was like everything was snowballing. I got sick and had to be hospitalized several times throughout the pregnancy, and then Bas was like a mental patient. Because we lost our mother and infant brother similarly, he went crazy. You think he was nuts with Abbi? That was nothing."

Just remembering those days made me shudder. Sebastian was like a warden, and I his prisoner. I knew he was scared, and I knew he loved me, so it was easier for me to understand where his actions were rooted. But to an outsider, the man had to have seemed certifiable. If Jake had been around at the time, there's no telling what would've happened.

"I'm a little worried about what Bas is going to do when he finds out Jacob is Vela's father. I think they've forged some sort of friendship while working together, but I've heard my brother level so many threats over the years." I shook my head, recalling random things I'd heard him say. "Yeah, I'm concerned for sure."

"You don't really think he'd hurt him though, do you?" she asked. "Not now, I mean."

"My brother can be very irrational when driven by loyalty and fear. In the moment, he justifies that he's doing the right thing because his fight or flight instinct still lies right beneath the surface. And unfortunately, the man has never been one to choose flight. Ever."

"Well, he's definitely an alpha kind of guy. But the actual truth of this whole matter is going to be your responsibility to explain to Sebastian. Or, at least, that's how I see it."

"I'm not following—"

"It's not actually Jacob's fault he wasn't here to help you, Pia. You made that decision for him. I think your brother needs to understand that, and I think you're the responsible party on this one. You're the one who needs to explain it to him.

Wouldn't that be the fairest to Mr. Cole?" Wren asked with the innocence and clarity of an uninvolved party.

"I suppose it would be, but I'm not sure how *fair* I'm feeling toward Mr. Cole at the moment. Especially if he's going to continue to insist on implanting himself in my carefully planned-out life. You know?"

Yes, I heard the words I was saying. Yes, I heard they weren't impartial or kind. And no, I couldn't bring myself to feel differently about any of it. I spent Vela's entire nine years of life doing what I had to in order to protect her. Sometimes that meant making hard choices or doing things I wasn't proud of. This would just be another one of those times. How bad could I really be expected to feel if Jacob had to take one for the team once in her damn life.

My friend sat forward and refilled both our glasses. After sliding mine toward me, she kept her stare locked with mine.

"Okay, let's come at this from another perspective. I feel like I'm in danger of overstepping, but..." She laughed a little, but it was more of an uncomfortable choking sound than one of humor. "Shit, when has that ever stopped one of us in this posse?"

"Right?" I agreed with a grin. "But seriously, Wren, you know you have freedom of speech in this house. You always have and always will. Not only do I trust you with my daughter's care and safety, but I value your opinion as my friend."

"Thank you for saying that." She smiled warmly and reached her hand out, and I gave it a gentle squeeze. With a fortifying inhale, she said, "Maybe instead of thinking about what fits into your life's carefully planned outline, you should look at what Vela wants and, on some level, needs. What she's been silently—and not so silently—begging for. What she's been willing to imagine about random men she encounters on the street who seem to be good daddy candidates."

Like a gameday drink cooler, that ice-cold truth was dumped over my head without mercy. At least Wren had the decency to wince afterwards.

My initial Shark instinct was to attack. Especially the mother Shark in me. But again, calling on justice to prevail with a calmer temper, my safest bet would be to let virtue guide me. It wouldn't be fair to have encouraged the woman to freely speak her mind and then lash out at her for doing exactly that.

"Thank you," I said quietly and nearly gagged on the words. Emotion clogged my throat, and I felt like I swallowed a ping-pong ball. Feelings weren't things I dealt in very often. Usually, I avoided emotionally charged situations if it could be helped. Given the fact that, for the most part, I was raised by Sebastian and his two best friends, it was a wonder I was emotionally available at all. When I was a teen and Bas really started experiencing success, one of the first things he insisted on were weekly therapy sessions—for me, at least. He refused to go, of course. To this day, I rarely missed a session.

"You're thanking me for that? I thought you'd be throat-punching me." She breathed out a huge sigh of relief.

"Just because things aren't easy to hear doesn't make them untrue. At least not as a rule."

"You have a point. But you also know, as a rule, I wouldn't say something intentionally to be hurtful to you. Especially where our little queen is concerned."

I loved the twinkle Wren got in her eyes when she spoke about Vela. She started with us so long ago, Vela was deeply embedded in her heart.

Nodding, I agreed with her. "I do, I do. But do you

understand? I don't want to share her. That's just the blunt, bold truth. I don't want some stranger, because let's just call him what he is, waltzing in here and playing weekend warrior daddy and trying to make up for nine years of MIA daddy by going over the top. Not with grand gestures of affection and lavish gifts or heavy-handed discipline. Does that make sense? I mean..." My entire body shivered at the thought of either of those scenarios. "It makes me want to vomit just thinking about it."

"Is he that type of man?" my assistant asked simply.

"I don't presume to know what type of man he is anymore."

"Okay, fair enough. A good number of years have passed, and this is a capacity you've never witnessed him in. But what about the man you knew him to be before?"

Rephrasing the question by those few words was enough to make me pause and think. Had we ever talked about having a family? We definitely had done a lot of dreaming together. It was one of our favorite pastimes. Being broke college students forced you to find creative ways to entertain yourselves on dates. We would lie under the stars for hours and stare into the heavens and talk.

Jake was a deep thinker, and I loved listening to him theorize about anything and everything. He came from a really big family and would often tell me stories about growing up with nine brothers and sisters. When we had holiday and summer breaks, he would always invite me to go home with him, but I made excuse after excuse as to why I couldn't. By our senior year, we were so in love, we both stopped going home and spent the entire year in Northern California with each other. At that point, Sebastian was too busy with his infant company to worry about my school calendar.

"I really don't know the answer to that. We were babies ourselves, Wren. We had no business making a baby so young. But it happened. And I will never say she was an accident or a mistake. I don't think we fantasized about becoming parents—certainly not then—but I'm not sure we ever had a talk about the future of it either."

My friend launched another question as soon as I had finished answering the previous one. "Were you planning a future together? When he came back from that internship?"

"Yes, that was the original plan. But then I found out I was pregnant and started ghosting him. Since I never told him my real name, it was pretty easy to disappear."

It was surprising how much pain I still felt when paging through the psychological scrap book from that space in time. The emotions reignited from mentally thumbing through aged snapshots and rereading old journal entries carved into the surface of my heart. It felt as raw as the day we went our separate ways.

Even I could tell I stared off wistfully for way too long.

"I'm guessing those heart eyes aren't for Stoney?"

In legitimate danger of spraying wine through my nostrils, I hustled to the kitchen sink and burst out laughing while hovering over it.

When I settled down enough to speak, I reminded Wren about the guy I recently started dating. "It's Boulder. His name is Boulder."

Then it was her turn at the barking laughter. "Seriously, Pia." She sucked air in through her nose. "Who names a child after a rock?"

CHAPTER SIX

JACOB

Last night, instead of sleeping, I spent way too much time trying to come up with reasons why I would need to consult with Pia on the Edge project. Her designs were flawless, no matter how many times I looked at them.

Repositioning the pages on my room's little coffee table from one direction to another didn't net a different result, either. Everything the woman touched was perfect. It always had been.

Was that why she ditched me so easily? Maybe she realized I had no place in her perfect Shark kingdom. Maybe she knew if she didn't take out the trash herself, her brother would do it for her.

But that was the part of this mucked-up mire she didn't know about. Cassiopeia hadn't been the only one doing some creative pruning of the ole family tree whenever the topic came up. And from what I could remember, the topic didn't come up all that often. More than likely, we both steered clear of the subject in fear the other would ask too many probing questions about our bloodlines.

Because when you hid the most basic things about yourself, every question felt like a probing one.

Like Pia, when I enrolled in college, I used a surname

that would attract far less attention than my famous family's. I wanted to experience college life without the trappings that came with the privileged life I was accustomed to. I didn't want my fellow classmates to suffer from knowing me either. I couldn't imagine anything more unfair and disruptive to the other students in their pursuit of higher education. So, I kept my family's fame and notoriety a secret.

My parents—well, my mother specifically—had done an excellent job of keeping my siblings and me out of the media. Therefore, I wasn't recognized by sight alone. My father flat out refused to allow me to attend a university unless I had bodyguards on campus at all times. No one could offer a legitimate reason for the precaution, so it just seemed like paranoia. But I knew better than to argue with the man, especially about particular topics. Our safety was at the top of that list.

We came to an agreement that security would pose as college students, wear plain clothes, and live wherever I did. If that was in the dorms, so be it. If I ended up living off campus, they would move there too. All in all, it worked out well. Outside of my brothers, those men were still some of my closest friends.

Speaking of my brothers, the one I had the closest relationship with called and interrupted my mental stroll down memory lane. The lyrics from one of our favorite songs while in high school, "Just a Dream" by Nelly, blasted from my phone to announce the incoming call.

"Hello?"

"Why do you always do that?" my brother Lawrence asked with a laugh.

"Do what? And good morning to you too," I said with an

edge of annoyance. But just an edge because he knew I could never truly be mad at him.

"You say hello like you can't see who it is on the caller ID. Like I could be a telemarketer wanting to talk about your expiring car warranty."

"How would you like me to answer the phone when you call, brother?"

"I don't know—like a normal person. Like, 'Hey, Law, what's goin' on?'"

"Hey, Law, what's going on?"

"See? That wasn't so hard, was it?"

"Jesus Christ. Are you doing drugs again? I don't think our mother will live through a second round of that bullshit."

"Fuck off. No, I'm not. And smoking weed hardly constitutes doing drugs, Jacob."

"Cut the full-name crap, man. You were doing more than smoking, and we both know it. But anyway, what's up? How's it going on your side of town this morning?"

"Not too bad. Can't complain, really. Dude, I met this smoke show last night. Oh my God, I think I found the mother of my children."

"What about last week's mother of your children?" I teased my brother. "Won't she be upset when you tell her?"

"Nah, that chick ended up being a little too crazy, even for me—and before you say it," Law interrupted himself, an endearing habit he had, "that's saying a lot."

I laughed with him for a minute then sobered. I had to tell him about Pia before he took off on another topic.

"Dude, you're not going to believe what's been going on around here." I glanced at my watch and realized I needed to get moving to work. I'd spent way too much time in the clouds this morning.

"Actually, are you free for lunch?" I asked instead. "I think we should have this conversation in person, not over the phone."

"Hang on, let me look at my schedule." The line was quiet for a minute or so until my brother came back on. "I can do something a little later, like one?"

"Yeah, okay. That should work. If something comes up, though, I'll text you. Cool?"

"For sure. Talk to you later, man. Can't wait to hear what all this is about, though. You never have good dish anymore. Frankly . . ." My brother let his husky laugh slip out, and I knew he was about to bust my balls about something. "You're damn boring, Jake. I just didn't want to say anything."

"Well, thanks for sparing my feelings, Lawrence," I answered dryly, even using his full name to sound extra square. "You know how fragile I am."

"Oh shit, the office is calling. Talk to you later." And just like that, he was gone.

But the smile on my face stayed in place for a long time after we hung up.

I had made some decisions overnight. At least I got some things accomplished, even if sleep wasn't one of them. Before finding Pia, I was really unsettled about what I'd wanted to do with my career. Did I want to settle in Los Angeles or move back up north? I wasn't overly fond of the Bay Area the way I was even a few years ago, but to be honest, I wasn't sure how I'd fit in in this town either.

Now that my woman and child were here, though, this was where I wanted to be. The decision was made for me. I needed to find a permanent place to live as soon as possible. I didn't think buying would be in my best interest before I knew how things turned out with Cassiopeia, though, so renting seemed like the best plan on that front. Still, getting a Realtor involved would be the route I'd take since I was unfamiliar with the city and didn't have time to investigate all the little subdivisions on my own.

Sebastian kept nagging me about putting down roots, so he'd be the first person I would ask about a Realtor recommendation. I was sure the guy had one of every service professional at his beck and call, so he'd likely be able to point me toward someone reputable.

The second half of the decision was either to join an established architectural firm in town or to become an independent contractor. Up to this point, I'd only worked for other firms, and that had always been fine. I was a solid team player, and I didn't mind not being the one in charge or going home with all the headaches at the end of the day.

While I trusted my talent would keep food on our table, I had no knowledge about running a business. But I had to admit, there were aspects about it that were enticing. There were also basic reasons why staying with a firm was the smarter way to go. If my day got swallowed up by tedious things like health insurance, payroll taxes, and expense reports, when would I have time to do the architectural design I felt so passionately about? I just didn't see how a business owner got around those required provisions, even with as few as two employees.

Like last night, I was no closer to an answer on that portion of the dilemma now than I was then. But that was all fine too. The Edge had at least another year until the project wrapped up, so I'd stay busy with that. Other clients were already starting to make inquiries because of my work on that site, and once it visibly became nearer to completion, those requests would ramp up substantially. At least, that was what I'd experienced on other buildings I'd designed in the past. Nothing beat word of mouth, and my design spoke for itself.

My thoughts kept drifting to Pia. When we were in school, she was always up at the crack of dawn. I wondered if she was still an early riser. She probably had to be to get the little one up and ready for school. What grade would she be in? I did some quick calculations and figured she must be on the far side of eight, if not nine. That would put her in third grade, like my niece Stella.

Tossing my phone from one palm to the other, I thought about what to say for a few minutes and decided to keep it simple.

Good morning. Still an early riser?

A few minutes went by with the message not being read and then a few more after the status changed. Finally, the little throbbing ellipses appeared to show she was responding. Not that I was captivated by the little three-by-five-inch screen or anything.

Hard to be anything else when you have a child to get to school on time. Stop texting me.

Want to have lunch? A girl can't live on milkshakes alone.

Sorry, already booked. Stop texting me.

Dinner, then. Pick you girls up at six.

Have a great day, Star.

Jacob, no. I'm serious.

See you at six.

There was no way I was backing down. She'd be ready by five thirty p.m. She couldn't possibly think I'd forgotten all her little quirks. Just because she shut me out of her life didn't mean I'd shut her out of my heart or my memory.

Every single day, I thought about this woman. Every single one. In one way or another, she crossed my mind. Granted, they weren't always pleasant thoughts or well-wishes. But she was always right there. Pia Shark wasn't just my first love; she was my only love.

When we were together, it was so good. We were *that* couple. The couple everyone looked at and wished they were a part of. Sure, everyone said that about their own relationship, but we set serious couple goals. Maybe finding someone so perfect right out of the gate was the curse? I still couldn't figure out where it all went wrong. The woman I loved would not have hidden a pregnancy from me. Why would she have thought I wouldn't have stood by her side through the whole experience? Why would she have thought I wouldn't want to have shared every single moment of that experience? Why would she have robbed me of that?

The more I thought of those questions, the more my anger and frustration grew. And I knew damn well those feelings didn't belong here. They wouldn't help solve anything now because it was all water under the bridge. If I wanted to be a part of these ladies' lives now, I needed to approach this whole situation with an open heart and an open mind. I had to find a way to leave past hurt there. In the past. I wasn't sure if I could do it completely. I was almost sure I couldn't, quite frankly, but I would put in the work and try.

Maybe I'd try to find a therapist in the area to work with. Hell, if this was going to be my new town, I'd need to find all sorts of new professionals. Might as well start there.

Since Shark was my main client at the moment, I'd been leasing a small office space downtown near the Shark Enterprises' building. I couldn't work effectively from that hotel room—there just wasn't enough space, and it wasn't professional if I wanted to meet with prospective clients.

I arrived at my office around ten, already feeling like half the day was gone. I spent so much of the morning in my head and then on the phone with Law. After speaking with him, one of my other brothers, Wade, called, and then my mom phoned too. I loved my big family, I really did, but they could really suck up a lot of my time. For some reason, no one took the fact that I had a job seriously.

A few of my siblings were still in college, and the youngest two were still in high school. Like me, Law worked for a living, and two of my brothers just lived off the family money. That was probably the hardest to digest of all of my siblings' life choices. I couldn't understand how they were content not contributing to society. Going to social functions and hobnobbing with other rich people seemed to be their definition of contributing. It was a conversation I steered clear of after trying once and getting absolutely nowhere.

The office space I rented had three other adjoining offices, and we all shared one receptionist. The concept was similar to a WeWork setup but on a much smaller scale as far as the number of people it could accommodate. Also, the offices themselves were much larger. It was perfect for long-term but not permanent setups like mine.

"Morning, Tabitha. How are you today?" I asked the receptionist. She was a nice girl, always very cordial when I walked through the lobby.

"Good morning, Mr. Cole. Getting a late start today?" she asked, smiling.

I wasn't sure if it was impressive that she was so keenly aware of my habits or if she was ribbing me because I was getting in so late. Really, what business would that be of hers? Quickly I decided she was just being friendly and observant and held on to my good mood with emotional fingertips.

"Yeah." I faked a laugh. "Much later than I'd prefer, actually. Do I have any messages?" Better to just change the subject and move on.

"Yes, a few. These are for you." She handed me several pink notes with her bubbly printing on them. If they had been printed on a computer, the font would be called *Teenaged Girl*.

While taking the notes, I told her, "Thank you. I don't have any scheduled appointments until one, so I'll be in my office until then."

"Sounds good." She smiled and turned back to her work, and I walked down to my office.

Just as I was unlocking the door, my phone signaled an incoming text message. I got inside the door and set my laptop bag and drawings down on the desk and drafting table before I pulled out the device to see who was reaching out.

Of course, Pia's face was filling my mind's eye the entire time. She better not consider canceling our dinner plans. Not that she'd ever agreed to them in the first place, but the woman always responded better to my firmer demeanor than anything else. Instantly other parts of my body grew firm with those memories too.

Not now, man. Not here. Just—yeah—no. Not an option.

I'd jacked off at least five times last night, and I still couldn't get her out of my mind. Her and all the memories of the things we used to do. That woman was a—well, a shark in bed. I don't think she had a limit I didn't test. And obliterate.

It was probably another reason losing her was so damn hard. Going from all the wild, unadulterated, carnal, sensual fucking and gentle, soul-melding lovemaking we used to fill every day and night with to nothing at all was like quitting a serious addiction cold turkey.

The first six months in Barcelona would have been unbearable if I hadn't been so busy with my studies and work. The firm that gave me the internship viewed the position as a career-changing opportunity, and I was sure they were right. I had to view every moment of their time as valuably as they did, or I would be excused from the program. Not only would it have been a huge hit to my pride and dignity, but it would've been career suicide as well.

The text message was from my oldest sibling, Cecile. Her daughter Stella was the one I guessed to be about the same age as Pia's. Shit . . . same age as *mine*. A grin spread across my face as that thought really settled in. I had a daughter. Stella was going to be so excited to find out she had a cousin.

Hey, Jacob. I need a huge favor. Can you pick up Stella after school?

Hey. Umm, not sure. What time?

She's out at 3:20 p.m.

I stared at my phone, trying to calculate the commute across the city. My niece went to a private academy near my sister's home, but it was nowhere near the stupid extended stay hotel where I was living currently.

Maybe if I got ready at her house for my date and picked Pia and Vela up from there, it would work out. I just didn't know where Pia lived, and that was the giant X-factor here. If she lived near downtown, I was fucked. I'd never be able to fight rush hour traffic to get to her by six p.m.

Don't worry about it, Jacob. I'll figure something out. I can ask a neighbor or something.

I could hear my sister's edge and disappointment all wrapped up in those two short sentences. Maybe some of that was my own guilt... Okay, so *most* of that interpretation was my own guilt, because Cecile rarely asked for my help. I hated to let her down on the uncommon occasion when she did.

No, you can count on me, sister. I'll be there. Will Stella know to look for me in the loop? Also, I have a date tonight and won't be able to make it back to my place in time to get ready. Can I get ready at your place and leave from there?

Only if you give me all the details about the date before you tell Law. You will have

*to park in the visitors' lot and sign her
out in the front office. They've changed
procedures for non-parent pickups again.*

OK. I'll be there at 3:30 sharp!

*3:20 Jacob! Please don't make her wait!
You know how she gets.*

*I was totally messing with you. I'll be
there on time. XO*

Shit. I definitely would've been late had I not reconfirmed the time. To be extra safe, I set an alarm on my phone for when I needed to head in the direction of Stella's school and another for three twenty p.m. so I wouldn't screw it up. Cecile would never forgive me, and worse than her, neither would Stella.

When my sister's no-good ex-husband walked out on his family, my niece started getting into a lot of trouble in and out of school. Even though she was very young, the divorce affected her in unimaginable ways. She started hurting herself and her classmates as well as some of the kids she played with in their neighborhood.

After a few months of therapy, it came out that her father had been physically abusing her in clever ways that didn't leave marks, and he'd probably been doing it for her entire life. Now, she and my sister were both in counseling, and I suspected neither of them would ever be the same.

The world could truly be a fucked-up place.

My desk phone's ringing brought my attention back before the usual rage that spun up when I thought about that whole situation had a chance to gain too much momentum.

"Jacob Cole," I answered in a professional voice.

"Mr. Cole, hello. This is Craig, Mr. Shark's executive assistant."

"Oh, hello," I answered coolly but immediately started freaking out.

She'd told him. She'd told him I fathered her child and left her to go halfway around the world, never to be seen or heard from again. And now he was calling to remove me from the project. Well, he was having his assistant do his dirty work for him, but wasn't that how most big shots normally handled dirty work? They got someone else to do it for them?

"Mr. Cole, can you please be at the office today at three for an urgent meeting? I realize it's late notice . . ."

I knew he expected I would bend over backwards to be there.

Sorry, Shark. Not today.

"Oh, sorry. I'm already booked. I won't be able to make it. Please give Mr. Shark my regrets and tell him to feel free to email any design concerns I can help with."

"Pardon?"

A few really long beats of quiet stretched between Craig and me, and I finally couldn't stand it any longer.

"Was there anything else? I was just about to head out to my next appointment. You barely caught me." I kept my tone firm but respectful.

"Uh, no, that will probably do it for you. Take care of yourself, Mr. Cole," Craig said as he hung up.

What the hell was any of that supposed to mean?

CHAPTER SEVEN

PIA

"Isn't that my father?" my daughter asked while pointing across the small school campus.

"Vela, please," I began to say, but she yanked her hand from mine and stopped in her tracks.

"And what is he doing with her?" she asked with an amount of venom I didn't know she was capable of.

Now I tracked her gaze to the walkway that meandered from the front door of the school's office to the visitors' parking lot. Sure enough, Jacob Cole strolled along while smiling down at an adorable little girl with a mop of bright-orange hair. My goodness, she was precious, but seeing him hand in hand with another little girl our child's age freaking gutted me.

"Let's just get in the car, Vela. We don't want to hold up the loop and get in trouble," I said while applying pressure to her shoulder blades to move her along faster.

Oh—wrong move, sister.

My daughter snapped.

Vela twisted out from under where my palms had been touching her back, doing her best imitation of a Sunday parishioner who had fallen to the tent's dirt floor and was about to speak in tongues.

I wasn't sure if it was the exact top of her lung capacity,

but if it wasn't, it had to be damn close.

"I don't care about the fucking loop. This is bullshit! And it's your fault!" The profanity-laced tirade was complete with a tiny eight-year-old index finger pointed aggressively toward my face, in case any of the uptight parents who stopped to gawk weren't sure who she was bellowing at.

Folding in half at the waist, I got right in my little queen's face and said through gritted teeth, "You better get in the car immediately, or I will call Uncle Bas before we leave this property. Do you understand me, lady?"

Vela scampered into the back seat and slammed the door so hard I was shocked the window remained intact.

Holy hell, I was about to tan this girl's backside if she didn't check herself. Of course, I would never do such a thing, but I remembered hearing my own mama say that to Sebastian when we were little, and if a threat could make that little devil stop misbehaving, it must've been a powerful one.

We drove for a few minutes, but watching her cry in the back seat was both dangerously distracting to my behind-the-wheel abilities all while tearing my own heart from my chest. I turned into a shopping center parking lot and put the vehicle into park before it had come to a complete stop.

My SUV lurched violently forward and then rocked equally as hard backward, repeating the process until all the unspent energy was absorbed through the brake system and we were still. When I turned in my seat to face my daughter, I could only imagine how I must have looked.

"Why did you pull in here?" Vela asked between sniffles. "Can we just go home? Please?"

Pinching the bridge of my nose, I replied, "I'd like to talk about what just happened."

"No, thank you."

"Vela. Look at me."

Finally, she lifted her red-rimmed eyes to mine.

"Who was the girl holding Jacob's hand? Is she in your class?"

The tears picked up their pace, and she nodded and sniffed harder.

"What's her name, baby? Do you know her?"

"That's Stella, Mama."

Wait, that didn't make sense. I could feel the scrunched-up face I was making and tried to relax the expression before asking, "Stella Masterson?"

"Yeah. B-B-But why was he holding her hand? Is he her daddy too?" Her voice broke on the last word, and with it, so did my heart.

I couldn't sit here and watch my daughter's emotions get run up the flagpole at the hands of her own father, when none of us even knew what the hell was going on. While Vela sobbed, I frantically dug through my handbag for a tissue or something suitable for her to use as one.

Last year, with her mother's permission, all the parents were sent an email about Stella Masterson. Her father was being investigated on some sort of child abuse charges, and apparently the poor little girl had been acting out in class.

According to the pickup loop gossip I overheard, she'd even gotten physical with some of her classmates. It was right around that time the email was sent home, so something had escalated to the point that the school felt the parents needed to be made aware of what was happening.

When I asked Elijah to look into it to ensure I was handling the information dissemination with Vela appropriately, he could barely find two facts to string together. The family was likely doing their best to keep the whole situation quiet because they were very well known and wouldn't want their dirty laundry being aired in the media.

Everyone knew the last name Masterson in one way or another, though. They were one of those families who had their hand in the consumer sector, similar to Johnson & Johnson.

"I don't know what's going on either, little star."

"This is your fault!" she bellowed.

"Listen, Miss Shark." I widened my eyes at her until they felt like they might fall from their sockets and roll across the floorboards of my SUV. That crazy mom face normally cut through the crap pretty quickly, though, and this time was no different.

"You've been completely out of line today. The profanity in the pickup loop, for starters." I ticked off her transgressions on my fingers as I went. "The volume at which you are speaking to me." I bent a second finger back with my other hand until the knuckle popped, and her eyes widened farther, probably thinking I was willing to break my own fingers because I was so fed up with her shit. "Thirdly, this demanding Shark-style temper that I will not put up with. Do. You. Understand. Me?"

"Mama, you're scaring me. You look crazy. Do you need me to call someone?"

"Yes. Here. Knock yourself out." I handed her my phone and stared at her.

"Can you unlock dis?" She handed the device right back with matched attitude.

"*This*," I repeated while tapping in the four-digit code to unlock my phone. I handed it back to her because I really could not wait to see what stunt this little shit pulled next.

I watched her sounding out the names in the contacts list, using her little finger to follow along beneath the letters like they were taught, until she found the one she was looking for, selected the name, and then pressed the Call button. I was actually very impressed she could make a phone call so easily. I had no idea she could without relying on Siri.

I could hear the line ringing in the quiet car, and then the call connected. I thought for sure she would call my brother, but surprisingly, she'd called Elijah.

"Hey, Pia, what's going on? How are things with Cole?" he teased.

I winced.

I could hear his words crystal clear, and Vela raised a brow while staring at me, watching my reaction.

Talk, I mouthed and pointed to the phone, and she remembered she was still the one driving this bus into the ravine.

"Hey, Uncle Lijah, it's Vela, not Mama. But don't worry, I already know all about my daddy, even though Mama is trying to tend it's not true."

"Pre-tend," I corrected.

"Annnywaaaay…" My daughter dragged it out with a fresh eye roll for me. "I really need your help with something. Can you come get me at my house?"

"Okay, that's enough," I demanded, holding out my flat palm. "Give me the phone."

"Stay out of this," she growled while glaring at me.

"Vela, not cool, little lady," I heard Elijah admonish. "You can't talk to Mom like that."

"We're having a fight right now, and she's acting cray zee."

"Give Mom the phone, babe. Now," I heard Elijah instruct

my saucy daughter. Until he added that last command in that particular voice, I wasn't sure she wouldn't argue with him, too.

When I got the device pressed to my ear, I quietly breathed, "Hey."

"What on earth is going on?" he asked just as softly.

"I don't even know where to begin." Pressing my forehead to the steering wheel, I continued, "But we're all going to have to have a really long talk. My brother is going to lose his shit, I know that much. But in the meantime, this child is driving me to day drink, Elijah."

His deep, husky laugh wrapped me in warm, familiar comfort.

"Don't you laugh. I hope you have eight girls and they're all some stunning combination of the two of you. You'll never get another wink of sleep again for as long as you live." We were both laughing by the time I finished issuing my evil hopes for his future parenting experience.

"You know what, Dub? I hope you're right. I can't wait to find out what we're having. I know it's early, but I'm already obsessed with the whole idea of being a father. We all drew such shitty father cards in life, you know? Well, not Han, but the four of us." The man grew silent for a beat before finishing his thought. "I just want to do my best."

"Elijah, you're going to be an amazing father. I'm sure of it. I can't wait to watch it all happen."

"So, back to this talk we all need to have. When do you want to do that?" he pressed. "And are you going to let Junior be there?"

"I haven't given it that much thought, but there was just an incident at afternoon pickup." My phone was quiet while he waited for me to tell him more, but all I could manage was a whimper.

Finally, knowing full well he wouldn't know what I meant and that I could be opening myself up for more questions, I said, "It's going to be unavoidable after this evening anyway. And no, I don't think she needs to be there. She's already confused about how much say she has in certain conversations."

Elijah barked out a laugh so sharp I had to pull the phone away from my ear momentarily. "I meant Jake."

"You guys call him Junior? Oh, that's hilarious. If he heard that—well, yeah, that's just funny." I paused for a moment, not sure if I should say what I was thinking, but then thought, screw it, why not? If he was going to be a part of my landscape, I didn't want these boys thinking they were going to kick him around like their shiny new toy.

"You know… he's not all that different from the rest of you."

"What does that mean?" he asked curiously, not defensively.

"Exactly what I said. You should all get along just fine while you're pissing on things. Okay, I need to get up the hill and get ready for a dinner meeting with the aforementioned Junior. I'll reach out about the other meeting though and be in touch."

Before either one of us disconnected and hurried off to our next obligation, I paused to really be sure my friend heard my words.

"And Elijah…" With a big inhale, because after so many years, being able to depend on these men was never something I took for granted, I said with my whole heart, "Thank you so much. I'm really sorry if we bothered you with all this today."

"You know I always have time for my two best girls." His rich tone was as good as any hug.

"It's just…yeah." I sighed again, as uncomfortable with emotional displays as my big brother on most days. "Thank you. Love you."

"Love you too, Dub."

My phone took a little hop across the seat where I tossed it after hanging up. We really needed to get home and cleaned up for our dinner date if we were going to still make that happen. I just didn't know how to approach the subject with the little powder keg in my back seat. Maybe waiting until we weren't in a confined space together was the better plan.

Wren was there to give me a break when we got in the door, but before they scurried off to do their thing, I needed to see if my daughter still wanted to join Jake and me for dinner.

"Vela, before you go to your room, I need to talk to you, please."

She rolled her eyes and let her shoulders drop so low, her backpack slid down to the crooks of her elbows. "Restriction?"

"Well, yes, but that's not what I wanted to talk to you about. Earlier this afternoon, before all of that happened…" I would just leave it there for now. Neither of us wanted to open that can of worms again so soon. "Jacob texted me and invited us to dinner."

Her young voice and face pitched higher with interest. "Both of us?"

"Mm-hmm. Originally, I thought you'd be ecstatic, but if you want me to give him your regrets, I can do that."

"My what?" she asked, not understanding the terminology I used. But this was the best way to teach anyone new words— by using them.

"If you don't want to go, I will tell him for you," I explained. "I'm still going to go to the meeting, though, and you can stay with Wren."

That was the plan. She could choose to come along or stay home. But it wasn't bargaining time, which she typically tried to pull. I could strangle my brother every time because of his art-of-the-deal-style influence on her behavior.

"Why isn't it called a date if he asked us to go to dinner? Why are you saying you are going to a meeting like you are going to work?" She slowly shook her head while considering me. "You're so confusing today."

Wren, bless her soul, stood quietly on the other side of the kitchen, badly pretending to be shuffling some mail. My assistant wasn't usually so out of the loop with major events like this and was likely trying to put together the pieces of my afternoon from what she was overhearing.

"Tell you what. Because I know it's a big decision, especially after all that just went on"— again I made the gesture that would be my new hand-sign for the clusterfuck of the day—"you go get a bath, or shower, and please make sure you rinse your hair well and think about it. I'll peek in and see what you've decided while I'm getting ready."

"I already know I want to go. I want to go wiff you."

"*With.*"

"With you. Please."

"Go shower. Maybe we can get ready together? I'd like that if you would," I offered cautiously. I wasn't up for rejection, because where this child was concerned, my tender heart felt like a wounded soldier.

"Yes!" She held up her little hand for a high five and skipped down the hall to her room.

"Be there in a few, Star," Wren said. "Let me catch up with Mama, 'kay?"

"Ooohhhh-kaaaay." Her voice drifted away as she went deeper into her own en suite.

I leaned way back to peer down the hall, making sure I heard the water come on before even making eye contact with Wren.

When I went to the refrigerator to see if there was an open bottle of wine left from the night before, she said, "This is going to be good. I can already tell. And we killed that bottle last night, remember? Shit, was that last night? Night before?"

"Okay, we need a new, emergency, hard-and-fast full-stop on all the cussing around this kid. I know it's not you. It's the boys, but they are going to get a big earful, trust me."

"Oh dear ... Do I dare ask?"

"Do you remember Stella? The adorable little Annie-looking classmate?"

Immediately Wren identified the child. "Sure. She was the one whose father—"

"Right." I cut her off there because I didn't want Vela overhearing any of that.

Obviously, Jacob had some sort of ties with the Masterson family that he was able to take Stella from school. Damn straight I'd be getting to the bottom of that by the end of the night, but I didn't want my daughter saying something unintentionally hurtful or insensitive.

I continued with the low-down. "So, we were in the loop today, I got the hand-off from the teacher, and we were walking the ten feet to the car," I started to explain, but already, my friend's stare was growing, and it pulled me up short. "What?"

With concern, she asked, "You got out? Of the car? In the loop?"

This was a sacred school pickup and drop-off no-no. I knew it, she knew, even the kids knew it. But I had to skip giving my opinion of that rule-heavy school at the moment and press forward.

"They were really backed up. I don't know what the holdup was, but anyway, for reasons I don't yet understand, Jacob was leaving the front office, hand in hand with Stella."

"Oh, no."

"Oh. Yes. And she lost her fucking . . . sorry, freaking mind. Wren, she went batshit. I mean, sorry, she really lost it. Yelling obscenities at me." I bugged out my eyeballs just remembering the way it played out.

"She was saying it's my fault and that he's gone and found a different daughter now. Oh my God, the mouth on that girl. Where is she getting this language?" I drummed my nails on the kitchen island surface, waiting for her input.

"You've already hit the nail on the head, I'm sure. When she was younger, they were so much more careful. I think now they figure she knows better, and they've gotten looser with deploying the F-bombs."

Honestly, I trusted her opinion with things like this because there were a lot of hours Vela spent with her nanny. This woman knew what my daughter was exposed to.

I went through the quickest version of the events at Vela's school, in the parking lot of the shopping center afterwards, and on the phone with Elijah. With all the supporting details in place, I asked her opinion on my little one's latest mood shift.

"Are you surprised she still wanted to go to dinner?" I asked.

"Not at all."

"*Hmmm.*"

"Think about it, Pia. She's been building up the fantasy of her father for years. One little slip-up with Stella Masterson isn't going to tear that asunder."

"Good point, good point. I need to get ready because he's supposed to be here at six. What time is it?"

We both turned to look at the small clock display on the microwave and audibly gasped. Under an hour. He'd be here in under an hour, and I had to get us both presentable in that short time.

"Okay, can you help? I've already canceled piano for today, so after we leave, you will be free. Do you have plans right now?"

"I'm totally waiting up for you." She smiled slyly and nudged my shoulder as we walked toward our bedrooms.

I laughed. "I'd expect nothing else. Let's not expect anything fancy. Clean jeans without holes and whatever shirt she picks will be fine. A casual dress at most. No tights or any of those things that just cause problems. Good?"

"You got it," she said and gave a quick knock on Vela's door to let her know she was coming in. Vela didn't have a lock on her bedroom door at this age, or I'd be worrying about that too right now.

In my own bathroom, I went through the most abridged version of a shower, leg shave, and face wash possible, and then out to my bedroom, where I heard the other two ladies.

"Mom said this isn't a fancy date," I could hear Wren say. "Let's put this one back in the closet for a special date."

"This is special!" Vela shouted, and I swung my door open so fast they both froze.

"You will stay home, so help me, Vela. Andromeda. Shark. I will not tolerate you behaving this way. Are we clear?"

My stern and resonant voice did the trick.

"Mammmma, please. I want to look pretty," she whimpered. As more damn tears rolled down her red cheeks, she finished with, "Prettier than Stella."

Dropping down to my knees, I pulled her into my chest and held on with all I had. This man was going to have his balls as an amuse-bouche at the current rate. Making my daughter cry over him twice? Not a good first date, and he hadn't even arrived yet.

"You listen to me." I held her at arm's distance so we could keep each other's gaze. "It is not the dress you wear that makes you beautiful. It's what's in this amazing, abundant, beautiful heart." I lightly tapped the general spot kids thought their hearts were on her chest while giving her my most sincere love and support. "And it's what's in this gifted, talented, creative mind," I vowed while stroking her silky chocolate hair back from her warm skin.

Wren knelt down in front of my daughter too then and scooped up her little hands. "A woman's wardrobe is not her worth."

"But Mama." She bounced her glassy blue stare between her caregiver and me. "You always say it's better to look good than to feel good. I heard you say dat to Auntie Abbi."

"*That.*"

My daughter actually growled out her frustration that time and wiped her watery nose with the back of her hand.

"Sometimes adults say things that are meant as jokes, honey. You know that. I was teasing Auntie when I said that. Do you remember what happened after I said that to her?"

I waited for Vela to scan her memory.

"You both giggled and then hugged," she said with

confidence. The child, as most did, had a lock, stock, and barrel memory.

"That's right. Because we were just being silly. Now let's get ready, or Jacob will have to wait for us on the very first time he invited us out. How rude would that be?" I stood up again and squeezed Wren's shoulder in gratitude.

"Mama." Vela grabbed both my forearms with gravity. All tears gone now, she said, "He made us wait almost nine years. Ten minutes won't kill him."

CHAPTER EIGHT

JACOB

Because I got ready at my sister's place, I was already in Calabasas. When I typed Pia's address into my car's navigation system, I checked, then rechecked again for accuracy. The women weren't neighbors exactly, but only a few master-planned communities and surface streets separated them.

Christ, I was nervous. Thankful I didn't have a trying afternoon, I got ready at a casual pace but still arrived much too early. So, I sat in front of my girls' place and stared at the digital clock on the dash, setting my breathing to the throbbing colon between the hour and minutes on the display.

Fine. I had some weird habits. Over the past five years, I'd had to learn a lot of mental strategies to conquer—well, things. I wasn't placing blame for every single thing that went wrong in my life on the woman who resided behind that tall, cobalt-blue door, but her dumping me was definitely one of the defining moments of my life.

Being alone in a foreign country, homesick and heartbroken, I spent a lot of time alone and inside my head. Now, especially at times like this when I wasn't quite sure what the best way to handle something was, I skittered right back to those dark days and my expert ability to overanalyze things.

So, I sat here waging an internal war with myself. Should

I wait a few minutes past the hour, ensuring I didn't look too eager? Why would it be negative to be eager, though? Would it look better if I went to the door early? Of course, then I risked them not being ready, but it would highlight how punctual I was. That one was a draw because an argument could be made for both sides at the same time. Was this the right house? I checked the address again, knowing damn well it was. The blue door, when every other front door in sight was stained wood, was clue enough.

No matter what, I wasn't calling Law for guidance. Or any of my other brothers or sisters, for that matter. I'd never hear the end of their merciless teasing. Everyone in the family knew I was a terrible overthinker.

But I knew Pia damn well too, despite what she would argue. Certain things didn't change about a person, no matter how many years has passed between us. There was no way that a perennial early arriver would now be the woman who kept others waiting. I also knew this woman kept tight control of everything she could.

From what I knew of the man, Sebastian and his sister were very much the same. It had been difficult to shake thoughts of Shark for most of the afternoon. After that odd exchange I had with his assistant...who knows? Maybe it wasn't odd. Maybe the guy just said something in an unusual way, and I was reading too much into it.

And I completely circled the wagons. Overthinking was hardwired into my brain. Too many years trying too hard to please everyone else.

After I rang the doorbell, I could hear the same sounds I heard from behind the closed door at Cecile's—little feet running back and forth and overly loud, excited whisper-shouting that didn't afford anyone the privacy intended. Regardless of the big blue door separating us.

"He's here! Mama!" I heard the girl report.

It was so precious that she called Pia *Mama* instead of *Mom* or *Mommy*. It fit my girl so much better than one of the ordinary tags.

"Stand back, honey. Let me open the door," another female voice said, but it definitely wasn't Pia.

The stately front door was pulled inward, and Pia's assistant greeted me.

"Hi," she said with a warm smile and offered her hand. "We haven't met officially. I'm Wren. You're Mr. Cole, right?"

"Please, call me Jacob. Or Jake. Either is fine."

"Please come in. The ladies are just finishing up. Can I get you a drink?" she asked over her shoulder as we moved deeper into the home.

"No. Thank you, though." I leaned closer as if to share a little secret. "I'm so nervous, I don't think I could hold a bottle of water without spilling it right now."

We both chuckled, and it felt good to be real with someone and expel some of the extra energy that had built up while I stewed in the car debating if it was too early to call at the door.

"We're definitely used to spills around here. No one would even notice." She gave me a conspiratorial wink before quietly adding, "They're both pretty excited too."

Hearing some shuffling, we both turned, and the other women of the house appeared. The moment was breath-robbing.

The physical similarities between the two when standing side by side were uncanny. But had I been struck mute by some magical spell? Every attempt I made at greeting them got hung up somewhere between my heart and my tongue.

My heart. That damn thing felt like a red superball at the moment. A rubber ball with its own mission, apparently, as it felt like it was ricocheting off my chest walls. The sensation compelled me to reach up and rub at my sternum because seeing these two extraordinary females standing in front of me did things that both hurt and felt more joyous than anything else I'd ever known.

Was that possible? How many emotions could one person physically experience at once? Because I felt like I was running the emotional gamut.

Vela clutched her mother's hand, and every ten seconds or so, I could see the muscles in Pia's forearm tighten like a rubber band, then go slack again. Maybe they were quiet reassurances to her child—*our* child—or to herself? Maybe her muscles and nerves felt like mine? Live wires touching wet pavement, then dancing wildly up into the air only to touch down again a few seconds later.

Maybe it had been so long that I'd felt those arms around me—whether in comfort or ecstasy, it didn't fucking matter— that I was imagining all of it? Maybe I'd finally snapped and lost my damn mind from so much time denying myself intimacy?

"Hello," I said like the squarest square that ever had four sides. The mayor of Squareville, really.

"Hi." Pia smiled shyly, and that damn muscle in her forearm jumped again.

The physical cue spurred the child into motion.

Our perfect little human took a cautious step forward and offered her small hand. "Hello. I'm Vela. It's a pleasure to meet you."

Habitually, I shook the little hand thrust so bravely

toward me. Though first, I dropped down to one knee so I was at eye level with her, and I could feel that bell-clanging traitor heart of mine throwing itself violently from left to right just behind my ribs. I was afraid to open my mouth and have the whole room hear bells toll.

Ding ding dong.

Get a grip, man.

I truly heard a deep resonating gong and thought I'd given up my last fingertips' grasp on sanity. Right here.

Ding ding dong.

I knew this moment would be powerful, but I didn't expect to actually hear bells. It was more like a gong than a bell, though. Maybe the cosmos was showing me a sign. Or maybe it was the ... doorbell?

Ding ding dong.

"Are you expecting anyone else?" Wren asked Pia but then looked to me in a panic as I rose to my full height.

My beautiful woman twisted her face with curiosity. "No, and I made sure to cancel piano."

Vela's eyes went twice their size with panic. "No, Mama. Please don't make me do lessons now. I said I was sorry about the loop. Please don't do dis."

"*This*," Pia corrected, and our daughter was not impressed with the impromptu speech therapy. "Listen, I just said I canceled. We're all going out as soon as Jacob touches back down to earth." She smiled at me pointedly. "Isn't that right, Jacob?"

"Absolutely," I overcorrected, breaking through the fog with an enthusiastic smile.

"Oh. My. God," Wren muttered while peeping through the hole on the door.

"Please tell me it's not Sebastian." Pia begged the words to her assistant but had her eyes fixed on the ceiling like she was calling in the big guns.

Wren stared at her boss, desperate to manifest telepathy, but Pia just tilted her head to one side, continuing her end of the wordless conversation.

Those were my hints. As much as I wanted to stand beside her and square up with her brother if I had to, I did the right thing socially and asked, "Would you prefer some privacy? Vela, do you want to show me your—" I looked to the women, willing one of them to fill in the blank with something appropriate. I didn't think asking her to see her bedroom was my place on our first seven minutes of officially being introduced.

"The backyard!" Wren shouted, and we all gaped at her like she sprouted a red clown nose.

"Ohhh kay. The backyard would be a great place to go right now," I said, slowly pronouncing each word and giving someone—hell, *anyone*—the opportunity to come up with something better.

"We have a pool!" Vela announced, clueless to what was going on around her with the adults but now totally embracing her new tour-guide duties.

"You do? You are so lucky! Show me?" I started following my daughter as she zipped ahead. I laughed. "Wait for me! I don't know where I'm going." My smile spread as she doubled back.

"Sorry," she apologized, then stopped all that abundant, energetic movement for a profound second, and it was like the earth stood still and breathed with us both.

Vela earnestly admitted, "I'm so excited you're finally here."

And she was off again, skipping ahead around the pool deck with the jabbering picking right back up like we hadn't just shared that special moment.

But hell yes we had, and I would cherish it forever.

"Do you like to swim? I do. And I can do the backstroke, and my Uncle Lijah is an amaaaazing swimmer. He taught me how," she said with a dip of her chin, decreeing what she claimed to be law. Obviously, Elijah Banks was popular with the mini lady crowd too.

I gave a look over my shoulder and into the house just as Pia opened the door.

What the fuck?

Another man, encumbered with a huge floral bouquet, charged in and swept her into a twirling hug.

Yep. Backyard tour over. "Okay, I think your mom's ready to go now," I insisted. But I might as well have been chirping with the birds in the overhead branches of the stately palms dotting the SoCal weather friendly landscape of the backyard.

"You didn't see the best part!" she said, halfway across the lawn on the far side of the pool. "You have to come here. We'll just be a minute. She'll be okay. Dis was her idea," Vela reminded me with an impatient eye roll.

Was it my place to correct that speech thing? Probably not without talking to Pia first, but I wanted to get back inside as soon as possible and see who the guy was. And what was he thinking getting handsy with my woman? With me in the same house?

Yeah, things were going to change around here real fast.

I hurried after Vela while she prattled on about the pool, the barbeque her uncles argued about while putting together, and nearly everything else just shy of the gutters and downspouts. My goodness, she barely came up for a single gulp of oxygen by the time we made our lap around the beautiful backyard.

I was especially captivated by the grotto built into the pool's hardscape and had to bite my cheek a few times to keep my thoughts appropriate for the audience. I'm sure I could rig up some sort of restraint in there for her mother, though.

Back inside, I slammed the glass slider home in its frame with a bit more force than intended, and the couple still congregated near the front door jumped.

I bent down to address our daughter. "Will you please find Wren and make sure you're all set to leave? We have to drive about twenty minutes, so you may want to use the bathroom before we go."

"Good idea." She nodded soundly, giving me a high-five as she bounced down the hall the women first came from in that magical moment earlier.

Time to take out the trash.

"Ready to go, Star? Our daughter is using the washroom before we head out. Traffic...you know?" I kept Pia's gaze while thrusting my hand toward the schmo in her foyer.

"Jacob Cole," I offered in a friendly enough tone. "How's it going, man?"

"Yeah, hey." He barely lifted his chin in my direction, also not offering his name. Hopefully, we could end this before the child returned.

"Look, guy. You seem like a nice enough person. Maybe a little dense, though, so I'm going to spell this out for you and do it quickly and quietly because our daughter is only a few rooms away. You've reached your expiration date in this woman's life." I motioned to Cassiopeia then snuck her a fast wink.

"Do not call her. Do not ever, seriously dude, *evvv errr*, drop by this home, or her office, without calling first and receiving permission from my woman and me. Take care of yourself and drive carefully."

"Jacob—" Pia gasped but did nothing more to stop what was happening. That gave me the green light to finish this.

The guy just stared slack-jawed between her and me, so I strode over to the blue door and *whooshed* the thing open in a grand gesture.

"Off you go, now. And, buddy, I get it. She's hard to get over. Been there." Shaking my head in commiseration, I gave the dipshit two hearty smacks on the back as he passed by, and he aggressively threw his shoulder to dislodge my palm.

He still clutched the now-crushed and sad-looking bouquet in his meaty hand.

"Dumbass."

The door *thunked* shut behind him the moment he cleared the jamb, and I turned to rest against it, schooling every chest-beating, caveman sentiment that sprang to mind.

With no sincerity in my tone, I commented to my shoes, "He seemed nice."

"Ready!" our little girl sang as she hopped back into the room. "Oh..." She looked around, then to Pia. "Where's Stoney?"

That was the final straw for me. A laugh that sounded much more like a bark escaped, and once I started, I couldn't stop. All the anxiety that had cranked up in the room leading up to that innocent child's question popped free like the cork in a shaken bottle of champagne.

While we all had a good laugh, Pia explained, "His name is Boulder."

That gem of information only served to make us all laugh more.

"Have fun! If I crash on the sofa, don't wake me," Wren muttered to Pia as they hugged one last time.

Christ, I was bringing them back after dinner. I wasn't kidnapping them forever.

Although ... the idea had merit.

At the curb, Pia helped Vela into the back seat, where Stella's booster was still in place from the after-school pickup.

"Oh, hey, this is just like my booster, right, Mama? Jacob, how did you know I would need a booster? Oh, you probably told him, right, Mama?" She fired question after question, not waiting for an answer to the previous one before moving on to another.

"Oh my God, this is insanity," Pia muttered into the cradle of her hands when we were all situated inside.

I, on the other hand, put the car into drive with the biggest, dopiest smile I could remember having.

When she finally sneaked a peek and saw my expression, she chuckled. "Is this amusing?"

When we got to the first red light after exiting the neighborhood, I finally answered. "This is happy," I said and gave her a quick study before the light changed and I had to drive again. "Thank you both for coming tonight."

"We're happy too, Jacob. Right, Mama? Hey..." She waited for one of us to acknowledge, and out of habit, I thought, Pia took charge.

"Hay is for horses. Did you want to interrupt a conversation and ask something, though?" She looked over her left shoulder into the back seat, and I just watched her.

Years made my college girl a goddess. She was beautiful

when we were in school, of course. But motherhood and life added so much wisdom and character to her features. I couldn't wait to have her beneath me again so I could stare down into those endless, imaginative eyes and try to work my way back into the memories fluttering behind her chestnut lashes.

Pia wore very minimal make-up on her flawless skin. I noticed our daughter had the smattering of freckles I'd had when I was a child, and it made me smile softly. The girls were still chatting about something I'd tuned out while greedily reacquainting myself with Pia's beauty, and it wasn't until she said my name with a bit of impatience that I realized they were waiting for an answer.

"I'm so sorry. I zoned out. Can you repeat the question, please?"

"We were wondering where you were taking us," Pia supplied.

"I can go to adult restaurants," Vela interjected from the back seat. "Right, Mama? It doesn't have to be Crap Donald's or Toxic Hell."

"Vela," Pia admonished. "What did I just tell you about the profanity? Not three hours ago."

"That's the name of the place. Uncle Grant calls it that all the time. He loves the tacos that smell bad and make him—"

"That's enough." Pia clipped her off right there. "We don't need to hear about Uncle Grant's iron stomach that only Taco Bell can topple."

Pia hid her face in her palms again, and I grinned. But this time, not thinking, I reached over and squeezed her thigh so she'd look at me.

Shit, though, when she did, the heat coming off her features was measurable from my spot behind the wheel. I just couldn't tell if it was from desire like the inferno inside my body or anger. Always such a fine line with the lady.

"Don't," she whisper-hissed, then shot her indigo glare over her shoulder.

Okay, got it. Not in front of our daughter. And she was right, we didn't need to confuse the kid more than she already was.

"Ease up, though, yeah?" I said quietly. "She said *crap*. The world isn't going to stop rotating, Cass."

"You have no idea the day we've had," she muttered. "And the cussing is just the start of it."

We both took turns looking back while talking about Vela while she sat just three feet away.

In a tone Vela could clearly hear and know she was being invited back into the conversation, I suggested, "There's a tapas place I've been wanting to try. How does that sound?"

Pressing her lips together, Pia answered, "That might be good."

"Do I like paws? I don't know if I do," our passenger added, and pressed a little index finger to her chin.

A smile lit up my woman's face, and it felt like I was basking in sunlight. Parenting was such an interesting and challenging role. Constantly setting the right stage and monitoring the literal and figurative language yet finding joy in it all too. It was like watching someone juggle butcher knives—thrilling and life altering with every decision or misstep.

"Tapas it is!" I decided for the group because I sensed we would get to Highland Avenue before everyone agreed on anything else.

In the restaurant, the food wasn't the only thing grilled. The way they were firing questions at me made me suspicious the two of them staged their attack. One would lead off with a seemingly harmless question, then the other would go in for the kill.

This child of mine was much smarter than I first gave her credit for. And with absolutely no disrespect to Cecile—because Lord knew that woman had her hands full with so many other gigantic marital problems for much of Stella's young life—but Vela was head and shoulders smarter than my niece.

She maintained adult conversation better than some adults I knew, and I reminded myself to mention my amazement and gratitude to Cassiopeia. So many things the little girl said were words taken right from her mother's playbook. When that happened, a particular unstoppable grin spread across my face, and I'd get the side-eye from Pia.

"What?" I asked after one of those looks.

"I'm trying to figure out what's setting off that grin every few minutes." She smirked, having caught the grin fever too.

"She's so much like you. Like a little you. It's doing things to my"—I rubbed the center of my chest—"insides. She's wonderful, Pia. Thank you."

Vela was busy playing on an iPad that Pia produced from thin air, and we finally had some semi-private conversation.

"Why are you thanking me?" she inquired, and that made me smile even more. Loving this woman had always been so effortless. As easy and natural for me as breathing. Having her enjoying a meal with our daughter and me was so much more than I would've dreamed possible. Even as recently as this week, when we first saw one another after so long and I first found out I was a father. All the hurt that had been stored away for nine years mucked up the interactions we tried to have.

This. This right here, though, was what I wanted from our reunion. Our connection, even if it had to come in glimpses for now, I'd take it. When we were younger, we were convinced our love had been written in the stars. A love everlasting—for each of us, our one true love. I still believed that about the stunning woman currently waiting for me to say something and not just stare at her with cartoon love hearts coming out of my eyes.

"I'm sorry, what did you ask?"

"Are you on medication or something?" She chuckled when asking, but it wasn't a real laugh.

"What? Why are you asking me that? What am I doing? Are you going to eat this last bite?" I held up one of the small square plates, and she shook her head.

Pia lifted her shoulders then dropped them softly. She wasn't being confrontational, just inquisitive. "You zone out a lot."

"Trust me, I'm not normally like this." I laughed because I couldn't be alone in this. We couldn't have gone from star-crossed lovers to little or no feelings or physical chemistry. "There's just no way."

"No way *what*? See, this is what I mean. If you aren't staring off into space, you're randomly saying things that have nothing to do with the conversation we're having. Does that not sound like a person taking some sort of mind-altering medication?"

"It's you."

Pia stared, saying nothing.

"You're the drug. You're the one doing this to my brain, and Christ, girl, what you're doing to my body is another conversation completely. My God, it's been so long, you have no idea." I let my eyelids droop closed and thought about fucking her. "Seeing you, smelling you, being in the car with you. It's like my brain is getting fried on some sort of drug, all right. It's called lust, or longing. Or hell, if you really want to freak out, we can go for broke and call it what it really is."

"And what is that?" she asked, leaning closer with every low, seductive comment I made, like I was reeling her in on a fishing line.

Our foreheads were leaning toward each other like we were moments from kissing. We were, right? *Should we be?* I could just move in a bit closer while I dropped the last part of my thought.

I rasped, "Love."

CHAPTER NINE

PIA

"Are you kissing?" Vela asked in a vocal cocktail of glee and outrage.

"No, we're talking quietly. Like you should be. Please use inside volume, honey."

So many things were becoming clear to me this evening. The two big standouts, of course, centered around the little queen sitting across the dinner table from her father and me.

Jesus—talk about words I never thought I would combine in the same sentence.

For one thing, I now understood why women waited to introduce their date to their child until well into the relationship. Not like that was an option with Jake, but we wouldn't be taking her on a date with us again anytime soon. In my own defense, I wasn't actually expecting any sort of date vibes during this meal.

Secondly, I had to be very careful with Jacob. Feelings were alive and well between us, and it was scary. I thought I might have been in some sort of safety time zone—like the amount of time that had passed between us would act as a buffer. Dulled, if not killed, all the feels.

I was wrong.

Jacob and I broke up by design. A design I created and

then crafted. Every element of that design was in the vein of self-preservation and the wellbeing of our child. None of it—not one single thing—had to do with my feelings for him burning out.

But now with so many years having passed, there were a lot of holes in our collective story. They were gaps that needed to be attended to or we would fall through them over and over again. I was already seriously considering keeping a small journal handy to jot things down that he said in passing that either didn't make sense or that I wanted to touch back on later when we could have a private conversation. Granted, this was our first civil meeting since reuniting, but the list was already getting too long for me to mentally track.

I waited for Vela to go back to the game she was playing before I reengaged in conversation with Jacob.

"This was delicious," I said to my date. "You've never been here before?"

"No. I've seen it driving by, and of course I miss the food from Spain. I miss a lot of things about that place, but I've been wanting to try this spot. I'm glad we got to do it together."

Immediately, pangs of jealousy zapped my stomach. And that was a feeling that had no place at this table. But my naturally curious mind hopped right over the warning guardrail in my head and heart and continued tormenting me.

Was it a woman in Barcelona he was missing? Or *women*? This man had an incredibly voracious sexual appetite. Or at least he did nine years ago. I'm sure he sampled the local fare plenty. But I had no right to ask him about any of that, especially since he hadn't mentioned Boulder once since the incident at the front door.

Served that dipshit right, though. Showing up

unannounced and uninvited the way he did. I never took visitors in that manner and didn't plan on changing now. Whether it was controlling of me or not, people owed me the courtesy of letting me know when they were coming to my house.

I knew my brother was the exact same way, and I wasn't sure if it was yet another scar from our childhood. We had to hide from social services when they came by our house, which was supposed to be abandoned, so they wouldn't take us away.

Bas instilled a fear in me of that happening that was bone deep. It was a miracle I ever got to the point where I could let my own child out of my sight and not be paralyzed with fear that she'd been taken from me.

Vivid memories from my childhood of the way my mother had scurried around the house, cleaning up after my father before their friends or family were coming over, fed the preference too. He'd always had empty bottles lying around somewhere.

The man was such a slob, from what my little brain recalled. As an adult, it was hard to understand why she stayed with him as long as she did. Or even more confusing, what was she thinking creating a third child with the man?

If she hadn't done that—if she hadn't risked her life in another pregnancy—maybe she would still be here today to help me understand the world better than I did. Maybe she would still be here to help me teach my daughter how to be a strong and brave young woman in this world.

"Now who's zoning out?" Jacob teased.

"You're right," I said with a shy smile. "My apologies. There's so much swimming around in here." I tapped my temple with my index finger. "You know?"

"Oh, believe me. I know." He paused after supplying that but looked like he wanted to say more.

"What? That sounded like you cut yourself off. Ask whatever you want, Jake. Whatever it is. There's no use hiding things from each other, especially if we're going to co-parent a child."

"I want to ask you every question that pops into my mind. And there are so many. I want to spend days just listening to you tell me about everything. About the years I've missed, and I don't want you to skip a single detail."

He was as excited as his daughter when she learned something new. I never realized she got that from him. But as I sat and listened to him jabber on and on, all I could think was how much she was like him.

We'd all vowed that Vela was a Shark, through and through. Again, that was by my design. I created the small person she currently was by teaching her my mannerisms, my way of doing things. But sitting here, getting reacquainted with her other biological contributor, I could see what an amazing mix of the two of us she was.

"I won't change her name," I blurted in a panic. "She's always been a Shark."

Would he expect her to change her name? I couldn't just let go of all the years she and I built together. We had to fight to make our way alone, and I couldn't just step aside and let him start calling the shots.

"It would just be weird to give her Cole now," I continued. "Confusing, you know?" I motioned between him and me. "I don't want her to be confused about what's going on here."

"Let's agree on something from this moment forward," he offered. "I think it will save us both our sanity."

His declaration sounded like a PowerPoint introduction. This wasn't a business deal or a design contract. What the hell convinced him that talking about our child and her emotional wellbeing should sound anything like laying out the groundwork of a corporate merger?

The panic I felt over changing her name ballooned. I didn't want to make any sort of agreement about anything right now while I was so anxious. Was he rushing me to agree to things on purpose? Was he trying to take her away from me? Already?

"What do you mean?" I retorted, trying to ratchet down my anxiety a few notches.

"Let's just take it one day at a time," he said. "I don't want to overstep. I'm not trying to barge in and take over as if I know better. The last thing I want to do is disrupt the obviously very well-behaved, very well-adjusted, very loved human you've been working on."

He waited for me to say something or give some sort of visual cue that I received his words as intended.

I gave a quick nod that would hopefully encourage him to continue if he had more to say, because he just pulled the rug right out from under me with that offer. By the way he came out of the gate, the notion was the opposite of where I thought he would go.

"My deepest hope right now is that you are patient with me and that you can make some room for me in your busy lives." Again, he waited for me to respond, and I noticed our daughter was all ears now, too.

Vela put the iPad down with a bit of a clatter. There were so many little plates all over the table with various stages of food debris on them, it was hard to find enough space for the device. She was around the table and standing beside my chair in a moment.

"May I use the restroom, please?" she asked along with an urgent foot-to-foot weight shift.

"Of course. Let's see if we can find it really quick," I said, already standing and grabbing my bag from the back of my chair. I swooped across the table and grabbed the iPad, stuffing it in my bag while telling Jacob, "Be right back. Please let me treat?"

He guffawed. "Not on your life. Do you want a drink? Coffee?"

Over my shoulder I called, "No thank you. Be right back," and hustled behind my daughter, who was almost jogging now that she had the restroom in sight.

Inside the bathroom I said, "You doing okay?"

She went into the stall to do her thing, and I waited just outside the door.

"Yep!" she chirped. "I think it's going well, don't you?"

I burst out laughing, as I sometimes did when she said things so strangely adult for her age.

"Uh-oh," she replied, and I stopped laughing immediately. That was a word you didn't want to hear while your kid was in a public restroom.

"What's wrong?" I asked quickly.

The toilet flushed, and she was off to wash her hands, me following right behind.

"Why did you say 'uh-oh'? Is there anything that needs to be dealt with?" I pointed back to the stall, wondering if she had a bit of an accident.

"Nope! All good. I was saying that cause the way you laughed. That usually means not good things." She schooled me via our reflections in the mirror behind the line of sinks.

"I was laughing at how incredibly smart you are. That's all.

And to answer your question, yes, I think it's going fine. What about you? How do you think things are going?"

But instead of answering my query, she hit me with another one of her own. "Are you having a sleepover?"

"No."

"Are you going to make Wren move away? Please don't do that. I love her so much."

"I would never do that. And she loves you that much and then some. Facts."

"Can Jacob come over tomorrow?"

"Probably not tomorrow," I said over the loud hand dryer. I grabbed a towel from the dispenser and pulled the door open, but she wouldn't budge.

"The next day?"

"We'll see. Come on. I wanted to treat tonight, but we're going to miss the waitress because we're taking so long," I explained, thinking that might entice her. She loved doing the extra things when we went out, like paying the bill or holding the door for everyone.

"But Mama." Just like that, those blue eyes that held all my secrets and the answers to my world's most complicated questions filled with tears. "Stellllla."

Back behind the privacy of the restroom entrance, I promised, "I will get to the bottom of that, but Jacob is not going anywhere. You just heard everything he said through the entire meal. He will want to come over again."

The only thing I could do was wrap her in a warm, reassuring hug and repeat two more times on the way back to the table that he would come visit again another day.

On my mental to-do list, I added scheduling an appointment with Vela's therapist. And mine, too. Since starting that first mental list of questions to ask the man more details, I started a second one as well.

This list's items would be more challenging for me to conquer, I already knew it with complete honesty and accuracy. I knew myself well enough after years as an adult and as a single mother thrown in to boot; I had major control issues.

How would I let this man take my child out of my presence? What if he wanted to have a daddy-daughter. day together? And I knew my daughter had created at least twenty-three fantasies surrounding the guy already. Hell, they were in her little dreamer's head before the dude even showed back up in my orbit at the beginning of the week.

"We're all set here whenever you ladies are ready. No rush, though." Jacob stood to push our chairs in when we came back to the table. For my ears, he asked, "Everything okay in there? That seemed a bit long?"

He wasn't wrong. We had definitely been away from the table longer than a normal bathroom visit, but I still must have looked skeptical when cautiously answering.

"Fine. All good."

"What?" he asked when I kept my eyes trained on him when he sat down.

It took me a moment to organize my thoughts. I was doing my best not to be or sound defensive or suspicious at every turn. It wasn't always something I pulled off well.

"I'm trying to decide how you came to the conclusion that was a longer than average trip to the ladies' room. With a child, I mean." Keeping my features relaxed and as neutral as possible helped me believe I did a better job of it this time.

"I have a niece Vela's age. Or close to it. She's eight."

"I'm eight!" my daughter chimed in but quickly added, "but I'm going to be nine really soon. Right, Mama?"

"Yes." I smiled. "In a few more months."

"When is your birthday?" Jacob asked Vela directly. "What date?"

"You didn't see me happen?" Vela asked, puzzled.

"Well, I saw part of it. But it was early days, you know." He chuckled at his own dumb guy humor, and I groaned.

"Stop now while you're ahead," I tried warning the poor fool. "She picks up way more than you think." If he wasn't careful, he'd be having *The Talk* with his almost nine-year-old daughter by the time we got back in the car.

"Oh, I figured that out earlier. Like a sponge, I'm guessing." Then he pointedly turned more toward me in his seat, and I looked on with a bit of concern. Based on the look he was giving me, anxiety quickly mounted regarding what was about to come out of his mouth.

"You've done an amazing job, Cass. I'm in complete awe, and honestly, for the first time in my life, I believe it's possible to love another woman besides you."

"Yes," Vela muttered but kept her eyes on the table. A little smile kissed the corner of her mouth while she tried to contain her joy.

"You didn't tell me, darling. Your birthdate," he prompted our daughter while taking a pose of deep concentration. "I have to store it in my brain so I always remember."

"It's November twenty-first. I'm a Scorpio, but I don't know what that means because I'm also a Shark. My uncle Sebastian says that's the only thing I need to remember in my whole life."

I couldn't help but grin widely at that proclamation. Let's

see the man try to talk her out of the name. She had as much Shark pride as the rest of us. My brother made sure of it.

"Your uncle is a very smart man," Jake agreed. Did he sense the gloves would come off if he tried to say otherwise?

"He knows so many things, it hurts my head when he talks at his office," Vela said. "I have a baby cousin. His name is Kaisan, and now my auntie Abbigail is making another baby! Did you know that?"

"I did. Your uncle Sebastian and I do a lot of work together. I've gotten to know him a little bit over the past few months," Jacob explained after we all agreed we were ready to leave.

While we walked out to the car and I listened to Jake qualify his relationship with Bas to Vela, I had a thought.

"Why weren't you at the groundbreaking ceremony? For the Edge? I mean, it's your design. Didn't you want to deal with the press?"

"Unreal," he muttered and opened my door.

"What is?" With barely a pause, I asked my kiddo, "Do you need help with the seat belt, Star?"

"I got it," my daughter chirped from the back seat.

He waited until he was settled in behind the wheel and chuckled and shook his head again.

"What's unreal?"

"If I had been at that ceremony, I would've seen you. But that much sooner. I'm just kicking myself now."

"So why weren't you there? I'm just curiously prying into your life. Forgive me," I apologized awkwardly once I realized how rude I was being.

"You aren't prying. I told you to ask me anything. I meant it. I was in Barcelona. A bunch of us did an alumni reunion thing."

"Oh" was all I said at first, attempting to inject some brightness into the comment with a follow-up. "That sounds nice."

At the first light, he said quietly, "I would have rather been reuniting with you."

How should I react to these comments? Another uncomfortable smile and quick look over my shoulder to meet two very inquisitive blue eyes staring right back at me.

"Did you have a nice time at dinner, Miss Shark?" I asked Vela instead of dealing with Jake's comment.

"It was lovely, Ms. Shark. You?" my daughter replied in her best adult tone.

"I should say as well, thank you," I said in my best formal society lady voice. "Bed when we get home. No arguments, even if Wren went to the back."

"I know, I know," she grumbled.

"Went to the back? What does that mean? I feel like there's so much to learn." Jake laughed.

"Wren lives in a granny flat on my property. It's in the back of our house, so we've always just worded it that way."

"Oh, I see. I wondered if she lived in your house."

"Almost." I smiled. "She needs her own space every now and then, so I send her back."

"Has she been helping you for a long time? You two seem pretty close."

"Yes, she started babysitting for me when Vela was just a baby. I needed a nanny, but she was so young, and I had to"—I looked heavenward, trying to find a tactful expression to use—"strongly encourage her to stay in school until she graduated."

"I'm not following."

Jacob Cole was definitely going to have to step up his fill-in-the-blanks game if he wanted to hang around my nosey kid more.

"Her mom is the meanest of all mean meanies," Vela interjected, and I nodded.

"Yes, that." I thumbed over my shoulder. "I gave her the opportunity to leave a very abusive home once she was a legal adult, but there were times"—I shook my head, remembering the condition in which she would show up to our house—"we weren't sure she was going to make it out alive."

"Why make her stay in that sort of environment?"

"No, I made her stay in school, not in the home. Big difference."

"I should say. I misunderstood you there. Sorry about that." Jacob took in the landscape from his window and then out the front windshield again. He even ducked down to see the name of the street on the sign swaying above the intersection.

"This is Archibald?" he asked, mapping a line out the windshield from left to right.

"Yes. It's two more lights in this direction. Sorry, I should've been paying closer attention." Why would I expect him to know how to get back to my house without guidance? Maybe because he seemed so familiar with everything else in the area.

"No, that's not what made me ask. My sister Cecile lives off Marquette. It's right in this neighborhood, if I'm not mistaken. I know I drive on Archibald to turn into her community."

"She lives in Calabasas? What a coincidence."

"No, I mean she lives in one of those houses." He gesticulated toward the homes that were visible through the windshield. "We're that close."

"It truly is a small world," I commented and then felt

like an imbecile that it had taken that long for the pieces to snap together. The Stella mystery was unraveling with that new information, but I still wanted to have the confirming conversation with Jake without Vela in earshot.

Every time the topic of any of her classmates was even hinted at, her physical demeanor shifted. A call to the director went on the mental checklist because I needed to be completely sure there wasn't more going on at school. While I could appreciate their desire to handle unsavory behavior on the spot and not get the parents involved until necessary, I felt compelled to ensure what I was seeing at home wasn't a byproduct of a larger problem.

Additionally, I didn't want to upset her again. And speaking honestly, I didn't want Mr. Cole here to know the kind of emotional and psychological hold he already had on her. If he witnessed one of her little fits of jealousy, I'd be mortified.

Her exemplary behavior was always a source of personal pride for me. Her uncles and I worked continuously to teach her what was and wasn't appropriate behavior, especially in public. These recent meltdowns were new territory for her and me.

Nothing wrong with getting some reassurance from the pros. While the thought was private, apparently my stamp of self-approval was out front and center.

"What?" my date asked, and I giggled a bit thinking how many times one of us asked that of the other tonight.

"That's going to be our new motto at this rate," I explained.

"I don't want to miss a thing. Now or ever again."

With that bold declaration, Jacob slid the car into park and shut the engine off. He put his index finger against his lips and directed my attention to the back seat. All the excitement had finally taken its toll on Vela, as she was sleeping awkwardly with her face mashed against the headrest of the booster.

Now what? he mouthed.

I wanted to laugh. How many options were there?

He asked his next question, but I couldn't make heads or tails of what he was saying, so he motioned me closer across the armrest.

"Will she stay sleeping if I carry her?" he spoke into my ear, and the sensation was so similar to a lover's caress of breath, goosebumps prickled across my arms and thighs.

It was doubtful, and my expression must have conveyed that. Jacob motioned me close again to whisper his next question.

"Thank you, incredible woman."

I tilted my head enough to give him a side-eye of curiosity.

"You've done an amazing job with her, and I will be forever in your shadow. I know this. But I can't thank you enough for giving me the chance to get to know her."

A slow smile took over my lips, and I gently rolled my head from side to side to ease the tension in my neck. When I looked back toward him, Jacob was still staring at me, but he had shifted so our faces were just inches apart.

It would definitely be a mistake to let him kiss me. A big, big mistake. We had so much to sort through. Confusing things more by involving physical feelings would be bad.

Baaaaad.

I just had to keep telling myself that, or I'd get caught up in something. Something like how incredible he smelled. His cologne was intoxicating. It was the perfect mix of the ocean and fresh herbs. Maybe rosemary or sage? But on the man, it was so masculine and inviting. I wanted to run my nose along his throat and greedily inhale him. The scent would stay with me for the rest of the night, at least. Longer in my memory.

Jacob was more handsome now than when we were in college. It was unfair but true that men aged differently than women. Wrinkles around his eyes that deepened when he smiled or when he was deep in thought added to his manly appeal. Once boyish and fresh-faced, Jacob had a dark stubble that probably grew in by lunchtime, based on its appearance now that the moon was out.

"Can I kiss you?" This time when he spoke in my ear, his voice was not only low in volume, but the timbre was so dark and sex-heavy, I had to swallow a few times to find my voice to respond.

"I don't think we should" was all I could come up with. I didn't want to answer with a flat-out no because it wasn't how I truly felt. I wanted to feel his mouth on mine again after all these years. I wanted it more than anything else I could think of.

"I know I'm not the only one feeling this right now," he said with confidence. "I know it's been a long time and all, but some things don't change."

Yes, a subject change. Sure, it was very slight, but I seized the opportunity and answered quickly, "I think we've probably both changed quite a bit in nine years."

"What I'm saying is I know how to read the air in this vehicle right now. We both want the same thing." He patiently looked on, almost daring me to deny it with his confident stare.

He'd definitely gained a lot of patience since we were in college. Where he was once a bit of a hot head, especially when he wasn't getting his way, he now merely shifted in his seat to intensify his focus.

"I don't want to confuse her," I blurted adamantly. Or, as much as one could while whispering.

"Fair enough. I don't want that either. Let me help you get her inside, then I'll say goodnight." Jake motioned with his chin toward the house and suggested, "Why don't you make sure the door is unlocked."

He set the plan, and together we accomplished the goal. It was so natural to follow his lead, I just complied. I couldn't think of another person who ever had that influence over me.

Maybe we could find our way back through all the dust and cobwebs. Just like time was the ultimate thing that stood between us, time would be the only thing that would tell if we could love each other again.

I wasn't fooling myself, though. At least I didn't think I was. As I hurried in front of the man who carried our child so tenderly in his capable arms, I reminded myself that his good nature could only last so long. Eventually he would demand an explanation. A long, honest conversation about why I cut him out of her life for so long. Why I thought I knew what was best for all of us and made that choice without giving him a say.

Jacob deserved that, too. So far, he was being very patient and considerate through all of this. Granted, it hadn't been a full week since we'd found each other again, but some people would've wanted the whole saga on the spot.

Where did you go? Why did you leave? Why did you cut me off like we never mattered? Why would you choose single parenting when we could've been a family?

All those questions would come, and he deserved the answers. Every single one. The thing I was most concerned about, though, wasn't not being brave enough to have that hard conversation with the man I once called my everything.

It was looking into his eyes after I gave him all the answers. Sometimes, people wanted mysteries solved but then were sorry they'd pressed so hard for the resolution.

Other times, no matter how you told and retold your story, the bottom line was the same. People made mistakes. People made bad decisions every day. Could I lay my heart at his feet and ask for forgiveness? Was that really what I needed from all of this? It didn't feel that way inside, or I would've made things "right" a long time ago.

That wasn't to say I hadn't been living with regrets about the way things transpired. My natural inclination was to blame my brother more than anyone, including myself. Which was utter chicken-shit and not at all fair to Bas.

Yes, he'd had a lot to do with why things snowballed so fast when I found out I was going to be an unwed mother. And I'd done enough self-examination and hours with my therapist to understand where my brother's heart lay when he railroaded my life and my decisions. It was the role he was used to playing. Sebastian was a fixer. All the guys were. While their hearts were filled with the best intentions, they tended to completely steamroll whoever was in the way of the most thorough, tidiest solution to the problems they faced.

From the doorway, I watched Jacob lay our daughter in her bed. He was so careful and gentle with her. Watching them made my heart ache, but in an even combination of happy and sad ways.

Wren hovered in the hallway to go in after we left to get her situated. The woman was such a godsend. I never had to ask her to do things. She was always right there to help me. We ducked back out as quietly as possible and made our way back into the living room.

"Thank you for a lovely dinner. I'm glad we did it," I said, not sure what to do with my hands while I spoke. I ended up fussing with a pillow on the sofa and then setting it in the exact spot it had been.

"Can we hang out a bit? Unless you're too tired. I don't want to keep you up past your bedtime." He treated me to an easy grin and a quick wink, and my stomach actually fluttered like a teenager's. How had I forgotten how charming Jake could be?

Shyly, I responded, "Sure, I think I have a little gas left in the tank. Think I'll have a cappuccino, though. Would you like one?"

He followed me into the kitchen, where I got busy with the machine on the counter. Grant had given me the appliance for my birthday a few years back, and I hadn't had a plain cup of coffee since.

"A beer sounds better," my date answered.

"I think you might be in luck. Let me see what I have in the other refrigerator."

Jacob offered instead. "I can help myself while you do that. Point me in the right direction?"

I directed him toward the laundry room, where I had a second refrigerator for entertaining and daily overflow. Likely because of my father's alcoholism, I didn't like a lot of adult beverages in the same fridge my daughter went in and out of. Probably silly, but it was one of the many unexplained weird habits I had. But for so long, I was the only adult with a say in the house, so I did what I wanted, the way I wanted.

By the time he found his way back to the kitchen, I had my steaming coffee in hand. "Join me outside on the deck? I think it's a pretty clear night."

He gave me a knowing smile because I was obtusely rekindling an old favorite activity of ours. We used to spend hours outside under the star-filled sky. Talking, laughing, kissing—all the things you do with a lover when it seems like you are the only two people in the world. We would never recapture the innocence and freedom of our hearts from that moment in time, but we had a lot of catching up to do regardless.

We got comfortable on the sumptuous lounge furniture I had arranged by the water's edge. I spent a lot of time out here in the warm months, and when it cooled down, I had a great firepit that was easy to use and gave off ample heat. We both sank into the cushions of the same sofa and angled our bodies toward each other.

"She's just so amazing, Cass. I can't stop grinning. And smart as a whip, huh?"

"Oh, dude. You don't even know the half of it." My smile grew as I spoke about Vela. "I'm always so proud of her, but then there are times that I think she's growing up way too fast, and I want to freeze time so I can get my fill of her at every stage."

"Yeah, I guess she probably changes every day. Like what she's into and that sort of thing. My niece is like that too."

"Can we talk about your niece for a little bit? I have a sort of confession. I just didn't want to get into it with the queen present."

"Of course. I told you earlier, and I meant it. Ask whatever you want to know. I'm hoping I can have that same freedom with you?" He said that part as a clear question, so I started nodding before saying a word.

"Yes, I think it's best. Full disclosure on all things."

"It's a deal," Jacob said and raised his bottle for me to tap with my cup.

"But I have to warn you ahead of time..."

He looked at me with a worrisome twist to his lips, so I reassured him. *Kind of.*

"I think as we rehash some things that happened in the past, bad feelings might come up." I held up my hands in ready surrender. "And I don't blame you. Not for a second. I just wanted to say that. I'm dealing with the fact that I have nine years of explaining to do. I'm not kidding myself thinking by tomorrow we're going to be LA's hottest new couple."

"Full disclosure, right?" he asked.

I nodded resolutely.

"Just show me where to sign up. I'd commit right now, Star. I'm not wanting to pressure you or freak you out with that. I know we have a lot of time to make up for. But I never stopped loving you. Not for one day."

How do I react to that?

I couldn't stop the grin that spread across my lips after his declaration. But I didn't want to add more fuel to the fire, because he was right, we did have a lot to work through.

Deep down, my heart knew it wouldn't take much to make the same sort of commitment he just vocalized. Yes, it had been nine years. Still, when I sat there looking at his handsome profile in the calm, balmy night, my heart felt like it had been nine minutes. It would be so easy to dive right back in since we both were feeling the same way. So easy to sweep the whole nine-year mess under the rug and carry on like nothing ever happened.

But I knew that over time, that pile of unanswered questions would start leaking from the threadbare places in the rug. Whenever a weakness was revealed, unresolved issues or unspent feelings of resentment—whatever he was feeling— would poke through the thin spots and hurt our soles. Our *souls*, actually.

"What did you say your niece's name is? Stella, right?"

"Yes, that's right. She's gorgeous. You should see her. She looks like a little doll with a shock of orange curls on top." He motioned in a circle above his head as if drawing a halo. "And the biggest, most inquisitive green eyes I've ever seen on a child. The difference is remarkable, really. And I mean no disrespect toward my sister."

"What do you mean?"

"When I look at our daughter, whether she's listening to you tell her something or she's prattling on about something, she has such wisdom in her eyes. Like she knows things in here"—he tapped his temple—"in her mind, but maybe she hasn't discovered she knows them yet. But it's all in there. She's so intelligent." He shook his head and chuckled. "I know I keep saying that."

"I understand what you mean, though. I think from being around more adults than children most of her life, she has an element of maturity that doesn't belong in her eight-year-old body."

"My niece is different. When she talks, plays, listens to Cecile, there is a wonder in her stare like she is literally learning as fast as her mind can take it all in. Whereas Vela seems like she'd be the one doing the teaching."

I almost choked on my cappuccino while laughing. He wasn't that far off the mark with his early assessment, either.

I set my cup and saucer on the table beside the sofa and said, "Just don't say things like that around her. Goes right to her head. She takes after Bas that way."

We both laughed at the comment, but again, it was the complete truth.

"So what is this confession? I have one myself, but you go first."

"No, you first." Coyly, I said, "You are the guest, after all."

"I want to hold your hand while we talk."

Well, I asked for it. I thought I was being clever, prolonging telling him about the after-school pickup today, but he'd caught me completely off guard.

I offered my hand after a moment. I really wanted to lie in his arms or with my head on his strong thigh the way we used to. But he was right, hand holding was a much better place to start.

"Thank you," he said quietly. His low, rich baritone blended with the night sounds and blanketed me in comfort. Until a sneaky grin took over half his face. "Your turn."

No sense prolonging it. "We saw you and Stella today at school. Vela and Stella are classmates at Benning Academy."

"I heard you make a few comments about after school while we were having dinner. Did something else happen? And you should've said hello."

Christ. How did I explain all of this to the man? Honesty—it was all I could offer. When I exhaled heavily, his demeanor shifted to one of concern.

"What?"

"I'm trying to figure out how to say all of what is knocking around in here." I motioned to my head. "And here, if I'm being honest." I finished with my free hand over my heart.

"Okay. Take your time. Just please, be up front with me."

"I vow I will. In everything that concerns my daughter—"

"*Our* daughter."

"Yes, sorry. Our daughter. You have to be patient with me on that too. It's been a long time of just the two of us, so please know if I say the wrong thing, it's not with the intention to hurt you. I know I've done enough of that to last a lifetime."

"Possibly two."

Quiet settled between us after that remark. Would I be apologizing every day from now until she was twenty-nine? Not sure I had that in me. I made a strong daily effort to live in the present. To not fret about my past—or there would be days I wouldn't get out of bed. Rehashing the same transgressions over and over would take their toll on me, even if I deserved it. Living in the past went against everything I worked on personally.

"Vela has been missing a father figure in her life for a while now. Boulder was the first man I dated, and even that was in its infancy. Over the years, the guys have been so good with her, and me, to be honest. But recently, she's really been fantasizing about a dad in her orbit."

"That's probably natural, no?"

"Her therapist says it is, and for the most part, there weren't actual problems because of it."

"For the most part? What does that mean?"

"Well, today for example, when we saw you with Stella. And she is adorable, you're right." I smiled in agreement with his assessment of his niece. "You were walking from the office to the visitors' lot, hand-in-hand. Vela spotted you first." I closed my eyes for a few seconds, conjuring the bravery to keep going with the story. "And she lost her little mind. She had a complete meltdown, yelling at me, telling me it was my fault you went and found a different daughter now because I wasn't letting you come over."

Jacob sat forward and pulled me into his arms. Whether he sensed my distress from recounting the crappy scene at school or just needed to be closer to me, I didn't know.

And it felt so good. It felt so good with his arms banded around me. The way he kept me tight against his warm body. For a few moments, I allowed myself to escape there. I could pretend someone had finally come to rescue me from having to do everything alone all the time.

Dangerous thoughts in a vulnerable moment, but I didn't care. I stuffed my nagging conscience into the corner of my brain and allowed my heart and soul to be nurtured.

He felt so good. So safe and so strong, and I nestled in closer. A sort of hum vibrated through his chest, and I felt him inhale with his nose in my hair.

Eventually, I sat up and pulled out of his arms. It felt like the night air temperature had dropped fifty degrees when I was no longer in his embrace.

"I could've fallen asleep there," I admitted.

"I won't stop you," he said quietly. When I felt courageous enough to meet his stare, I saw raw hunger and need.

My own features were probably a mirror to his. It had been so long since I'd been with a man.

Since *this* man.

"Can you imagine what that would be like? Getting caught by Her Highness all snuggled in each other's arms. My God, she'd be picking out flower girl dresses by noon."

"Uh-oh. Does she have her mother's love of shopping, too?" he teased.

"Umm, I'd say she loves getting things, but not necessarily shopping for them. Not yet at least. But I want to finish with today's events. I won't bore you with the gory, profanity-riddled details, but—"

"Profanity? At Benning? That could *not* have gone well."

"Fortunately, we were out in the loop, so they weren't responsible for her discipline at the time," I explained. "We drove off school property, and I parked in a shopping center up the street so we could talk."

"I'm so sorry, baby. I'm sorry you had to go through that, and I'm sorry you've been shouldering all of this alone for so long," Jake said and situated his frame closer. "I've seen how rough single parenting has been for my sister, and it kills me knowing you've been going through the same things."

"From what I understand, your sister is better off alone than with the man who was in the picture?" I couldn't help it. A big part of me wanted to know if all the school gossip was true or not.

"Well, yes, she is. The guy is as low as they get. If any of my brothers and I ever see that guy while he's out and about..." Jacob threatened darkly, and I understood why.

Based on the way my own brother behaved regarding my single-parent status, if he found her father was then causing her harm in some way ...

Dude would already be dead and gone.

"Is Vela doing okay now?" Jacob asked. "She seemed happy at dinner."

"When we got home, I was feeling lower than the dirt on her shoe. Both for the way she treated me and because we're in this situation in the first place. She's too young to understand why I made the choices I did. Plus, not every decision I make has to involve her, you know?"

He nodded. "There's a lot I don't understand, and I'm the adult in the story," the man added plainly.

"I know, Jacob. I know I've been unfair to you. I'm

exhausted suddenly, and we can't sift through nine years sitting here in an hour. This is all going to take time."

"Don't you doubt for one minute, though, that I want to be here with you. I plan on showing up for every difficult decision, every happy celebration, and every normal day in between," he vowed solemnly. "I can promise she won't have to worry about having a father anymore."

I had no doubt he meant every word he said.

"I can't thank you enough for how patient you're being," I repeated.

"I already know the gold at the end of this rainbow will be worth every ounce of patience I have."

God, how I wanted him to be right. First, we had to weather the storm of the past nine years.

CHAPTER TEN

JACOB

What a night. In my loneliest hours, I never allowed fantasies of what reuniting with Cassiopeia would be like. There were so many things about our new first date that I couldn't stop thinking about. Even now, three days later, I had a hard time staying on task at just about everything. There was a good possibility the dopey grin on my face was starting to creep some people out, though, judging by the side-eyes I was catching at the office.

The night of our tapas dinner, I had to lecture myself for five minutes in her guest bathroom about not making a move on her when it came time to say goodnight. Even with all the self-talk and internal discipline I'd cultivated over the past years, I couldn't keep my mind straight when it came to the memories of the things we used to do.

The last impression I wanted to give Pia, though, was that I expected to jump right back into a physical relationship like we once had. Not without winning her back first and making her want me with the same hunger and desperation with how I wanted her.

The Stella story, while flattering in a way, broke my heart in other ways. After all the things my ex-brother-in-law did to that sweet, innocent child came into light, my entire family became wildly protective of her.

Knowing there was still so much gossip going on at that damn school she attended made me furious. Worse than the whispers was the notion she was a threat to anyone—ever. In ways I didn't know were possible, my heart actually hurt when I let any of that toxicity ride shotgun in my brain for too long.

And that was way different than the suffering I felt when Pia ghosted me in college. Hell, that had been heartbreak in every way, shape, and form. Relentless sadness. But back then, I didn't know I had a child. Looking back on that era now, I was grateful for that. Missing both of them or feeling the loss and emptiness without them both might have been more than I could have handled.

We'd covered some ground after our daughter was tucked in bed but didn't begin to unwind the tangled ball of yarn that was our past. I wanted to understand the reasons why she'd made the choices she had.

When I thought longer on just that aspect of our separation, I could tap into a significant reservoir of anger. She'd made decisions for me that were so outside of what I would've chosen for myself, I wondered if she knew me at all. That brought up legitimate concern on top of the anger. What if this whole thing was a load of one-sided feelings? I could exist amid unrequited love for only so long before problems erupted.

Confidence and positive self-image had never been a problem for me before ... until she'd left me and couldn't be found. Then I spent a lot of starless nights wondering where I'd gone wrong. When the other half of my soul wasn't around to lend support, it became easier and easier to fall into the morass of self-loathing.

I was pretty sure the kid was my biggest ally in this whole

mess. The assistant seemed incredibly loyal to Pia, but she wanted her to be happy, too. I'd have to work on charming her a little more next time we were together. I'd seen my sister's best friend's level of support and influence when Cecile left the dirtbag, so I was confident getting in Wren's good graces would only help my cause. Maybe she would eventually take up my agenda too and the three of us could mount a solid, strategic takeover of my star's heart.

Wasn't that what all of this was, really? One big competition? At every sporting event I'd ever attended, the home field advantage was a live, breathing component of winning. It made the most sense to get everyone in that household cheering for my team.

Because I planned on winning. And there'd be no sweeter victory than officially becoming a family. Pia and I had always talked about getting married. It was something we'd both wanted. Now, I wondered if that was still true.

By ten o'clock, I'd officially waited as long as I could. I had to see her, or talk to her, smell her, or touch her. Kiss her. No other options. I simply had to bask in my star's light one way or another.

Good morning. How does lunch sound?

I decided to go for friendly and cool, no stress about a thing in the world.

Hey! Mmm, can't today. Booked all day.

Not the answer I wanted, but I could work around it. She

had to eat at some point, so I would pivot my plan a bit and go to her. I doubted she'd turn me away if I came bearing her favorites.

> *Bummer. Just wanted to say hello. Have a great day, Star. Thinking about you.*

Thanks, Jake. Call me later?

> *You bet.*

I wrapped up the small project I was working on and sent the proposal to a potential client. My head wasn't in the details, and neither was my heart.

I sat for a few minutes, second-guessing what kind of sketch I'd just sent. There was no way I could let my burgeoning love life encroach on my trade. I'd worked too long and hard to have that sort of unprofessionalism attached to my name.

But I had to give myself a break now and then, too. Could it be helped that the excitement in my veins and the passion in my heart were currently from just one muse? There was no point beating myself up over phoning in that proposal. I would make it up to the client with better concepts if I landed the contract.

Multitasking while I was working, I ordered lunch from a great Mediterranean place a few blocks away. I was due there in twenty minutes to pick up my food, so I freshened up and stopped by Tabitha's desk on my way out.

"I have a lunch meeting, and I'm not sure if I'll be back this afternoon or not." I'd already spoken to Shark first thing when I arrived at work, so he was handled for the day. Little did he know, he was going to be the topic of our lunchtime discussion.

Lying to the man felt so wrong in my gut. But I wasn't outright lying to him, necessarily. I just wasn't telling him what was going on and what my role in the whole thing was.

He'd asked me several pointed questions about how his sister and I were getting on, and I was completely honest there. Pia was the one who needed to fill in the gaps for her brother, though. Not me. I tried looking at it from every imaginable side and still arrived at that same conclusion.

My woman needed to buck up and have an adult conversation with the bossy guy. I didn't want to go past the end of this week without it happening.

"Sounds good. Enjoy your day, Mr. Cole," the girl said brightly.

"Thanks. See you later."

Less than an hour later, I stood in front of Pia's receptionist, asking to see the business owner.

"Do you have an appointment?" she asked skeptically. The woman probably knew Pia's schedule inside and out and was well aware I didn't. However, I wouldn't be deterred.

From my vantage point, I could see Pia's closed office door. Deciding it would be more hassle to set all of my food bags down, I disengaged from the conversation and beelined for my woman.

"You can't just barge in there," she blurted after me.

Over my shoulder, I called back to the secretary, "Of course not."

A huge, mischievous grin spread across my lips, and I said, "I'll knock first." But when I lifted my arm to do just that, two of the bags slid down my arm and knocked into the door. Instantly I became the guy in the hall causing a lot of commotion.

Pia swung the door open before I could juggle all the things I was holding and accomplish a proper knock.

"Jacob!" she greeted in surprise. "What on earth is all this? Let me help…"

"Maybe just point to where I can set this down?" I sheepishly replied.

She shuffled ahead of me and cleared a decorative bowl off her coffee table, and I unloaded the bags.

"I know you said you have a full schedule, but I also know you have to eat, so I just popped in to bring you some Greek." I rushed it all out in a nervous jumble before remembering I'd also brought her a bouquet of her favorite tulips. "Oh, and these are for you too." Thrusting the flowers at her, I felt my face getting hot.

When had I become such a bumbling fool around the opposite sex? My brothers were all notorious ladies' men. If even one of them saw this performance, I'd be razzed for the next year.

"Will you join me?" Pia asked quietly and looked at her watch. "I have an hour before my next appointment."

"I'd like that, but only if you're sure I'm not encroaching. You look stunning today, by the way," I said, adding a warm smile.

"Thanks," she replied and looked down at her dress. "I found this shoved in the way back of my closet. I forgot I had it."

Pia's entire office was filled with the enticing aroma of grilled vegetables and lamb. My mouth was watering by the time we sat on the sofa, using the coffee table as our lunch top.

"I wasn't sure how big a risk this was," I admitted.

"The food selection? I love Mediterranean. I guess some things don't change."

"No. Just dropping in without a hard plan. I know you don't usually see people, at home or work, who don't have an appointment," I explained while handing her utensils. "I'm guessing that's another thing that hasn't changed."

"True, but I'm starving, for one"—she wrinkled her nose and continued—"and the protein bar in my purse has seen better days. It wasn't good to begin with, and now it looks even more unappetizing."

I shook my head with a grimace to match hers. "Uhh, yuck. I still haven't found one of those things that I can stomach."

Pia continued while dividing the food between our plates. "Well, in a pinch, it's better for me to have something in my body than to go hungry. That really messes with the insulin levels, you know?"

"Yes, of course. I'm glad you take it so seriously." I gave her a sideways look. "There was a time you thought you were indestructible."

"Me? Ha, that's funny," the beautiful woman teased. "I seem to remember picking up some pretty crappy habits from you, mister." She giggled with the taunt, and the easy flow between us felt so good.

So natural.

I decided to ask her about work, and hopefully from there I could transition into talking to her about Sebastian.

"So, other than the Edge, what big projects do you have going on right now?"

"My brother's building definitely takes the lion's share of my time. But I just signed a contract to redecorate the atrium at a studio's office building in Hollywood. I have a few other bids out right now as well." She inhaled deeply and sat back into the comfort of the sofa. "What about you? What are you working on?"

I took a drink of the iced tea I brought for us before answering. "I'm much the same in that the Edge is consuming most of my energy right now."

"Yeah, that's my brother's way of doing everything. If you're involved, he sucks you in and demands as much of your creativity and energy as he is putting in."

"You know, I'm glad we got on this topic. Sebastian, I mean," I said, but based on the way she winced, maybe that transition wasn't as smooth as I thought it was.

"Has he said something to you?" she asked and sat upright again. "About us, I mean?"

"No, he hasn't. But I was wondering if you have a plan in place?" I questioned.

"Explain."

"How are you going to tell him about our past and about Vela?" I inquired and then watched her fidget with her silverware for a few beats.

This couldn't have been the first time she'd thought of our situation and that controlling man. Maybe she didn't know the vehemence he held for the faceless father of her child. I'd certainly heard enough of his comments, and I had limited exposure to the guy.

"Every time I think about it, I get very tense and nervous," she began to explain.

Silently, I vowed to keep my opinions to myself until I heard her out fully. I could only hope we agreed on the need to tell him and the urgency of it.

"He certainly can be intimidating," I said. "When I first submitted a proposal to design his building, I remember being so nervous." I laughed a bit while thinking about everything that had happened in my life since getting back to Los Angeles.

"Those first few meetings we had are straight-up embarrassing to think back on now."

"I know this is a tangent, but I've been meaning to ask you . . . Why did you use a different name at school?" Pia asked pointedly.

And that wasn't a tangent. That was a full topic switch. This was a conversation we needed to have too, so I'd answer the question. I would ensure we circled back to Sebastian, though.

"Probably for a lot of the same reasons you did. I wanted to have a peaceful college experience, and I didn't want to be a burden on the other students."

"What do you mean by *burden*?" She looked at me with a puzzled expression before admitting, "I don't think we used aliases for the same reason, or this would be making more sense to me."

"It wasn't my intention to be vague. Sorry. I thought you would have put it all together by now. Especially after you told me you know my sister and Stella."

But by her continued perplexed appearance, I could see I was going to have to spell this out.

"When my sister married, she kept our family name. Stella also has our family name." Now I sat and watched the pieces of the puzzle click together behind her expressive eyes.

"Are you saying your last name is Masterson? You are from the Masterson *dynasty*?"

"Yes, that's what I'm saying. My name is Jacob Cole Masterson. Cole was my mother's maiden name, and she gave it to me as a middle name. Several of us have it as our middle name, actually. Which is sort of funny in a George Foreman sort of way, right? Although when you have ten children, maybe you just run out of ideas for names?" I shrugged because I never gave it a lot of thought. We were taught it was an honor to carry the names we had been given.

"George Foreman?" she asked with a little shake of her head. "I didn't realize your family was also in sports entertainment."

I gave a hearty laugh at her confusion. And I should have known better. She did not appreciate being the butt of any joke. Big or small. So I quickly explained, "George Foreman has ten kids, five boys. He named them all George Foreman."

She nodded then with a more relaxed smile. "Ahhh, gotcha."

Then it was my turn to ask, "And why did you use a different name when we were in college?"

Carefully, she wiped her mouth with her napkin and exhaled. "Like you, I didn't want to spend my college years fending off the media or defending my brother to idiots who didn't know him and believed what they saw online."

Obviously, that was the practiced answer she had probably given countless times before when this came up. But her pensive countenance clued me in that she was about to share a more personal reason.

"For the first time in my life, I wanted to just be Cassiopeia. Not the mighty Sebastian Shark's little sister. Shark Enterprises had exploded two years before I went to college. Bas was in the media constantly, and I just wanted to be away from it all. I remember being in the admissions office and having this opportunity"—she motioned in front of herself like she was fanning out a stack of papers—"to be whoever I wanted to be. So, I just wrote down my name. Ironically, also using my mother's maiden name."

Her shy smile reached right into my chest and gave my lonely heart a squeeze.

Then she shrugged and finished with, "And that's pretty much all of it."

We cleaned up the empty containers and packed up what food we couldn't finish. "Do you have a refrigerator in here?" I asked, twirling in a circle with two bowls in my hand. "Then, when you're hungry later, you will have better options than the sad protein bar."

With that comment, I gave a little wink, and her smile stretched. Her beauty took my breath away, and I had to stop what I was doing and give thanks to the universe for bringing this amazing female back to me.

"Thank you for spending time with me, even without an appointment. I think your assistant at the desk"—I motioned toward the front reception area—"almost fainted when I walked right past her."

"She'll be okay. She's on the newer side and still afraid of her own shadow." While she spoke, I noticed she had something on her cheek from lunch.

I stepped in closer and ducked down to wipe her face.

"What are you doing?"

"You have something, right here." I gently wiped her skin and lingered for a few seconds longer than necessary. She was silky and smelled so feminine and alluring. Instantly, hormones stirred in my body, and I parted my lips to inhale more of her scent. I was so hungry for intimacy, the tingle quickly morphed to a painful drumbeat.

"Can I kiss you?" My voice was low and raspy, and she must have been feeling her own chemical reaction, because her nostrils widened with the full breath she inhaled.

Eventually I'd stop asking permission and just do it, but I was so concerned about overstepping. I didn't want to chase her off when I just got her back.

Pia didn't use words to answer but tilted her chin higher and let her eyes close and open lazily. I moved in closer, until she spoke.

"I don't know if we should—"

"The child isn't here this time. Just once. I'll beg if that's what it takes."

"You don't have to beg," she whispered.

I slid my fingertips along her jaw, then back farther to cradle her face in my palm.

Pia made a needy, breathy sound, and it was my undoing. Yet somehow I still managed to maintain control and slowly moved in closer. Our lips were a moment from touching, and I was trying to give her every opportunity to say no. Why? I wasn't sure. I was starting to question if I was a closet masochist. Then convinced myself more of the possibility when I considered the years of celibacy I'd endured in this woman's name.

Finally, our lips met. Warm and delicate, the feel of her mouth against mine kicked up my need to devour her completely. But I went slow and lingered with each movement. There wasn't a moment in her presence I wanted to rush. I tried to memorize every catch of breath, every nerve ending's tingle, every desperate grip of her fingers in my shirt sleeve. *Just in case.* In case I was daydreaming or this was the only time I got away with kissing her in truth.

When we parted, I couldn't move away more than a few inches. With one kiss, the rapture of physically loving her reignited. Remembering the creative ways I'd once mastered her body, mind, and soul had me craving more.

"More," I growled, and it might have shocked us both.

Pia widened her eyes in surprise, and another primitive sound rolled up my throat and past my lips.

But she protested. "Not here. We shouldn't be doing this here."

"Where, then? I need you so bad, Star. Just that one small touch has me on fire right now. Do you remember how good we were together, baby?"

She dipped her chin down, effectively tearing her gaze from mine. Her shyness made me want to defile her.

Suddenly I had an idea. I had tucked this side of my psyche far away since she'd ghosted me. Allowing myself to have her physically—even in this small way—reignited the desire to dominate her completely. All I could hear in my mind was one thought on a repeating loop.

Punish her. She should be punished for her lack of trust and faith.

I looked down at her, feeling like I'd added two inches to my height just by making a solid resolution. She would feel me again.

Crowding into her personal space, I caught her attention immediately. Her glassy blue eyes were riveted to my commanding brown ones, and I was very deliberate with my next moves. I slid my hand along her jaw again, like I just had when I kissed her so tenderly. This time, however, I moved all the way to her nape and gripped on to a fistful of her thick brown hair. Tugging her head back until her chin was almost pointing at the ceiling, I bowed my frame over hers.

"It just hit me like a storm, lady. I know what we both need here, and I've waited damn long enough to have it. Don't you agree, Star?"

Her throat constricted with her anticipation and apprehension.

"Every time I have to ask the same question will be another stroke for you. Assuming you're still the pain slut you've always been? I can't wait to take the past nine years out on that milky white ass," I warned in a deep, husky tone. "You're not going to sit comfortably for the rest of the month."

"Jack—" She moaned, and my cock actually jumped in my pants.

"Fuck me, woman. That sounds so good. I'm going to figure out where, and I'm going to decide how, but you will submit to me again, won't you?"

She gave an automatic nod, or what she could manage of a nod with the grip I had on her hair.

"We both need this, girl. Nothing has ever felt more right in my bones than that realization." I watched her gulp again and couldn't help but take a kiss from her parted lips. This time, I thrust my tongue deep into her accepting mouth and completely pillaged my way through the connection.

One last instruction, and I would leave. She would have a lot to ruminate after I departed, and it was exactly where I wanted her. I had done more examining and self-assessing than any one person should have in an entire lifetime. It was her turn to take some time and sit with what she did to us. To our family.

"When I leave here, you figure out a way to talk with your brother about this mess. I will gladly stand by your side while you do it, if that's what you decide. I'm leaving it in your hands to tell me that. Are we clear now?" I gave her another quick kiss and paused a moment with my mouth on hers. "Say you're with me, baby. We need to get back on track. As always, the power is in your hands." I released her hair and stepped back one step but kept her prisoner to my stare. "Tell me."

The silence was interminable. Her motionless body wasn't any better. I vowed to wait her out, though. Watching her pulse hammer in the vital artery in her slim neck, I was positive this was our way out of Perdition.

Pia ran her fingers through the hair I had been pulling and smoothed her dress down the front of her thighs. Measured breaths in and out accompanied the regrouping before she finally met my waiting eyes.

"Jesus, Jacob. Unexpected . . . but . . . yeah . . ." she said and blew out a long breath through pursed lips.

"You haven't played with anyone lately?" I shamelessly fished for how many men she'd shared her body with since me.

"No. Not at all. I—well, yeah. No." She waved a hand through the air, too flustered with the whole topic to speak about it, maybe.

The blood that should've been nourishing my brain was currently throbbing in my cock, so it took a moment longer to organize my thoughts. While she studied me with those fathomless blue eyes, I thrust my hand down the front of my slacks to rearrange my erection.

"Please let me know when you come up with a plan, then?" I posed the comment like a question so she would know I needed her agreeance. After a quick assenting dip of her chin, I said, "Thank you for sharing your lunch hour with me." I grinned and strode closer to her.

"No." She put her hands out in front of her. "No more. Not while we're in here. I have a client in"—she looked at her watch—"shit, she's probably waiting in the lobby."

"I'm simply going to hug you goodbye, Star. Settle down."

I couldn't help the cocky grin that spread across my lips after she admitted the effect our exchange had on her.

When I wrapped her in my arms, she sagged into my comfort. I pressed my nose into her hair and inhaled. Yet another thing I'd never get enough of.

With a quick peck on the top of her head, I left her office.

"Have a great day!" I bid her receptionist as I strolled by her desk.

"Thanks, uhh, you too," the woman said, still not knowing my name.

While I walked to my car, I quickly scrolled through my email. Nothing too urgent leaped out at me, but I was curious to see a reply to the proposal I sent before I left for my impromptu lunch date.

With day-glow ink, I made a mental note to surprise my woman as often as possible. She was way more raw and real when I caught her off guard than when she had time to prepare an agenda and erect emotional walls.

It was comforting to know very little had changed. With either of us really. Definitely not between us. We just had to find our way back to all the things that made us so great.

CHAPTER ELEVEN

PIA

"What time will he be here?" my assistant asked, trying to shuffle Vela's backpack contents back into the bag. It was always a magic trick if everything that came out of that carriable disaster zone fit back inside.

She asked just as I went into the kitchen pantry, so when I came out, I jumped right back into the conversation with an answer. "He just said after work. You know my brother, though. That could be in twenty minutes or two hours."

"Are you sure you don't want me to whip something up for dinner?" the young girl offered. "I don't mind, really, and Miss Judy canceled piano again."

"Nah, he said he had a late lunch. My nerves are so bad, I don't think I could eat a thing." I grimaced and clutched my upset stomach. Anytime I was overly anxious, my tender stomach was the first to suffer.

"Well, I don't need to nag you, but I'm going to." Wren smiled warmly. "Please don't skip the meal altogether."

Giving her a quick side hug, I quipped, "Yes, dear." It was touching that she worried about my health on top of everything else she did in my house. "Jacob surprised me with lunch at the office today," I threw in at the end of our quick embrace.

She set me back by an arm's length but still clutched my

hands. "Really? Do you want to tell me more about it?"

Here was another amazing attribute of my friend. She never pried or injected herself into matters she wasn't invited into or that didn't concern her.

"How am I so lucky to have you in my life?" I asked her first.

"What brought that on? I mean, thank you, I feel pretty darn lucky to be a part of your life, too." Then a shudder wracked her entire body before she said, "I can't imagine where I'd be right now without you."

"Please know I mean that from my heart. I wasn't saying that to force you to shower me with gratitude."

"Pia." She just stared at me.

Finally, I said, "What?"

"We know each other better than that, don't we?"

I answered while nodding, "I'd like to think so, yes."

"Okay, good. Now, stop beating around the bush and tell me all the things about your lunch date."

"You had a date? With who? With my father?" Vela appeared seemingly out of the ether.

"Oh, here we go," I muttered and dropped my face into my palms. I didn't want to tell my daughter about seeing Jake today and get her hopes up that things were on some sort of fast track with the man or have her pissed that she wasn't included. The latter was the stronger possibility.

My daughter peppered me with questions. "Mama? Did you see Jacob today? How is he doing? Is he coming over? Does he want to see me too?"

"Darling, yes, I saw Jacob today. I'm sure at some point he will come see you again. Probably soon." I added that last part because her little face was falling into crushed-heart territory with every word I carefully uttered.

Damn it! This was so complicated. I had always vowed to be honest with my child. She needed to understand things in life weren't always sunshine and rainbows. But I completely caved in the moment I watched her expression go from hopeful excitement to crestfallen disappointment within one sentence.

I must have recovered better than I thought because she clasped her hands in front of her chest and confessed, "I've been hoping and praying with all my good thoughts that he would come back."

"Climb up here for a minute. And seriously, just a couple minutes because Uncle Bas is coming over and I want our conversation to be over by the time I have to talk to him, okay?"

She crawled up on the counter-high stool at the kitchen island and said, "I'm with you, whatever you need." Vela proceeded to stare at me, waiting to hear what I wanted to say.

Times like this, when she spurted the most grown-up sounding comments, I couldn't hold back my laugh. Quickly, I explained, though, because she was also increasingly sensitive about people laughing at her.

"You're growing up too fast, Miss Shark."

"Don't women get new last names when they make babies?" she spouted out of nowhere.

"No, traditionally, a woman takes their new husband's last name when they marry," I explained, opting for fewer details rather than sticking my foot into another gooey mess I didn't have time to handle at the moment.

The answer seemed to satisfy that curiosity, because she was on to another question back-to-back. "So, what did you want to tell me?"

"I want to be sure—well, I hope you understand..." I paused again, trying to get my wording right. This was an important one.

Vela put her little hand over mine on the island and gave it a couple pats. "Take your time. Just try."

A smile took over my face again because she was repeating word for word what I'd said to her when she was flustered and having a hard time expressing herself.

"Can we hug?" I asked sheepishly.

"Always!" She catapulted herself into my arms from her stool, and I buried my nose between her neck and shoulder.

After we hugged, I pressed my face in farther, and she began to wriggle out of my embrace. I knew her most ticklish places.

"Mama!" she squealed with delight.

We settled down then, and I told her what I'd been trying to say. "It's very important that you try to keep my friendship with your dad and you getting to know him separate. That's probably confusing, right?"

"I'll say!" she answered with a hand to her cheek.

"I've known Jacob for a long time, honey. And now, years—nine to be exact—have gone by where we haven't been friends. So at the exact same time he wants to learn all about you, he's trying to learn about me too. But those two things don't necessarily have to go together."

With the most innocently confused expression, my daughter said, "I don't know what you're saying."

"He and I have a lot of things we need to work through. Grown-up things. So, I want you to understand that my not wanting to hang out with him every day and night is no reflection on how much he wants to spend time with you. Does that make more sense?"

"But Mama." She studied me for a moment, then said, "How can we be a family if you guys don't wanna like each other?"

"We just have to take it slow. He and I. One day at a time, and see where things go. And families don't always have a mom and dad, right? We were a family before he came around, weren't we?"

"Yeah, we were. But I really want a mom and dad," she admitted with an edge of whininess.

"I know you do, honey. And I promise, I'm going to try to be friends with him again."

"Gretchen has two mommies," Vela blurted.

I rolled along with the subject shift. "You're right, she does. How lucky is she?"

"Okay. Can I go start my piano?"

"Yes, my love. Thank you for talking to me. I love you so much, Star." I leaned in for a peck.

"I love you too," Vela declared and came closer so I could land my kiss on her perfect little nose. Then she hopped down, no worse for the wear from our talk, and I exhaled loudly.

I didn't realize how much stress I was holding on to over that.

Now, if things went as well with Bas, I might actually get some sleep tonight.

★ ★ ★

Almost an hour later, my brother and I settled into the sofa, each with drink in hand. I'd already drunk a glass before he arrived, trying to calm my nerves a bit. It was ridiculous to be so worried over his reaction. This was my life. God forbid he was just happy for me and kept his opinions to himself if they didn't line up with mine.

"Thank you for stopping by. I know you have a family at home waiting, so I will try to keep this as brief as possible."

"Abbi never complains about us spending time together," my brother replied. "She actually wanted to come along, but I knew you wanted to talk about something specific, so I told her I'd try to set something up before I left tonight. I think she's missing family connection."

"Oh, I'd like that. How is she? How is the pregnancy going this time?"

"I'm not sure if it's because it's the second time we're dealing with all of it, or if the symptoms are actually lighter this time, but she's doing good. The day-long morning sickness is still a big issue, but she said some of the tricks she learned while pregnant with Kaisan are helping."

The smile on my sibling's face was so heartwarming, I couldn't help but smile too.

"It's probably a combo of the two things, I would think?" I suggested, and he nodded while I spoke.

"Yeah, you're probably right."

I took a big breath and dove in. Any more small talk, and I'd go mad. "We probably should've had this talk years ago, brother. But I think if I admit this to you, it will be a good start at explaining why this conversation has been so long coming. When I was younger, I was too scared. It's that simple. So many things were changing all at once, and I took the coward's way out and let you steamroll right over me and take control of my life. I know now—well, I've known for a lot of years, that was wrong."

"Dub, what the hell are you talking about?" he asked impatiently.

I pointed at him. "Exactly that. Can you put on your peaceful hat for a minute and just listen? If I can get everything off my chest, there's a good chance most of your questions will be answered."

"I hate conversations that start like this," my big brother griped. "Grant and Elijah do similar things, and I hate it. I can feel dread bubbling up in my gut already with a preamble like that."

"I know, but there isn't a non-shitty way to spill nine years' worth of dirt at your feet and not expect to have a mess to clean up."

"Nine years?" He thought for a quiet moment and then stood abruptly. "Is something wrong with Vela? Is that why she was acting so strident the other day in my office?"

"No, Sebastian, other than she's growing up on all of us. Way too fast. Sit down, please. She's fine. Over-the-moon happy, as a matter of fact." My secret knowledge as to why made me grin.

My skeptical brother plopped back onto the sofa with so little grace, the cushion I sat on bounced too. "Fuck, Dub, don't scare me like that."

"Sorry," I offered quietly and patted his muscular shoulder.

"No, I'm sorry for overreacting like that. Right after you asked me to chill out, too. What's going on, sister? Tell me already—rip the damn Band-Aid off."

"Jacob Cole is Vela's father. I dated him for almost four years at school."

Yep. That ought to do it.

Bas's calm demeanor had always been scarier than his agitated one. I studied his face where his brows knitted so tightly, they looked like black Sharpie hash marks.

"Come again?" he finally said through gritted teeth.

I just stared at him, knowing damn well he'd heard every word. Then I started rambling and was pretty sure I didn't stop for almost eight minutes. I told him every detail about how we met, why he went to Spain, and then I tried to explain why I never sought him out to be an active part in my daughter's life.

My brother sat with his focus directly on me the entire time. When I finished talking, his motionless stare was a combination of anger and bewilderment, and if the whole topic wasn't such a cluster fuck, it would have been comical to see the great Sebastian Shark reduced to wordlessness.

But I knew better than to laugh or go for comic relief in any way. I needed to let him consider everything I just word-vomited in his lap and let him lead the conversation from there.

"When did Cole find all this out? Did that bastard know this whole time? So help me—"

"No!" I went on to defend Jacob because this was one of my biggest fears. "No, he didn't. The day in your office? The day you introduced us for what you thought was the first time? That's when he saw her for the first time. That was the first time we laid eyes on each another in nine years."

"Don't fuck with me to protect him, Dub."

"I'm not, Sebastian. I swear," I said accompanied by a raised hand in oath. "I've never lied to you about anything, and I have no intention of starting now."

He stared blankly, seeming to have detached from the conversation in a split second.

"Please don't lash out at Jacob. You know the whole story as it happened from when I came home after graduation. You know that I made the choices I made based on my best ability at that time, but there was more. I was in love with him. Crazy in love with him."

"I know *that*," my brother remarked quietly. "I remember it all like it was yesterday. I might not have cared at the time, not understanding the power of a love like that or believing you could either, but I knew you were struggling with missing the guy."

Then a completely unexpected grin stretched across his lips, and he went on. "Now that I have Kaisan, so many memories hit me—every day of when she was his age. We were all so young and had no idea what the hell we were doing with a baby. My whole approach to everything is so different now. It's like seeing the world through a new pair of eyes, as ridiculous as that sounds."

I put my hand on my brother's forearm, and he quickly leveled his stare to mine. "It doesn't sound ridiculous, Sebastian. It's beautiful. And I am so happy that you've allowed Abbigail and the baby into your heart fully. It would be sad to see you rob yourself of the joy that comes with the full heart of parenthood."

"Okay, enough with the touchy-feely stuff. I'm still me, and I have my limits, you know?"

With an easy chuckle, I said, "I know. I get it. You did good, though. That was a lot for you."

I gave him a quick wink, and his expression was one I'd never seen before on his stern face. Bashful? Maybe . . . But as quick as it came, it was gone. There would be no more examining that feeling, either.

"So where do you go from here? How is Vela doing? You said she was happy as could be. Because of him?" Bas looked and sounded incredulous. "Already?"

And I could predict what was going to come out of his mouth next. I also knew it was a giant masquerade to cover the real feelings that were probably threatening him right then.

Proving me right, he started in on Jake. "Is he good for her, Dub? I mean, he's basically a stranger. People can change a lot in eight—or nine, I guess—years. Are you sure he should be around her already?"

"Bas—" I tried to cut him off before he ramped up.

"Where is she? Normally she's out here bouncing off the walls excited to see me."

"She was supposed to be practicing piano, now that you mention it," I supplied. "And I asked her to give us some alone time to talk."

My brother laughed his reply. "Shit. And she listened?"

"Will wonders ever cease?" I laughed too.

There was one more information bomb I needed to drop on my sibling, and I couldn't begin to predict how he'd respond. Like before, I had butterflies dive bombing in my stomach until I got the courage to spill the facts.

"There's something else I need to tell you about Jake. Maybe it's relevant, maybe it's not. But like I just said, I've never lied to you before, and I don't want to start now."

"Ohhh . . . kaaay," he dragged out with trepidation.

"Sorry. I know you just told me you hate those lead-ins."

"Yep, still true. Just tell me, Pia. What more could there be? Fuck me . . ." He paused and looked at me suspiciously. "Are you knocked up again?"

"Sebastian! No. And if I were, wouldn't you be happy? Especially if I were happy?" I asked with a bit of expectant demand in my tone, warning that he think about his answer and make sure it was the right one.

"Of course I would. I think I would. I just can't forget how hard it all was, the pregnancy and managing the diabetes and then with our little queen when she was literally the fussiest baby ever born. I don't wish that on anyone," Bas said with authority because he was in the trenches with me so often back then. "When the boy cries, I think how the hell did we make it through those first two years?"

"I know, right? I think it made me stronger, that's for sure. And very, very tired." We both laughed briefly, but then Bas steered us back to the subject at hand.

"Sorry, I derailed us there, but go ahead." He motioned in front of himself like *bring it on.*

"Okay, when I first checked in with the admitting office, I changed my name so I wouldn't be followed around by reporters and stuff. SE had just gained major media attention, and . . . well, you remember all of that, right?"

Out of nervousness, I was regaling him with information he already knew. In the back of my mind, I figured if it was reasonable for me to have done such a thing, he shouldn't feel suspicious of Jacob for having done the same. I didn't want to start out our renewed relationship on the defensive with these bossy men in my life that smothered me with their love and protective shit.

"Sure. I remember. It also turned out to be a good thing when you came back pregnant and didn't want the guy to find you. Since you'd been using an alias, if he did try to look you up, it would've made it harder to find you." My brother agreed with me so far.

"Exactly. At the same time, it made it impossible to know this entire time, while you've been working together and openly talking about Jacob Cole, that he was the same man who was my one and only love."

Bas screwed up his face in confusion. "Explain."

"Jacob comes from a very prominent family and was using, or is using, a different name as well. Still, now."

"Do I know this family? Fuck me, Pia, tell me he's not tied in with Viktor Blake somehow." With that one question, I watched the color drain from my brother's face.

"No." I laughed. Of all the conclusions to draw, how the hell had my brother connected those dots? Always thinking worst-case scenario first, and anything better than that seems manageable, maybe?

So, I continued to explain. "Jacob's last name is Masterson. Yes, of the Mastersons you're thinking. I never knew that until a few days ago when Vela and I saw him at her school picking up his niece"—I gripped my brother's forearm again before dropping the biggest part of this—"Stella."

"What the—?" He stared at me for a few beats then said, "Seriously? That little troublemaker in Vela's class?"

"You know the backstory. Don't say that about her. She's been through an awful experience with her father. It sounds like the entire family despises the guy now."

"You think? I mean, can you imagine?" Bas nearly gasped at the thought.

"No. I don't like thinking about it because it's so heartbreaking. But back to Jake. His mother's maiden name is Cole, and it's his middle name. He's been using it in business now, too. He doesn't want any unfair advantages from anyone who may have loyalty to his family." I tried to relay the details similarly to the way Jacob explained his reasoning to me.

Bas rolled his eyes and said, "Gee, how noble. I mean, I get it, but at the same time, I can't help but be a bit pissed. The guy's basically been lying to me for a year—no, longer, from the time I first looked at his designs and considered hiring him."

"And none of what is happening in this house should interfere with the working relationship you've forged with him. I'm hoping that's not too much to ask," I said with raised brows. Of course it was a lot to ask . . . I knew it was.

"I'm not going to make any promises on that, Dub. I'll see how it all plays out, I guess. But let it be known, whatever working relationship I've established with the guy is also not going to make me accept him into your lives just like that." He snapped his fingers to display the short time interval.

Then something else flashed in my brother's eyes, and I'd seen this look before. His brain was really juiced up now, and he was tying up mental loose ends.

"Okay, but this doesn't make sense. The Mastersons are here in town. I know several of the others from business and social—places. Why is he living in a hotel like a nomad? That's always bothered me, and I couldn't put my finger on why."

"I don't have an answer to that. We've only spent time together twice—no, actually three times, since that meeting in your office."

I shook my head and fought back a grin. "Oh my God, Bas, the first time we spoke was a disaster. I was so confused about what the hell was happening. Talk about feeling like a big giant prank was being pulled on me!"

Apparently my daughter decided she'd given us enough time and chose that moment to stroll cautiously into the room. She looked between the two adults, waiting for some sort of cue that she was allowed.

"Where is my hug, Miss Shark?" Sebastian asked, and she bound into his embrace.

"Hi, Uncle Bas. How are you? Did you bring my cousin?" she asked, pointedly looking all around his body as he sat on the sofa.

"Not today, Star. I came over right from work, plus"— Sebastian checked the time on his watch—"he's probably already in bed for the night."

"Why do babies sleep so much?" she asked.

"He's very busy growing right now," I explained to my ever-curious child. "I bet the next time we see him, he will be noticeably bigger."

Vela looked bewildered and said, "Really? It hasn't been that long, Mama."

"You'll see what I mean. Little babies grow very fast in the first couple of years. Think about how much bigger he is now compared to when Aunt Abbi first had him. And really, it hasn't been that long."

"Oh." She nodded a few times and then added, "I grow a lot too."

"That's very true," my brother agreed. "Tell me what's new? How's school?" Bas engaged her in conversation while I excused myself to use the bathroom.

Honestly, I wanted to give them a little time alone, too. Vela always knew she could confide in her uncle if she had something on her mind that she didn't want to talk to me or Wren about. A lot of times, Bas ended up roping me into the conversation anyway, but I always thought it was good for her to know she had more than one adult she could turn to.

I wondered how or if their relationship would change with Jacob in the picture. I knew my brother better than anyone else knew him, and he would struggle with feelings of replacement if we weren't careful. The last thing I wanted, regardless of how this new dynamic played out between Jake and me, was for any of the people in my life to get hurt.

Why couldn't life just be easier? A lot of the complications we dealt with were self-induced, for sure. It would be up to me and no one else to ensure we didn't create more problems in an already difficult scenario.

With firm resolve, I thought a life with Jacob Cole Masterson in it would be worth the extra work. Anything worth having was.

CHAPTER TWELVE

JACOB

It was the day of reckoning. Judgment day. Or at least it felt that way as I walked into the first-floor lobby of the Shark Enterprises building.

Two nights ago, Pia called and told me about her conversation with her brother and seemed pretty optimistic about his reaction. I had to bank on the woman knowing the guy better than anyone did. If that was her assessment of their conversation, then I believed her.

Typically, these meetings were pretty laid-back. They used to be, anyway. I truly enjoyed the budding friendship I had with Sebastian Shark. I hoped we could slide right into our easy companionship and not let this get in the way.

But—this was Sebastian Shark, after all. The man had a notorious take-no-bullshit reputation. Even if his demeanor had shifted slightly to the more agreeable side since Abbigail came into his life and gave him a child. I didn't know him well before those life-changing events happened, but that was what those closest to him reported.

Up on the top floor, I checked in with Craig, Bas's executive assistant, and then dashed down the hall to the restroom. After a few splashes of cold water on my face, I gathered my wits about me to go take my medicine.

It frustrated the hell out of me, though, that I was putting myself through this kind of mental anguish. I was the victim in the whole situation, and for whatever reason, that seemed easy for everyone to forget.

As much as I didn't love that moniker either, it was better than thinking of myself as guilty. If I had known my girl was having our baby, I would've been on the first plane back across the Atlantic Ocean. It was that simple.

"He's waiting for you," Craig said quietly and ushered me through the heavy door and into the executive suite.

"Morning!" I said brightly, but Shark couldn't be bothered to look up from his computer.

I'd seen this bit of his enough times to understand it was a power play he pulled, so I ignored the slight and went to the conference table where we normally looked at my drawings.

Today there were a few changes to review, but a big deadline for the next floors was just around the corner. Originally, the next twelve levels were slated to be residential, but at our last meeting there were some mentions of changing those initial plans. So, I'd held off on further complicated work until I knew the exact specs he wanted to fill.

Finally, after I had my prints laid out, the other man stood from his desk and came over to join me.

"How are you?" I asked and offered my hand to shake. That wasn't out of the ordinary—we'd shaken hands countless times before.

Shark studied me and my outstretched hand for painfully long moments. Just when I was feeling like an ass and about to retract the greeting, he met me halfway, and we shook.

"Masterson," he addressed in greeting but then cocked his head to one side. "Why not just tell me?"

"Honestly, it never came up between us. I've been using Cole for so long now, it just never crossed my mind. It certainly wasn't to deceive you." Those were the true and simple facts. I had nothing to hide or hold back from the man.

"Before I met Abbigail, I used to frequent some of the same places as your brothers, Vaughn and Law," the man admitted.

"Interesting" was all I said. It seemed like letting him dictate the course of our conversation was the best action plan.

"In what way?" he asked as he moved a blueprint close to the edge of the table and bent to get a better look at something that caught his eye.

"I'm surprised our paths never crossed socially, then. Although, a few of the places they go are a little more ... public than I prefer."

I watched him carefully while I answered, ready to pivot on the spot. It wasn't every day you admitted to your woman's brother that you were wired as a dominant man. Conversely, that painted his little sister as a submissive, and maybe that was the part he was struggling with.

Sebastian crossed his muscular arms over his chest, and the fabric of his dress shirt pulled at every seam. He paced along the conference table, looking at the other drawings, but didn't comment.

Finally, he faced me and said, "These look great, Jake. As always. I have to be honest, though. I really struggled with the decision regarding dissolving our contract at this juncture or seeing this thing through with you leading the design team."

I rubbed my tense forehead and reminded myself to remain confident. The difference in body language between Shark and me at this exact moment was titanic, and there was no reason for it. I didn't want to come off as weak or stressed, so I stood up a bit taller and casually slipped a hand into my slacks pocket.

Nodding thoughtfully, I said, "Of course. I can imagine it was a lot to digest. I have moments where I want to pinch myself, and it's been more than two weeks." I paused, waiting for him to add to the conversation.

Instead, he let the silence balloon.

"Finding out I have a child and that I've missed almost nine years of her life was mind boggling."

"As a rule, I don't mix my business dealings and my personal life. How do you propose we proceed?" Sebastian asked the hard question and then let it sit between us like a giant boulder.

Just thinking of that word made me spurt a quick laugh, and I realized he thought I was laughing at his question. "Sorry, I just thought of that dipshit Cass was dating before I found her in your office here. Have you met him?"

"No." The man grimaced through a visible amount of concern. I was reminded how close Sebastian and Cassiopeia were. I'd heard them both talk of the other with an intense level of devotion and protectiveness.

"Vela mentioned him a few times. Well, she mentioned her mother had gone out on dates, but no other details." An incredible grin spread across the usually stoic man's lips, and he chuckled then too. "She tells me the most irrelevant details about every single subject but the one I would've been interested in hearing."

"You didn't miss much, trust me," I said and shook my head a bit. "The guy dropped by unannounced the other night when I went to pick the girls up for our first date."

"Oh, bad move, Junior," Shark said. "Pia hates drop-bys as much as I do."

"She always has," I commented. Happy to sneak in a trait I knew about her without him imparting the information. "Well, I let him know he shouldn't return."

"Oh, man, how did my sister deal with that?" Sebastian inquired with gleeful interest. "You butting into her business like that."

"Even if for some hell-has-frozen-over reason we don't work out, that guy was completely wrong for her. She was totally selling herself short with the man."

Before we got into any deeper conversation about his sister's love life, though, I decided to shift to the blueprints sprawled out before us. "So, these drawings complete the current phase, and I wanted to touch base with you on the finer details of the residential phase before I work on those. Is that something you have time for today, or do you want me to schedule on my way out when we're done here?"

Maybe if I set a good example of how easy it was to transition back and forth between our two new relationships, he would follow suit. I was confident I could maintain complete professionalism.

"Okay. Let's see what we have here and if there are any changes that need to be addressed, and then I'll know what my time is looking like. Fair?" He swiveled just his head with the question.

"Yep. That works. I'm completely at your service. Just like I've been through this entire process. Personally, I don't think there's any reason why we can't finish this building together."

The man turned his entire body toward me, and I stood from where I was bent over the last drawing. He was a mountain. Unmovable. Impenetrable. Non-negotiable.

"You know, Cole, for almost a decade, I've completely despised the faceless father of my niece. I did everything I could to help Pia raise her up to this point. We all did." He studied me as he finished his thought.

I could only assume he was talking about his two best friends, Grant Twombley and Elijah Banks. I nodded along while he spoke but yielded the floor to him completely. Hopefully, he would say his peace, and we could move away from any ill will.

"It seems my sister has been carrying around a lot of glossed-over truths this whole time," he admitted. "And part of that is my fault."

That comment took me by surprise. "I'm not following."

"Cassiopeia explained the reasons behind many of her decisions regarding being a single parent and remaining alone. That little girl is her everything. Outside of her daughter, she's barely existed other than work. For so many years, she's stifled her own personal happiness for the sake of her child."

Thank God. She must have finally gotten through to him. Vela not having a father all these years was a conscious choice she made. He was clear that I was the victim of those choices.

Of course, I also knew that her original good intentions quickly snowballed to the prolonged, unnecessary situation we'd all just endured. That her take-charge brother here steamrolled over her free will and dictated how things would go. Something told me she probably left that last part out, and I wasn't going to open that can of worms while we were trying to reach a happy medium regarding our own relationship.

"Have you and my sister discussed working together?" he asked. "Is that going to present problems?"

"No, we haven't discussed it directly. But honestly, I don't foresee any issues. She and I have always enjoyed creatively bouncing ideas off each other. We even dreamed of a future where we had one design studio. We would offer our clients a one-stop-shop kind of experience. I could design the structures, and she could decorate them."

The formidable man responded curtly. "I see."

"It makes perfect sense, right? Our chosen fields really go hand in hand."

"Yeah, it makes a lot of sense," the boss commented before proposing his next thought. "For our next meeting, let's loop her in as well. She might be the hold-up on her portion of my project. Especially now that we're getting into the residential floors. She's a perfectionist. And while I admire that trait in the people I work with, it can also be maddening."

We spent the next ninety minutes addressing the changes I'd made on the last prints, and Shark signed off on all but two. Now and then, we would touch down on the topic of Pia and Vela, but for the most part, it was the Edge that took center stage. I felt so proud of the way the building was coming along, but I was also reaching that inevitable phase of a project when I started losing interest.

Of course, my clients never knew I felt that way. I gave one hundred percent until the customer had the front door keys in their hand. Even afterward, I made myself available to them in case an issue arose.

I was rolling up the blueprints to store in the tubular carrying case when Sebastian leveled me with a long stare.

"What's up?" I asked, doing my very best to corral my nerves. One day this guy wouldn't make me feel so worried with just a look. Or the exact way he exhaled. Or the nosey questions he asked.

"Your whole family here in town?" he asked.

"For the most part, yes. We have one sister, Darian, studying abroad at the moment, and my oldest brother, Park, lives on the East Coast, where he heads one of the company's most successful brands."

He just nodded, but I wondered why he was asking. He never came off like he was gathering information to gossip with. Every word the man spoke and every move he made physically seemed predetermined. Sebastian Shark's confidence was part of what intimidated a lot of people. The man knew how to use it like a weapon, too. Like so many things, when you find what works, you stick with it.

It was the concept behind my family's fortune. Year after year, we were one of the top name brands in customer loyalty and satisfaction. We found a business formula that worked and stuck with it. When we launched new product lines, the concept was usually a large part of the marketing campaign. Loyal customers will try almost anything that you put in front of them.

"Jacob, I have to be up front with you about something that doesn't sit well with me." He let out a heavy breath and leaned against the edge of the table. "It hasn't for a long time, and I just can't get past it. Especially now, when I recognize that starry-eyed look my sister's already sporting."

"Okay. What's on your mind?"

"Your whole family, just about, lives right here in LA. Yet, for a year, you've been living out of a suitcase in an extended-stay hotel. Why? I just don't get it." He kept his piercing blue eyes trained on me but gave me the impression he wasn't done yet. "Why such an aversion to putting down roots? And is something going to spook you, and next thing I know, I'm picking up the pieces of my sister's heart and soul again?"

"You know, Sebastian, you're an amazing big brother. Pia is lucky to have so many people in her life who care so deeply for her. That makes me happy." I paused for a moment to consider how much I wanted to tell this man and how much of my life was no one else's business.

I went on. "I left UC a couple of weeks before commencement. Obviously, I graduated. I just didn't stay for all the ceremony. The internship I was awarded in Barcelona was with a renowned architectural firm, but the man I worked with day in and day out was very minimalist. He wanted everyone around him to live the same way. Especially since I stayed with him when I first arrived. He was incredibly gifted, and it was a privilege to study under his tutelage. So, he basically dictated all the rules. He believed keeping your surroundings simple and free from clutter allowed the creative brain to grow and dominate in a person's existence."

"Oh, for Christ's sake. And what if you wanted a flat-screen TV?" Shark asked. "Then what? They sent you home because you wanted to play Xbox?"

I shrugged and chuckled. "I don't know. I certainly never tested him. No one else did, either. But the reason I started there with my response was because when I got back here, to Los Angeles, I was used to living in that manner. Currently I own very few material possessions. It made perfect sense to stay in one of my family's extended-stay hotels until I found a place. I've been perfectly content there, and it's free! A total bonus with rent so sky-high in this city."

"What about now, though? How are you going to have Pia and Vela over to your place when it's probably smaller than this office?" he asked immediately, and I couldn't understand why he was making this his business.

But I continued to explain myself. "It's definitely too small for a family, plus that's no way to live with a child. It just came down to not needing anything more up to this point. I've actually been meaning to ask you if you have a Realtor you could recommend."

"I don't. It's been years since I bought my house. Twombley, on the other hand, keeps his Realtor on speed dial. He's definitely the person to help you. I'll walk you out to Craig, and you can set up your next appointment and get Twombley's info too."

"Perfect. I really appreciate it." I stopped fidgeting for a moment and held eye contact with the formidable man and said, "I feel really good about all this. I'm glad we met today, and I can't wait to dig in on these drawings. I have so many ideas I want to surprise you with."

That made him double take, one inky brow raised higher than the other.

"Trust me?" I asked.

"Isn't it obvious that I do? First I hand over my lifelong dream, and now I'm giving my blessing on my one and only family member. If I didn't trust you, Jake? You'd be driving home already."

"Thank you, Sebastian. For both. From the depths of my heart, thank you." I stopped there. I had to leave with some of my manhood intact.

"Just don't fuck me over, Junior. I'll destroy you if you do. I don't care who the fuck your family is or what guru you studied with. You'll never work again."

Well, okay.

What does one say to all that? So, I just let it all hang in the air between us like the rancid miasma that hangs over the downtown streets after a holiday weekend.

At Craig's desk, I collected Grant's contact information and set up my next appointment with Shark. After closing the calendar app on my phone, I scrolled through my emails and text messages. The first one I always looked for now was Pia's.

How did it go? Call me when you're done.

And then another an hour later, almost to the minute. Someone was watching the clock.

I hope Bas wasn't a jerk. Call me. I'm
starting to worry.

My sweet little worrywart.

The smile on my face must have told a thousand things, because Craig spoke up.

"You must've been waiting for that one. You look like a kid on prom night with that grin."

I didn't have something clever ready for a response, so a genuine laugh burst out. My cheeks instantly felt hot, hoping that wasn't as loud as it sounded to my own ears.

"I'll see you in ten days or so, Craig," I said to the man. "Try to stay out of trouble."

"Always, Mr. Cole. Always!" His smile was as wide as mine, and goddamn did it feel good to be happy. In the elevator, I shot a text back to my star.

Just finished up. All's well. Don't stress.

The reply bubble opened before I hit the lobby, and soon her text arrived.

Truly? You wouldn't just say that, right?

> *No, darling. Just honesty from me. That's a promise you can count on. Can we get together tonight?*

There's a little girl who would love to see you. If you're up for it?

> *I'll be there with bells on. What time works? I'm done for the day. Do you want me to grab her from school?*

This time her reply took at least twice as long to come in. The bubble was there and popped twice before an actual text arrived.

Shit. Did I overstep? Go too far, too fast? My brain spun with sixteen possible transgressions while I waited for her response.

You'll put Wren out of a job. Appreciate the offer, though. How does six work?

> *Perfect. Does my daughter enjoy reading? I want to bring her something.*

You don't have to do that. She's going to be thrilled with your visit.

> *Cass?*

Hmmm?

Just answer the question, please.

Yes, she does.

See? Wasn't so hard. See you at six.

I fought every urge to tell her I missed her or put some sort of heart-shaped symbol at the end of the message. Instead, I decided text messaging apps should come with a warning for users dealing with anxiety.

This was stressful on a whole new level. Worrying if the reader could sense your tone, worrying if you overstepped, worrying that you sent it to the intended recipient. The list of stressors was endless. Maybe this was why the concept never appealed to me before Pia was back in my life. Now I thought I'd be willing to use carrier pigeons or smoke signals if it meant I could exchange a few messages with my woman throughout the day.

I made a pitstop at the bookstore on my way home and had just enough time to shower and change and drive up to their house. As long as the traffic gods remained on my side, anyway.

After I got situated in my car, I called the number Craig had given me for Grant. The phone rang four times, and I thought for sure I would be talking to voicemail when the friendly man picked up.

"Grant Twombley," he said in greeting.

"Grant, hey. This is Jacob Cole."

"Uhh, don't you mean Masterson?" he asked, and I didn't

know the guy well enough to discern if he was teasing or pissed.

And how the hell did he hear that information already? I didn't peg Shark as a watercooler gossiper, but he must have been on that phone the second I closed his office door.

"That is my family name, yes. I've been using Cole since I was nineteen, though, so that is the habit I'm in," I explained in an effort to defend myself. "I wasn't trying to pull one over on you."

"Chill, man. I was just busting your balls. Bas is going to flip when he finds out, though. So, word of advice, Junior? Tell him before he has to ask you about it."

"I appreciate the inside scoop on that. Unfortunately, his sister already told him most of the detailed story." I heard Grant suck in a breath with that information but reassured him, "Nah, it's all good. It needed to happen, and she and I both felt it needed to come from her and not me."

"That was probably smart," Grant said.

"I know what our reasons were, but I'm curious why you agree?" I asked him.

"Well, I've known that man for twenty-plus years now, and I don't think I've ever heard him so much as raise his voice to his sister," the friendly guy explained.

With a chuckle, I admitted, "That was Pia's number-one reason too. And we both thought since the decisions were solely hers in the past, she should take ownership of all of it now. I didn't want to throw her under the bus, necessarily. I just couldn't provide the answers like she could. Answers to the *why*s and *when*s and so forth."

Shark's best friend added, "Again, good thinking. Because Bas always asks those follow-ups."

I forced a quick laugh. "They're so similar. Kind of unnerving, really."

"So, Jake, my man, can I help you with something, or did you just call to chit chat?" Grant said, cutting the friendly banter there.

I could still feel the warmth of his smile through the phone line, though. "Yes, I'm told you have a Realtor you work with routinely and have had good luck with. Would you mind sharing his or her contact info with me?"

Quickly he answered, "Oh sure. Of course. I'll send you her contact card when we hang up. Tell her I sent you, would you? Maybe she'll slash some of her insane commission off the bottom for me." Then he grumbled, "I doubt it, though."

"Great. I appreciate it. I'm ready to get out of the hotel room and find a place my girls wouldn't mind visiting, you know?" I said, steering the conversation toward its conclusion.

"Makes perfect sense," the man offered. "I'll send it right over."

"Thanks, Grant. And thanks for the advice about Sebastian."

"Anytime, Junior. Good luck house hunting. The market is pretty brutal right now."

I hummed in understanding. "I'm trying not to think about it too much. Can't control everything, can we?"

Now he was quiet, and I wondered what I'd said that made him uneasy.

"All right, Jake. Talk to you later, man." And he was gone.

"Bye." I stared at my phone, feeling a bit bewildered. I hope I didn't just piss the guy off.

As promised, a Realtor's contact information was in my messages app within a few minutes. I had to leave her a voicemail, though, when I called. According to the recording, she was conducting an open house and would be out most of the day. I committed to my memory's calendar to call her again tomorrow if I didn't hear from her first.

The next stop I made was the bookstore a few miles from my current place. Ever since I'd found Pia, I'd really started despising the hotel. Life would be so easy if she just asked me to move in with them. The house was more than enough room for the three of us. Hell, even the nanny could stay and we would have more than enough room. But even I knew with my obsessed, fogged-over brain, that was a subject I wouldn't just bring up nonchalantly.

I went to the kids' section of the store and scanned the end caps for the books I'd seen Stella reading. That would give me a starting point, at least. Feelings of resentment sneaked up on me after I walked up and down the aisles four times before finding something she might like.

These were the moments I felt pissed that I'd never had the chance to know Vela. And I knew I could never go back and make up the special time I'd missed, either. In my limited experience, life didn't work like that. All you could do is live in the moment and look forward to the future.

There was no room in this already-complicated relationship for negative thoughts and feelings. I put my choices on the counter and smiled at the woman ringing them up.

"Special little girl in your life?" she asked casually.

"Yes, very. But we just met, so I'm hoping these are a good choice."

"How old is she?" the woman asked, turning one of the books over to read the back.

"She's almost nine. Going on twenty-nine." I laughed a bit and thought a saying never fit a child more perfectly.

"I think you made great choices here. And this one"—she tapped on the third book I picked—"is first in a series. So, if she does love it, you'll have future gift opportunities." She gave me another smile, and I quickly looked to see if anyone else had come up behind me in line.

Why would I feel guilty that a kind salesperson was smiling at me? I couldn't figure it out, but I'd always felt awkward when women flirted with me. In my heart, I'd always felt like I'd belonged to someone.

Even when she didn't want me.

Shitty thoughts for another time. Right now, as I headed out to my car, I had a few great gifts for my girl and just needed to grab something for her mama, and then, if I played my cards right, maybe Pia would feel so grateful she'd take some pity on me and let me touch her more.

I caught a glimpse of my enormous grin in the rearview mirror and burst out laughing fully. It felt so damn good to be happy. Excitedly optimistic felt pretty great too.

The same buoyancy remained for the entire drive to Calabasas later that evening. When I rang Pia's doorbell, I felt like I was truly floating.

CHAPTER THIRTEEN

PIA

Three verbal threats since I'd arrived home, and Vela finally finished her homework. A large part of me understood her lack of enthusiasm because she had just been in class all day. To come home and dig right into homework was tough on an eight-year-old attention span. Undoubtedly what would be worse would be trying to get her to do her homework after her father left this evening.

And he would be leaving.

Much to my daughter's disappointment, we weren't at the stage where I was comfortable having a sleepover with Jacob. Especially with her in the house to observe and then report on the event.

It had been so long since I'd slept with a man. Since Jacob, actually. Just the thought of having sex with him made my insides turn into a battle zone. The stress of it all—oh my God.

First, my body was nothing like it was when we were in college. Back then, I was reed thin from barely having enough food to eat my entire life, and the little bit on my bones was muscle.

We didn't have the comforts of life that most of the kids we went to school with did. We walked or rode bikes everywhere, sometimes even all the way across town if we missed the school bus.

The last thing we ever wanted to do was draw attention to our home life. When children were absent from school, the office nurse made phone calls to the parents to find out why. Since we were basically squatting in our dead parents' home and not one single adult would claim us as their responsibility, we did everything in our power to fly under the radar.

Now, for Jake to see me, after giving birth and discovering a woman's body in the process, would he be disappointed? There were lumps and bumps in places that were once smooth and creamy. Skin that used to be flawless was now marked with the racing stripe scars of stretching to accommodate another human.

We would definitely have to take things slowly and manage expectations. And for God's sake, keep the lights out.

In the quiet, lonely hours of the night, I could recognize that I longed for physical intimacy. My body and heart craved the affection and connection I knew he was capable of providing.

And my God—the memories of the sexual satisfaction Jacob could deliver were enough to flood my entire body with arousal. The nights I allowed those thoughts to invade my mind, I had to reach into my panties and touch myself. There would be no hope of extinguishing the craving any other way than bringing myself to climax. Every single time, it was his face I imagined above me and his name on my melancholy sigh as I fell asleep afterward. Alone.

Jake arrived right on time. Nothing new there. The man took punctuality to an obsessive level. At least he used to. I knew there were so many things we would rediscover about each other.

Vela raced to answer the door the moment the doorbell played its first note.

"Wait for an adult, young lady," I called from about twenty feet behind her. "You know better than that."

"I'm just so excited," she said, hopping from foot to foot.

My smile matched hers when I swung the door open and we greeted our visitor.

"Hi." Jake bounced his stare back and forth between us. Then he stooped down to be on Vela's level.

"How have you been?" he asked her, and I looked on with the fullest heart I could remember having.

In my wildest dreams, I never allowed myself to think this moment would happen. That my child's father would have an active role in her life. I always figured, and probably unfairly so, having witnessed his amazing attitude so far, that he would either be so hurt he wouldn't come around at all or would have moved on with his life so completely, he couldn't spare her, or us, a second look.

"I'm good. Happy it's almost the weekend. My friend Jessalyn is having a birthday party on..." She paused and looked to me. "When is the party, Mama?"

"Saturday."

"She's having a party on Saturday, and I get to go. Mama said they are having a roller-skating party, and I've never done dat, so I'm super excited."

"*That*," I repeated, for which I got an eight-year-old's death stare. I realized I might have embarrassed her in front of Jake, so I mouthed *Sorry*. But she was on to the next topic already, so crisis avoided.

"Oh, I can't wait to hear all about it after you give it a try," Jacob offered. "I bet you'll be really good at it."

Vela's eyes got saucer-wide, and she suggested excitedly. "You should come to the party too! Do you know how to skate? You could teach me!"

While the idea behind the suggestion was precious, I had to stop the runaway train before it went off the tracks completely. I hated always being the wet towel.

"Honey, it's impolite to invite people to a party you aren't hosting."

She looked frustrated, but then a spark lit behind her blue eyes and her expression shifted right back to excitement. "But *you're* going," she stated as fact.

"Yes, Jessalyn's mom needs extra help and asked me if I could pitch in. Is there a reason you're pointing that out? You look like some plot is unfolding inside that clever mind of yours," I accused playfully.

"My father could go instead!" she said gleefully.

"Vela," I said with exasperation and embarrassment. "You also can't volunteer people for things they didn't offer to do. Plus, Jacob doesn't know anyone from that group of friends."

"It's okay. I can introduce—"

"Vela. Enough."

I could not have been more grateful for Jake in that moment because he artfully changed the subject with perfect timing.

"I brought you something today. I'm hoping you like it. Do you want to see?"

"Why don't we move into the living room and sit down?" I suggested. We were all still hanging out in the foyer. "Sorry for the full-court press the moment you walked in the door," I said once Jacob stood to his full height.

"No need to apologize. It's great for my ego to have someone so excited to see me," he said to me after our daughter skipped away to the other room. "I don't think I've ever had that sort of reception."

He stopped walking and crowded me back into the doorway of the powder room on our way to the living room.

"What are you doing? She'll be back here in three seconds."

"I better be quick, then." He planted a firm kiss on my lips, and I was so shocked by the move, I didn't have time to voice all the reasons he shouldn't.

As quick as he started, he stopped kissing me and stepped back so we weren't touching at all. If Vela doubled back to see where we were lagging, it would look completely innocent.

In a very husky voice, he said, "I've been thinking about doing that all day." He let the words sink in for a few beats and then added, "I missed you today."

All I could do was stand there and grin. For one thing, that kiss, although lightning fast, was so delicious I was already calculating how many minutes until my kid's bedtime.

"Where did you go?" Vela called from the living room. With flat palms to his chest, I pushed Jake the rest of the way out into the hall and then followed right on his heels as he walked the length of it.

I watched from the sidelines while Jacob gave his daughter the books he'd picked for her. Giving the guy credit, he'd made really good selections. She was overjoyed with his gesture, of course, and insisted they sit down on the spot and start reading. Carefully, she pronounced each word while running her finger under the letters. I had to choke back tears at one point and excused myself to the kitchen to fix us a snack.

When I came back into the room, I nearly dropped the bowl of popcorn I was carrying.

Vela was snuggled against Jake's side, and he had his long arm slung casually across the back of the sofa behind her.

She was doing her best to impress him, evident by the look of serious concentration on her little features.

But the handsome guy lifted his gaze to mine the moment he sensed my presence in the room again. He subtly shook his head and mouthed *Thank you*, and I thought my heart would crack wide open. So many emotions were flooding me, I couldn't focus on feeling any of them.

Just when I had pulled myself together, a second wave of emotions from that scene swelled my heart until it lodged in my throat.

But why would he be thanking me? For selfishly robbing him of nine years filled with moments like this? For not believing our love was strong enough to endure the wrath of my brother? For disappearing from existence without a single word of explanation?

Oh yes, Jacob Cole Masterson. You're so very welcome.

I didn't deserve this man. I certainly didn't deserve to witness this moment between the two of them while their bond strengthened and their glow of contentment just from being near each other could've lit the room.

If Jacob made up half of everything that was our daughter, I wondered if they both felt a sort of completion while sitting so close together. Jacob and I always swore we were written in the stars. Our pieces fit together so perfectly—that was the only explanation for it. It was a cosmic connection that went supernova the night we created this child.

"Who wants a snack?" I offered when I was sure my voice was strong.

"Mama, can I stay up past my bedtime?" Vela asked and quickly added, "Please?"

"You have school tomorrow, honey. You know how cranky

you are when you don't get enough sleep. It will wreck your whole day."

"But I want to read more and hang out with my father," she whined.

Jacob interjected, and it was the first time he did so while I was parenting. I was nervous to hear what was about to happen. I didn't want to already be fighting over raising this child.

"Vela, Mom said her answer already, and that's her answer."

She looked at him quizzically, trying to figure out if she had to listen to him or not. I knew when her little brows slashed downward, she was about to sass off, and I was in a lightning-fast internal debate.

I could let the guy flap in the breeze and see how he handled her, in all her moods. Or I could head this off at the pass before her father had to see a side of her he hadn't yet dealt with. With that option, we'd also risk the whole night crashing and burning.

"Check yourself," I warned, and I could hear her suck in a breath from where I still stood across the room.

She shot a glare my way but wisely kept quiet.

I tilted my head ever so slightly, and she dropped her stare to her lap.

Thank God for small favors.

"Can I show Jacob my room?" The girl switched topics, and I let out a sigh of relief, knowing she already moved on.

I instantly felt frustrated with my own behavior because my daughter had been the most agreeable, well-mannered child I'd known. This hellraiser attitude was new, and I didn't appreciate feeling like a hostage to it.

I'd have to chat with some of the other mothers next time we were all standing around at practice or whatever school event we were roped into chaperoning to see if anyone else was dealing with this stage too. For some reason, knowing you weren't going it alone helped navigate new territory when you came upon it.

"I think that would be fine if he would like to see your room." I nodded with a gentle smile.

"Do you?" Vela looked to her dad expectantly.

"Please use your good manners," I reminded quietly.

"Excuse me, Jacob? Would you be interested in seeing my bedroom? I have a lot of neat things in there."

Jake sat forward on the sofa with enthusiasm. "Oh, yes, I would love that. Thank you for asking."

I didn't miss the wink he sneaked my way as they walked by and headed down the hall toward Vela's room.

"You coming, Mama?" our daughter shouted on the way.

"I'm going to pack your lunch first, if you're okay with that? Jake, same goes for you."

"You want to pack my lunch?" he asked with a chuckle.

"No, smarty pants. Unless you love peanut butter and jelly like the rest of the kids in class." I teased back.

"Actually," the man said, "I do love a good PB&J. Especially if the bread is squishy and fresh."

"That's my favorite too!" Vela squealed so loudly, I could hear every word from the kitchen. Then I listened while she proceeded to explain that one boy, Rider, was allergic to peanut butter, so he couldn't sit by anyone who had it in their lunch.

Jake was going to have a whole new appreciation for how golden silence really could be.

Even after I finished with her lunch, I lingered in the

kitchen and great room, trying to give them time alone. Eventually I wandered down the hall to see what they were doing. It had gotten very quiet, and I hoped she wasn't giving him a hard time.

Vela's door was open, so the moment I rounded the corner and saw them, I felt like I'd been kicked in the stomach. The two were propped against the overstuffed pink-and-white gingham headboard with the mountain of decorative pillows still in place. My daughter was snuggled against her father's side, and he had a protective arm circled around her. One's hand clutched the other's and they rested their joined palms on Jake's sternum.

On top of that was the book we'd been working our way through, apparently laid to rest when they couldn't keep their eyes open any longer. It was a chapter book she chose from the library on our last visit, and now I'd have to reread to find out what I missed.

My smile was so big, my cheeks ached. Not sure how long I'd been standing there watching them, I reached for my phone to check the time. I snapped a few pictures of the precious setup before me and thought if the low-light pictures turned out, it would be a nice surprise to text to Jacob tomorrow while we were apart.

There was so much I missed about having a relationship to nurture. I wondered if Jacob wanted that or if his interest in me was a secondary byproduct of getting better acquainted with his child.

I didn't think I was mistaken that we both felt substantial heat in my office when he kissed me. I was a little bummed that he was sleeping, actually, because I was hoping once she went to bed we might pick up where we left off.

And what did I do now? Let him sleep here until he naturally woke up? Wake him up and likely Vela too since they were intertwined so sweetly? She had school in the morning. That fact hadn't changed. Nor did the bit that she was an absolute bear to deal with when she didn't get enough sleep.

Deciding to leave them for a bit longer, I went to my room and undressed. If they were still sleeping after I took a shower, I would carefully wake Jacob so he could leave. No way were we ready for a sleepover.

The pounding hot water felt so good on my tired body, I wanted to luxuriate beneath the spray for hours. But, I had company in the house, and Wren had the night off, so she wasn't around to entertain my guest while I lazed under the water spray. No, I needed to get out. I turned off the faucet and pivoted to grab my towel from the hook right outside the shower enclosure—and came face to face with Jacob.

A startled yelp came out of my mouth before I could stop it, and I hoped it sounded louder bouncing around the tiled shower than anywhere else.

"Holy shit! You scared me," I said with my hand on my chest. My heart pounded wildly beneath my ribs, and I took a deep breath. "I was going to wake you when I got out. I couldn't bring myself to disturb you, though." I hurried and wrapped the towel he handed me around my dripping form.

"She's still asleep. I covered her, but she's in the clothes she had on," he offered in response. "I didn't know what else to do and not wake her."

I reached forward and put my hand on his forearm to reassure him. "That's all fine. Seriously, it's exactly what I would've done in that situation."

He grinned. "Really?"

"Yes. You have a lot of experience with Stella. You know what you're doing. Don't sweat the little stuff," I said over my shoulder as I shrugged on my robe.

Jacob's heated stare followed every move I made as I sat at my vanity to brush my wet hair.

"May I?" He stepped in behind me and asked while reaching for the brush.

"You want to brush my hair?" This was a first, and his gesture took me by surprise.

"Yes. I would've washed it too, all of you, if I had just woken up a little sooner," he said casually and parted my hair into sections.

"Mmmm" was all I could come up with when he started tugging on my scalp with each pass of the brush. Pinpoints of arousal skittered from the top of my head all the way down to my toes.

"Feel good?"

"Yeesss," I sighed. "So good."

My God, it had been so long since another person cared for me in a physical way. I was a greedy sponge soaking up every drop of his attention.

Jake worked quietly, moving around me as I sat on the bench in front of my makeup desk, as Vela called it. I alternated between watching him in the mirror and letting my eyes drift closed in pure delight.

"Have you kept your hair long all these years?" he asked.

"For the most part. Never really thought short hair suited me like it does some people." I thought about it for a second, trying to picture myself with a different look.

"Like Rio, for example, Grant's wife? She's adorable and sexy in that little pixie, but I could never pull that off."

"Darling." Jake sighed. "You could be bald and be the hottest woman in the room, no matter the company."

"Well, you might be biased, then."

"Regardless..." he answered, grinning. Then I watched as he gathered my hair and twisted it into one thick rope and laid it over my left shoulder. He bent over my right and softly kissed the exposed skin, starting just behind my ear. He moved an inch lower and kissed me there and, in a very low, sexy tone, issued compliment after compliment.

"You're more beautiful now than you were in school." Kiss. Then I felt the heat of his tongue as he connected the wet mark from that kiss up to the previous one and back again.

"I want to kiss every inch of this incredible body, Cass." Kiss, lick, bite. "I want to feel you beneath me." He paused there to bite the space where my neck and shoulder came together, and I gasped at the remarkable sensation.

I shot my hand up to his hair and instinctively grabbed a handful, and he growled.

"Hands down," he ordered, but I didn't instantly comply. I was out of practice with the command-and-response dynamic.

"Now," Jacob said calmly. So calmly, especially when compared to how wild I felt inside. That time his dictate garnered my immediate attention.

But now my thoughts were so scrambled as he heaped on the arousal. I couldn't remember what he issued in the first place. He slid his mouth all the way back up to my ear and spoke right into the pit.

"Hands in your lap, Star, or I'll use the belt from your robe to bind them together."

Well, shit. Now I couldn't decide which sounded better. And this man was the one and only man who knew how appealing his threat would actually be. I'd always enjoyed being restrained. No matter where we were when he did it or what he used to do it with. I loved being helpless but safe and cared for all at the same time.

A few long beats passed, and Jacob grew impatient. Sternly, he asked, "Have you heard a word I said?"

"Yes?" I smiled sheepishly. But we both knew I'd been daydreaming.

"Is that a question?" he teased.

"Is that?" I shot back.

He met my blue stare in the mirror and quirked a brow in rebuke. His Cass from nine years ago didn't sass back, and he seemed unsure of what to do with it now.

"Is topping from the bottom your thing now?"

"I don't have a thing," I stated plainly.

"You don't play anymore?"

"Jacob…" I sighed, not sure I wanted to have this conversation at this hour. Fine, at any hour. But I turned my whole body so I was facing him.

He took a step back to make room for my legs between us but stayed close enough to hover above me.

Deciding I wanted to be on even ground for this, I stood too and suggested we go sit and talk.

"Lead the way," he said and swept his hand out in front of us, inviting me to go first.

There was a small sitting area in my bedroom, but it was cluttered with Vela's crap. A lot of times, she did homework or other art projects while I got ready in the morning. Just so we could spend more time together.

"Would you mind if we sat on the bed?" I asked over my shoulder and immediately winced when I heard how the invitation sounded. I spun back to face him and could feel heat flushing my cheeks. "I'm sorry. That sounded so forward."

"Woman, be serious." He grinned, but when I just stared at him, puzzled, he reached out and gripped my hips to pull me into his body. "I've been inside this incredible body in every possible way."

He closed the last inch that separated us and kissed my mouth with a firm press of his lips before asking, "Do you remember how amazing it feels to have my cock inside you?"

I parted to speak—or breathe, more likely—and he dove in with his urgent tongue. Aggressive stabbing and twisting, licking and thrusting—Jacob did magical things to my mouth with his tongue, and my head swam with dizzying pleasure.

If he kept up the assault, we'd fall onto the bed, not sit. I had to stop him. Never mind how divine it all felt or how the sounds coming from deep in my throat sounded like a vocal green light.

"We should slow down," I panted.

"No, I don't think we should. Why would we?"

"It's too much. Too soon." I cradled my face in my hands. "I don't know."

"Darling." He pulled my hands down and held them in his stronger, more capable ones. "Why deny yourself pleasure?"

"It's not—" I stammered before he cut me off.

"How long has it been, baby?"

"What? How long has *what* been?" Why I was acting so incredulous now, I couldn't say. This was the exact conversation I wanted to have. But not being in control of it made me protest having it at all. Fuck me, this man had my brain scrambled.

"You seem nervous. I'm trying to figure out if it's me making you feel that way, or if you haven't been with a man in a while."

"Yes!" I answered and forced a nervous laugh.

Jake studied me for a bit and finally asked, "But why? For one thing, it's me." He thumped his chest once. Twice. "For another thing, how can you possibly ever have a dry spell? Seriously, woman. Ever?" Jacob accused lightheartedly.

On the bed, I positioned myself to be more comfortable propped against the headboard with some pillows. Jacob moved to join me, so I scooted over to make room.

"Don't go too far now. Can I hold you?" He looked hopeful—and hungry—and my stomach fluttered with anticipation.

"Yes, I would like that," I said shyly and snuggled into his open embrace. When he buried his nose in my hair, my eyes drifted closed, and I simply enjoyed his proximity.

"You feel so good, Jacob. I've missed this." The comment had several meanings. One was the obvious. I missed him. There hadn't been a day that I didn't think about him in some way. It couldn't be helped, and I wouldn't apologize for it.

The second, less obvious reason was simpler to understand. I was lonely. It wasn't anything more than that. Basic biological or human needs. I longed for physical touch and satisfaction. The remarkable thing was the two reasons meeting in the middle to eradicate each other's existence.

I didn't miss the irony that reuniting with the only man I ever loved would also cure these pangs of need deep within my body and soul created by leaving the very same man.

"Explain to me why a woman as beautiful, intelligent, kind, caring, compassionate, sexy, and witty as you, Ms. Shark, has been lonely. Does your overbearing and ferocious big brother still scare all the boys away?"

My guy chuckled at his own question.

"Adult…mmmm…relationships?" I pitched my voice higher on the last word, making it clear I wasn't sure how to label dating in my life. "Are difficult with an eight-year-old in tow. Also, with the Edge's planning the past few years, we've all been burning the candle at both ends to keep the project on schedule. You get that part at least, right?"

"Absolutely. Keeping Sebastian content is a full-time job for someone, I'm sure."

I smiled picturing that saint. "Yes, her name is Abbigail. She is the best thing that could've ever happened to my brother. Watching him learn how to love her has been nothing short of awe-inspiring."

"I love hearing you talk about each other," the man admitted. "You both are so devoted to each other, you and Sebastian. Honestly, I feel a bit jealous."

"But you have such a big, close family. That has to be amazing in its own right, no?"

"Yes, there are definitely positives," Jake answered but didn't offer more.

"Are you close with your siblings? How many of each do you have? Sisters and brothers, I mean." I pressed for more information. I wanted to learn every single thing about the man.

He stroked hair back over my shoulder and answered, "There are ten of us in total. Just two girls in the whole lot."

"Stella's mother? I think you said her name is Cecile?" I asked, and he nodded.

"And my other sister's name is Darian. She's the third youngest. Between Row and Key."

"Your parents chose such unique names," I commented with appreciation.

"Their names are Rownin and Keenan. But yes, other than mine, they're all pretty interesting names."

"What's wrong with Jacob? It's very noble. And classic. I love it," I said, pouring on the adoration.

"What is Vela's middle name?" Jake asked next. It made sense that he would follow our weird talk track to that spot.

"Andromeda," I said with a sly smile. If ever there were a person who would understand why I chose the unusual name for my daughter—our daughter—it would be this guy.

"Ahhh, so clever. But I bet no one understands." His grin was so bright, I felt like I was sunbathing in his approval.

"No, most people don't know that Cassiopeia was Andromeda's mother, so they don't know the correlation. Therefore, it's our little secret, hers and mine. And yours too now. Obviously." My smile matched his then, thinking of the delight Vela got in sharing this little clandestine connection.

Jacob stared at me for a long, quiet moment. Quiet with regard to conversation, but the air in the room shifted. The pupils in his dark eyes had grown to the point I couldn't differentiate the brown iris any longer. As he started taking deeper breaths in, mine matched the rhythm. What the hell was happening?

"Jake?" I croaked.

"I want you so bad, Pia," he declared shamelessly. "I'd do just about anything you asked right now."

I opened my mouth to speak, to challenge him to take this slowly, to give me more time. Be patient. But he cut me off before I could utter a word.

"Anything but wait another minute. I'm so fucking hard for you right now, it hurts. I know you feel the heat between us, too. It's all still right here between us, Star. Nothing's changed, no matter how many nights we've been cheated out of."

He moved so he loomed over me as I rolled a bit to lie flat on my back. This time, when his mouth met mine, we had matched appetites of need and desire. I didn't have a thought-out plan here, but I was sure of one thing: Every move Jacob Cole made involving our bodies felt way too good to tell him to stop. I just had to be able to look at myself in the mirror in the morning.

CHAPTER FOURTEEN

JACOB

If she said stop now, I seriously doubted I could. Or would. The animal that had been hibernating deep in the coldest, darkest, cave of my humanity yawned and stretched and was ready to stake a claim to every square inch of her body.

As I hovered over her with my weight supported mostly on my bent forearms, I said a quick and mental *Thank you* to my merciless trainer for the endless minutes of planks he made me suffer through.

Hell yes. Worth every bead of sweat now!

"I need to see you. All of you," I issued to my beautiful queen, and she swallowed roughly.

"I . . . I feel embarrassed," she whispered.

My confusion must have expressed itself, because immediately she explained.

"I'm not twenty anymore." She followed the comment with an averted glance somewhere past me and then an uncomfortable smile.

"No, neither of us are. But you're twenty times more beautiful than you were then. And woman, you're so fucking hot—your body has me so hungry to taste and touch you, I don't want to wait another minute, baby." I watched her for a few beats, and when she didn't respond, I added, "But I need you to say okay. It's been a long time, and I don't want to misread anything here."

We held each other prisoner in our stares, and I finally had to straddle her thighs and rest my weight down on the mattress. That was okay, though. It freed my hands for more pleasurable things. I pushed my face into the juncture of her neck and shoulder and inhaled her intoxicating scent before sucking on her skin. Mixing bites and licks in with the firm kisses, I traveled up to her ear to issue a few commands.

"I'm going to untie this mom robe of yours and see if underneath you're still the naughty girl I once knew."

"Jake . . ." She exhaled my name with a light huff. But still, not the answer I needed from her.

"Tell me yes, Star. Give me what I want."

"Yes. Please, yes." Pia whimpered and arched her back in invitation.

Fuck me. Finally.

At once, I was a man on a mission. Trying not to attack her like the beast inside was willing me to do, I opened the robe's belt with the care of a surgeon making his first incision.

"God, Jacob, why are you taking so long? I want to feel your mouth on my skin," she moaned.

"Patience, darling. I've been fantasizing about this moment for so long, I'm trying to commit every second to memory." A nervous laugh escaped because it had been a long time since I undressed a woman. My careful ministrations finally paid off as I worked the knot loose.

When I parted the two halves of her robe, I audibly sucked in a breath. "Cass," I said with reverence. "You're stunning. I've dreamed of your tits more nights than I can count. I have to see you." I backed down her body just a bit so I could admire her completely.

"Star," I breathed. "You're the most breathtaking woman I've ever seen." She closed her eyes as I praised her, and I decided that for now, that would be okay. When I was deep inside her body, I would demand she hold my gaze.

At that moment, all I could focus on were the perfect breasts in front of me. Boobs had been my weakness from the moment I'd discovered girls' bodies were different than boys'. They're the part of a woman that is so uniquely her own. No two were the same—not even on the same woman.

Enough with the staring, though. I moved in to touch and stroke, lick and bite. Pia's nipples stood as hard points while I lightly danced my fingertips across the tips. I shifted closer and covered much of her breast with my greedy mouth. Beneath me, Pia sighed and undulated. Not to pull away but to push more of the swell into my face.

"What is it, woman? What do you need? Tell me so I can make this good for you."

"It—it's already amazing. My God. It's been so long, Jake. So freaking long. I feel like I'm going to pass out."

"Well, breathe, darling. Otherwise you'll miss the good parts. Because honestly, I don't think I could stop."

She spurted out a laugh. "That's really romantic, man."

We both relaxed a bit with our chuckles. "I think that sounded creepier than I meant it to."

"Just exactly how creepy were you going for?" she teased while I concentrated on regulating my breathing.

"No, not creepy at all. I'm all jumbled up like a schoolboy. This is ridiculous." I shook my head and then swiftly kissed her. Instantly, my hunger for her was stoked to a throbbing urgency again, and I deepened our kiss.

When she was panting from my assault on her mouth, I

stood and loomed over her. Pia kept her eyes fixed on me while I hooked my thumb into my shirt's collar and whipped the thing over my head.

She sat up on the bed and reached out to touch my bare skin. "Oh, Jacob. Your body—" She swallowed so roughly, I could make out her throat's undulation in the watery moonlight filtering through her wood shutters. "This is so unfair."

"Unfair? What do you—"

"How do you look even better than I remember? Please, come closer so I can touch you," she begged, but I was frozen in place beside the bed, watching her.

"Well, you know they say boys stop maturing later than girls."

She dipped her chin. "Yeah, I've heard something like that. Can...can I?" She raked her hungry eyes up my body again, and I actually shivered in anticipation of what she was about to ask.

"You can probably do whatever you'd like, darling. As long as you keep looking at me like you are right now," I issued.

"Can I see all of you?" She gained some courage and waved her hand in an unorganized way toward the lower half of my body.

How I didn't come from her rapt stare alone was a miracle.

Pia watched with almost fascination as I slowly released my belt and went for the button and fly of my slacks.

An idea struck, so I asked her in the most seductive voice I could manage, "Do you want to do it?"

She began her answer by slowly shaking her head then finally said, "No. I want to watch you."

Her normally strong, authoritative voice had shifted to something different altogether. There was a lyrical quality to her tone, and I was flooded with memories of her soulful singing voice. How had I forgotten that? For so many years, I had to force myself to leave details by the roadside that did nothing but torture me when I was lonely.

"Do you still sing?" I asked with my hands stalling at my waistband.

A shy smile crossed her lips. She'd never grasped how talented she was, and no amount of praise would convince her.

"Not as much as I used to. I mean"—she picked at the blanket for a beat—"does the shower count? I sang a lot to Vela when she was a baby. The child was so fussy, I'd try everything I could think of to get her to settle." She looked wistful with the memories, and I found myself, once again, jealous of all the things I'd missed out on.

"I think the urge really hits me when I'm missing my mom," she finished with. When she met my gaze square on, she challenged, "Are you stalling?"

In answer, I stood and dropped my pants around my ankles and stepped out of them, holding her hostage with my glare the entire time. My erection hadn't relaxed in the slightest. In fact, her sassy mood shift made it pulse harder.

If that was even possible.

How *was* that possible? It felt like I'd had the same unsatisfied erection going for seven days. No matter how many times I jacked off, it came right back the minute she crossed my mind. Which was constantly... therefore, so was the everlasting woody.

"Let me see," she whispered, staring at my crotch. When she sunk her front teeth into her bottom lip, I was in danger of pouncing on her right then.

"That hungry look you have is doing crazy things to my

cock, darling." My throat had become so dry, my deep voice sounded even lower than usual. "Are we doing this?"

Some things were obvious, things we both wanted—hell *needed*—at this point. But I wanted to know if we were on the same page so I didn't get carried away and make things awkward and frustrating for us both.

"Isn't it obvious?" she replied with a little grin.

"No, not completely. For one thing, you still have way too much clothing on for what I'd like to think is about to happen. For another thing, while it hasn't been nine years of complete celibacy for me, it's been a very long time since I've been with a woman. I don't think I'm going to be able to stop if we get going here. I just want to be fair to both of us."

If that ended up sounding like a warning, it wasn't my original intent. Though, if we couldn't be honest with each other, what was the point of even trying to rekindle our relationship?

"I appreciate your candor. If you need me to spell it out for you, I can do that. But I'd rather just let things progress naturally. I hear what you're saying. Or warning, more like. And honestly, Jake? It's just making me want you more."

Immediately I wrapped my hand around my shaft and squeezed. The damn thing jumped when I made contact, and my groan turned to a hiss.

"Come closer," Pia said seductively, and I shifted so I was within reach.

"Now you," I issued, but she was so engrossed in watching the way I pushed the darker crown through my fist first, followed by the length of the shaft—again and again as I tried to relieve some of the strain in my balls—she didn't respond to my dictate.

"Cass." Using her old name got her attention, so I repeated, "Now you. Take that fucking robe off, or I'll do it for you."

Physically, I knew every shift she saw in that moment. I stood taller, feet set to the width of my hips, shoulders back so my spine was arrow straight. My normally nondescript brown eyes got darker from dilating pupils meeting shadowed irises. Usually gentle, open, affable facial features morphed into serious, attentive, and very demanding characteristics that told anyone nearby, *Don't fuck with me right now.*

I was the dominant man she knew and loved. Craved and did her best to please. It wasn't a hard swap to find this side of my psyche when I did. It just wasn't something I'd allowed myself to indulge in for a very long time. There was a tiny glimmer of this part of my personality in the conference room that first day we saw each other again. That day was like the first day of spring after a very long and cold winter.

She'd responded then . . . She'd respond now . . .

Pia skittered off the side of the bed, fumbling with the thick material of the robe.

"Easy, Star. Breathe, baby. No one's in trouble." Then I added darkly, "Yet." I muttered the last word, but she visibly took a steadying breath and dropped her robe to the ground.

Without looking to me, she hooked her thumbs into her sexy little panties but caught herself. She met my waiting eyes with a question in hers.

Do you want the panties off too?

"Leave them. I think I'd like the honor," I answered her unspoken question, and she put her hands down at her sides and trained her stare on my feet.

My heart and dick swelled in unison. She was breathtaking like this. Unlike so many other little things that had been shoved to the corners of my memory so I wouldn't be constantly reminded of what I'd lost, for years, very clear memories of Pia's submission lived and breathed in the forefront of my mind.

She was who I saw every single time I was alone and had to take the edge off my pent-up desire in order to remain sane. The name I gasped when I climaxed in my own hand, on my stomach, or in the sheets of my empty bed, was hers.

And her ass was still the one I planned on striping raw for ever leaving me in the first place. For not trusting in what we'd built together. For not believing in the strength of our love to show us the way through our chosen separation.

For giving life to another human and for enduring single parenthood when I would've swum across the fucking Atlantic Ocean to be by her side. I was never even given the choice.

But tonight there wasn't room for all that. Tonight, this reunion would be filled with intimacy and passion. My plan was to spend the night rediscovering her body and relearning ways to please her. Anything on top of that would be a bonus.

Right here, I was reclaiming what was mine. Internally, I vowed to spend the rest of my life making her and our daughter happy, keeping them safe, and supporting them while they chased their dreams. This time, I wouldn't wait to be given a choice. This time, I would take what I wanted, when I wanted it.

Invitation or not.

I walked around her in a slow circle and observed her from every angle. On the second orbit, I stopped behind her, stepping directly into her personal space. She still had her hair down from her shower, so I moved the bulk to one side and exhaled on the back of her neck, watching goosebumps rise across her body.

Inside my chest, there was a consuming need to bite her flawless skin. The more I denied myself, the stronger it grew.

"Tell me, darling," I growled in her ear. The name was endearing, but what I was about to do to her was not. "Do you still like when it hurts?"

With her gaze angled down, she only had about an inch more to drop her head until her chin met her chest.

"Was that a nod? Answer in words, Cassiopeia."

"I-I don't know."

"You don't know?" I repeated incredulously.

"It's been so long, you know?" she explained quietly.

"I hope you don't hold it against me for saying this..." I kissed her neck and nuzzled right behind her ear with my nose. "But I hope you do. Because I really want to hurt you, girl." Another kiss to her neck then connected the two spots with my tongue before giving in and biting. I finished the thought after releasing her flesh from between my teeth. "In all the best ways."

Her whimper was like a love song to me.

I squatted down behind her and, in one unexpected rush, yanked her panties to her knees. Thinking about just tearing them off made my cock throb incessantly, but I resisted that urge, too. I shifted my position to kneel for a steadier grounding and lovingly ran my palms up and down her legs. I stayed clear of her pussy but could feel the heat coming from her core when I got close.

A few times, I brushed against her folds with the back of my fingers, and I was completely gratified when I felt how wet she was. Watching her breathing, I waited for it to pick up.

"You're being so good, Cass. So patient," I taunted my trembling woman. "Does it feel good to be touched?"

Pia nodded urgently.

"Out loud, darling," I insisted. "You know better. After today, no more warnings on that one." I sank my teeth into her ass and clamped down until she stammered through her reply completely.

"Yes. Yes, it feels—shit—feels good to be—touched. Jack! Please!"

"Mmmm, what is it, baby?" She moved to rub where I left a mark on her one ass cheek, and I warned her with a low growl.

"It still hurts," she whimpered but kept her balled fist by her side.

To soothe the ache, I pressed my flat tongue onto the bite mark and warmed her flesh with my mouth. After a few moments, I fluttered my tongue around the same spot, fantasizing I was in front of her in this same position.

I stood and walked around the front of my gorgeous woman. Red splotches decorated her cheeks, and her forehead was slick with perspiration.

"Give me your panties and get your ass on the bed. Sit right on the edge."

Pia had a regal sleigh bed. The monstrous piece of furniture would consume my entire hotel room, it was so large and opulent. From my subtle scanning, I didn't see any rig points for future fun. I was a resourceful man when necessary—I was sure some improvising could be done. Additionally, if I bound her, I couldn't feel her hands on my body, and I was too greedy tonight to not experience that too.

When I stepped in front of her, her stare went right to my dick. The tip was wet from crying to be inside her.

I watched her wiggle into the spot I indicated on the bed and then gave more instructions. "Rest your heels up here on the bed frame and let your knees drop open."

Pia held my gaze while placing her feet on the solid wood structure of the bed. It was somewhere between shin and knee high for me, making her look like she was in the stirrups of a medical exam table.

I had to close my eyes and take a few centering breaths after that thought. When I opened them again and refocused on the inviting sight in front of me, I moaned her name in awe.

"Cassiopeia. My God, where have you been?" I leaned over her and took her mouth in a deep, demanding kiss. I moved one hand right to her full tits and made long strokes along the inside of her thigh with the other.

Pia leaned back on her straight arms for support, opening her body to me like a sacred offering. She let her head fall back until she was staring at the vaulted ceiling. Each time I neared her pussy, a ripple effect of tightening muscles went from that point of contact all the way up to her expression.

"Hand me a pillow, please," I said, and then I dropped it to the floor once she had. I followed it right down to kneel between her legs. If I were a praying man, this would definitely be the altar where I'd come to worship. "My God, woman, you're so fucking sexy. And wet. You're so swollen..." I commented inches from her sex. The reverence in my tone was so pure and honest, she had to know I was completely enraptured.

With all the treasure in front of me, I felt dizzy with arousal. It was difficult to organize my thoughts enough to come up with a strategy, so I gave in to instinct and touched her.

Immediately, she moaned.

"Quiet, darling," I commanded. "We don't need the young one in here spoiling our fun, do we?"

"No, no, definitely not. I'll be quiet, I promise. Please don't stop," Pia begged. "I'm so ready."

"I better make it good then, huh?" I smiled and shifted closer to her pussy.

Fuck yes. Finally.

I used my hand to spread her open and dove in with an eager tongue. Her taste exploded on my lips first, and then I couldn't stop. Couldn't get enough. I was possessed by her smell, her taste, and her almost silent moans as I worked her over.

"Feels good baby, doesn't it? You're so creamy and delicious. I've thought about this cunt every day for almost nine years," I confessed from my knees. "Somehow it tastes even better than I remember."

Rediscovering what she enjoyed and what really made her squirm would take more than one time together, but I was all in. Silently, I vowed to make eating her pussy part of my daily accomplishments. Even with that frequency, it probably still wouldn't be enough.

Pia had told me she hadn't had sex since the night we conceived our daughter. Her pussy was so fucking tight, even working my fingers into her body deserved care and consideration so she wouldn't be uncomfortable. Her abundant arousal was making the task easier.

I bit into her, and she jerked her body to move away.

"No, stop. You know you love it. And when I ask you a direct question, you know I expect an answer." Then I reminded her what I asked. "Doesn't it feel so good?"

"Yes, yes, it's so good." She grabbed into my hair with both hands. "But Jake? Jacob?" The second time she said my name, it was more of a sigh.

I let her tug my head away from her pussy and met her wild stare. "What is it?"

"Please. Please—I need you."

"I need you too, darling. I swear I'm never going to let you go again. I hope you've made peace with that," I said seriously. And right now, my cock needed her too. Every pulse that rocked through to my balls had teeth. I'd never felt anything so exquisite.

"N-No," she stuttered. While her panting did things to my male ego, it was making communicating at the moment a bit tricky.

"No? You haven't made—"

But my sexy woman cut me off. She found her words now, all right. "No, that's not what I meant. I need you to fuck me, Jacob. Please. I need to feel you."

I stood between her parted legs, and she stared up at me. Her chest was pumping up and down—not fast, but deeply—as though every breath she was inhaling was to fill her lungs to their absolute capacity.

"Are you sure? I can get you off with my fingers or mouth."

"No, I want you. I'm s-s-sure," she answered while pushing up to sit right in front of me. Her eyes were riveted to my erection, and she looked up the length of my body to find me watching her. She reached a hand out and gripped my cock. Slowly—my God, so torturously slow—she pumped the length in a firm fist.

I had no intention of stopping her this time or anytime she wanted to touch me.

Pia darted out her tongue to moisten her lips just as my painfully hard cock sprang free from her grip. When the air of the room wafted across the sensitive skin, I felt just how much

I was leaking for her. The entire head was dewy, and she made a quick look up to me again while inching closer.

"No."

How I had the control to halt her would be the mystery of the night. The primary reason for stopping her from wrapping that warm, wet mouth around my tip was the legitimate fear of blowing down her throat. I was so ramped up, it wouldn't take much. My balls were so tight they felt like someone was squeezing them with their hand.

The beauty on the bed pulled back and waited for me to explain. Instead, I just started toward her. Lifted one knee to the mattress, and she fell back beneath me.

"Scoot up so we are facing the right direction," I told her, and she inched along while I crawled over her. If we stayed sideways like we had been, I wouldn't have enough room on the bed. I wasn't obscenely tall like Grant, but at six feet, I needed to lie in the intended direction if I wanted to plant my feet on the mattress for leverage at any point.

"Do you want me to use something?" I asked.

"Are you talking about a condom?" Her twisted face didn't clue me in as to which part of the dilemma was hanging her up. "Yes. My God. Once bitten, twice shy and all that. You of all people shouldn't need the explanation."

"You mean to tell me our daughter has never inquired about a sibling?" I was grinning foolishly when I asked the question but had dismounted to get a condom from my wallet and didn't stick around to see her genuine reaction to my tease.

"Well, yes, she has. But in that same span of one day, she also asked for a motorcycle. By dinner, as I recall, it was a guinea pig. So I didn't put a lot of stock into it, you know?" Pia sassed back in reply.

She seemed a little ticked off, and it was clear at this point I should've just assumed she would want me to and not have asked. Hoping not to have ruined the mood completely, I hustled to get the damn thing rolled on and was back to her with the speed of an eager teenager.

"You'll have to forgive my stupidity just then," I told her and then kissed her. Gentle at first, but when we both had a moment to regroup, the kiss quickly turned to a passionate and sensual meeting of lips and tongues again.

"Ready?" I asked, positioned at her entrance.

"Yes, more than. Just, maybe go slow? This may be like my first time again."

"I've got you, baby. I'll take care of you," I whispered and began pushing inside.

It was like a vise in there. The squeeze was incredibly snug and warm. My God—so warm . . . and wet. Marveling at every nuance of the experience, I had to remind myself to check in with the captivating woman beneath me to make sure she was still present and enjoying the experience.

Flushed cheeks, wide, wonder-filled eyes, and inviting, parted lips told their own story. The connection must have felt as incredible to her as it was for me.

"You doing okay?" I whispered.

One quick dip of her chin was all I got at first, which earned her a reproachful look, and she added a few words. "Yes. My God, Jacob, where have you been?"

"Looking for you," I replied without thinking twice. Then with my face buried in her neck, I repeated the declaration. "I've been looking for you the whole time, Star."

CHAPTER FIFTEEN

PIA

For the past nine years, I'd tried convincing myself that the memories I had of this man were much bigger than the reality. Telling myself that the moments I stored away in my mind were much better. Much sweeter, kinder, and sexier than the reality ever could have been.

I lied. A lot.

Well...there was no denying the truth now. Living, breathing, throbbing proof of how intense and amazing we were together was imprinted on every inch of my skin. With every thrust of his hips, every circle of his pelvis when he hit that special spot he remembered with astounding accuracy, I knew there would never be another for me. Even if this modern reunion amounted to a father for Vela and that was all, I could never find another man to fill this one's shoes.

And finally, being honest with myself, I could admit I didn't want to look.

"Darling, I need you to come for me," he panted. "I'm dying here."

Perfect timing for both of us, because I was hanging on by my fingernails, too. I just didn't want it to end, so I kept sabotaging my own climax. But now, the sensations had coalesced into a bright, powerful bundle, and I lost the last grip of control I had. Hearing his desperation to orgasm always did it for me.

"I'm going to come. I'm—I—shit. Jake, oh my God!" I squeezed my eyes shut and saw a million stars dance in celebration right behind my eyelids. Every nerve ending tingled to the point of pain as we gripped each other in the tightest embrace while we exploded together.

He was up and off the bed, and I leaned over to watch his bare ass flex as he shuffled to the bathroom to get rid of the offensive rubber. He washed his hands and was on his way back when he caught me gawking at him.

"You're beautiful, Jacob. That was incredible. I can't thank you enough," I offered and decided to just shut up there because I felt like I was already rambling in awkwardness.

Much of the bedding had been kicked to the floor. Jacob straightened the top sheet to cover me and laid the rest at the foot of the bed. He finally found what I realized he'd been looking for and pulled on his underwear. When he picked up his slacks, I felt my heart sink. What the hell was happening?

"Are you leaving?" I asked with a voice that had climbed two octaves between my accolades and accusation.

"Are you inviting me to stay?" he asked in response as he leaned down to kiss me.

I just stared at him as he approached, and he planted a sweet peck on my forehead.

"Well . . . I don't know. I don't know how to handle all of this," I answered honestly because I hadn't thought any of this through. Me. The woman who keeps a to-do list to organize her planners.

"Well, I figured no matter what, the last thing we need is our sweet little one bounding in here and seeing me with my dick out."

Okay, so one of us was thinking, at least. I, however, was the fool sitting on the bed clutching the covers in a panic, thinking the guy I finally slept with was doing the old hit and run.

I hopped out of bed and went to grab my robe off the floor where I dropped it. As I passed him, Jake reached his arm out and caught me around the waist and pulled me into him.

"Now you." He leaned back from the embrace and surveyed my body from head to toe and back again. On a deep breath in, he said, "You should definitely walk around naked. Always."

"You're ridiculous." I grinned.

"You're so unbelievably sexy. My cock is hard again. Think you can go again?"

I winced and then really concentrated on the stinging throb between my legs to determine if a second round was possible.

"That sounds very tempting. My God, I don't know how I forgot how good fucking feels."

"You mean how good fucking *me* feels?"

Laughing, I responded, "Yes! That's exactly what I meant. I know it's late and you have to drive home if you're leaving. I kind of think that's the better idea, as much as I really would love to sleep in your arms."

"We probably need to give her some more time to adjust," Jake replied. "Get more comfortable with me being around for regular things like dinner and stuff."

"That's very insightful, Jake, and I appreciate you thinking with Vela front and center. Your instincts are spot on, in my opinion." God, that sucked to have to admit.

Not that he was right. That made me smile from all the

way down in my heart. Jake would likely slide into a parental role seamlessly. From what he'd told me, he'd had a good amount of hands-on time with his niece since her father was out of the picture.

The crappy part was having to say goodnight at the front door. Although there were a lot of kisses and whispered promises about the upcoming days and some thoughts about our future, there was a heaviness in my heart when I slid the deadbolt in place and set the security alarm.

Where did we go from here? Christ, back to bed at least once a day like we'd just enjoyed? Please and thank you! The idea made me grin, and I'd bet Vela's college fund her father wouldn't need too much convincing to repeat that escapade, either. Especially if I could trust the suggestive and lewd things he whispered in my ear between those goodbye kisses.

My practical instincts were telling me to slow down. Really, I'd waited all these years, so what was the rush now? We should probably date for at least six months and reassess our relationship at that point.

But my whimsical instincts were telling me to strip off my clothes and take a Polar Plunge with the guy. Why not? We were together for a long time when we were in college, so we knew we were compatible. Why waste more time apart when we could so easily be together?

And what about Jake? What did he want at the end of the day? He hadn't really talked about benchmarks—or anything similar—on the path to our end goal. Was our end goal mutual? As far as I assumed, it was. But other than the bossy man simply stating what he saw as the obvious and inevitable, there was no mention of the *how*.

Clearly, he and I needed to sit down and have a serious

discussion about all of this. The trick now was going to be not tumbling into bed every time we saw each other. Since we both had denied ourselves physical attention and satisfaction for so long, the thirst inside seemed unquenchable.

The last time I remember looking at the clock it was two twelve a.m. That was the exact same time Vela was born. With that memory warming my soul and bringing a sense of calm to my overactive mind, I finally drifted off to sleep.

Things would work themselves out. They always did.

* * *

Five days later, I strode into the Shark Enterprises building with renewed purpose. Purpose, attitude, my view on men in general—you name it, I had a new opinion about it all. Hell, I even went out yesterday after work and bought a new outfit to fit the hellfire mood I was in.

Jacob had called only once since the night we'd made love. *Or fucked, I guess.* At this point, I was starting to think maybe that was all it had been to the man. And, out of fairness, he did call—the one time.

But I hadn't seen hide nor hair of him otherwise. Text messages were left unseen for hours. Before we'd had sex, it seemed like he would respond before I could even complete my thought. I called him each day, thinking his excuses had been valid the day before and I was just being hard on the guy. But each call went to voicemail and was never returned.

How did I get it all so wrong? I really thought that night was exceptional. Maybe saving myself for him all these years was a big, stupid mistake. Well, that just made my skin crawl, thinking the word *mistake* along with any decision I made.

Also, placing the word *mistake* near anything that we shared felt sinful.

Then there was our daughter. My sweet, innocent child was much too young to have to already suffer heartache. She'd asked about her father coming over so many times since his last visit, I'd finally just made up a story that he had to travel for work. I thought that would get her off my back for a while— or at least until I could speak to him and clue him in on what he was doing to her by breadcrumbing his attention—but my child was nothing if not tenacious and asked to call him on his cell phone because surely he wouldn't go on a trip without that.

And that was when I stooped to a low I don't want to ever resort to again. I allowed her to make the phone call. When it went through to his voicemail, she looked to me for guidance.

I quickly told her, "Leave him a message if you'd like. I'm sure he'll listen to it as soon as he can." I knew the whole time I was using her as a conduit and completely loathed myself for doing it. Immediately after she hung up, I privately vowed to never turn to a tactic like that again.

No matter how wrong I knew it was, I still hoped it would work. Shame on him, though, if he left a child on the back burner like he seemingly had exiled me to. But shame on me for employing such an immature tactic as using our child to guilt him into doing something he wasn't naturally compelled to do.

So that left the question, would I even want to speak to him after all this nonsense? How much of the nonsense was mine and mine alone? I wasn't used to all these feelings, and admittedly, I didn't think I was completely capable of dealing with them. Evidently not in an appropriate manner, at least.

Having lost my parents at such a tender age, much of

my upbringing was left to my older brother. At the time, he was young, angry, and dealing with more emotional turmoil because of our parents' deaths than I could understand at such an age. The fact that now we were both emotionally stunted wasn't a surprise to anyone who knew our story.

Speak of the devil...

I finally pulled my head out of my ass as I strode into my brother's penthouse office. The moment I walked through the door, I noticed something out of place. Because I had decorated his office suite, I knew the layout and contents as well as if it were my own.

"Sebastian, what is this?" I picked up a small art sculpture from one of the end tables and pointed with an angry finger at the missing head of one of the figures. "Do you know how long I searched for this piece? It filled this space perfectly. Not to mention, it was an original. How did this get broken?" My tone was filled with ire and frustration.

Bas hung his head and pinched the bridge of his nose between his thumb and forefinger.

"I told them you'd notice. And you know what?" my brother asked a bit too casually for how expensive the sculpture was.

"What?" I barked.

My brother raised an eyebrow before letting quiet settle between us. Eventually he said, "You're in a mood. Anything you want to talk about?"

For a moment, I just stared at him. All the closest people in Sebastian's life saw the incredible changes in the guy since he became a family man, but it was still startling enough at times that I had to just take a moment to marvel at the transformation.

"Not really. But I'm sorry I snapped at you the moment I

walked in here," I replied. "You don't deserve the fallout from my bad mood."

"Dub," he said simply, and again, just waited. "How many times have I taken out my shit on you? Seriously, if you want to unload, go for it. Especially since it appears everyone else is running late today." His frustration cranked up a notch while he spoke, so his next question was in his more familiar tone. "Are we really the only two who know how to manage our time?"

Aaahh, there was more of the Sebastian I was used to.

"Who's coming?" I asked for clarification. "I thought it was just you and me."

"Well, I always tell the two dipshits what I have going on just in case they want to sit in on anything. We've learned it makes more sense to pin a person down together if we each have items to review rather than each of us requesting a separate meeting."

"That's very wise."

My brother just nodded stoically but then added, "Right now, decisions that need to be made on the Edge are getting to the crucial stage. Every one thing that happens in a day seems to affect five other things that are scheduled to happen tomorrow. If we miss one beat, the whole team is out of sync, and we thrust ourselves from crucial to critical."

I looked at him for many moments before he finally looked up from his relentless phone scrolling to see why I hadn't said more.

"I'm so proud of you, Sebastian. You really did it."

His grin grew wider the more I spoke. "Thanks, Pia. I certainly couldn't have done all this without all the input and help from everyone involved." He took a moment and then finished with, "But yeah, can you believe we've come this far? Sometimes it just blows my mind. Especially now when I look at my own son. It makes me miss our mother, though. I wonder what kind of grandmother she would've been."

"Having a child changes your view of the world, doesn't it?" He was already nodding before I even finished my thought. "I know what you mean about missing our mother. It's always made me a little sad that Vela doesn't have any grandparents in her life."

I wasn't just saying that to humor him, either. It was something I thought about often. Now that Jacob knew he was her father, I wondered if his parents would want to be a part of Vela's life too. And what about all those siblings? With Stella being the only niece at the moment, I wondered if it would cause anxiety for her or Vela to inject my kid into their worlds. The last thing I wanted was for anyone to be uncomfortable or treat my daughter like the intruder.

As I pulled my laptop from my bag, a knock on Bas's door ended our personal discussion, and really, not a moment too soon. I didn't want to end up having to talk about getting used and tossed to the side by the only man I'd ever loved because foolishly I was willing to open myself up to possibilities again.

My brother would be full of a bunch of *I told you so*s and *You should know better than that*s, and it was the last thing I wanted to hear.

But then I nearly choked on the water I just drank when Jacob came through the heavy door, not one of my bonded brothers like I expected. And why didn't my brother mention he was invited when he named Grant and Elijah? Now I was really thankful I hadn't spilled my guts to Bas. The last thing I was in the mood for was my arrogant, bossy, big brother interfering with my personal life.

Bas strode toward Jake to greet him with a handshake while I stood beside my chair and left the ball in our guest's court what our greeting would look like. My stomach dropped to my toes, and I really had to tamp down the urge to rush past them both and head to the public ladies' room out in the corridor.

Conducting myself in a professional manner was always top priority while I was functioning in a business environment. This meeting would be no different. Even if we sat here for the next two hours, I would not get into a personal beef with the architect. I repeated the pep talk in my mind and focused all my attention on my fabulous new shoes.

Until perfectly shined wingtips entered my line of sight astride them. Then came the voice. That damn voice that turned me inside out every time.

"Ms. Shark, you look exceptional today," Jacob said, caressing every consonant and vowel of the statement.

I lifted my gaze to find him waiting and sucked in a breath. "Jacob! What the hell happened to you?" I quickly shot a glance to my brother to see his reaction to my . . . my . . . shit, I didn't even know what he was, other than the father of my child at this point. Regardless of all that, why hadn't Sebastian commented on the way Jake looked?

Reading my confused expression as I darted my stare between the two men, my sibling explained, "We had a meeting earlier. I already got the scoop. I just assumed you knew." Bas took his turn with the tennis match stares—first to me, then to Jake. Back to me, then to Jake again. While we stood there, locked in a battle of shocked glares, Sebastian finally offered, "I'll give you a few minutes."

He'd only taken a few steps toward the door when I snapped out of the trance Jake's swollen features had me stuck in.

"No!" I said a bit too aggressively judging by their reactions. "Sorry. That came out much louder than expected. Please, Bas, let's just have the meeting. I know how valuable everyone's time is."

I took my seat and didn't look at Mr. Cole again. Or, directly at him, at least. His face looked like he'd been in a street fight—maybe with several opponents instead of just one. While I pulled up the design software on my laptop, I glanced at his folded hands resting on the tabletop. Even his knuckles were bruised.

I'd nursed Bas, Grant, and Elijah after enough physical altercations to know his current injuries were from a brawl. Concentrating on the work in front of me became increasingly difficult as I tried to quiet my racing thoughts.

"Cassiopeia?" My brother's deep voice broke through the buzzing static in my brain.

"Hmmm?" I said unconsciously at first but quickly added a more appropriate reply. "What?" I had to look up then because neither of them said a damn word after he got my attention.

"Okay, this is ridiculous. Let's reschedule this meeting for tomorrow maybe? Check with Craig when we can all be back here with our focus and attention along for the ride."

Sebastian stood up and stretched across the conference table to Jake. "Get some ice on that nose, Junior. And you two get your shit together if you both want to stay on this project." The men shook hands, and Bas strode out of his office, leaving me standing there completely furious.

"He's so fucking high-handed he makes me crazy," I muttered.

Jake heard me, though, and came around the table to sit beside me.

I finally got the courage to look at him again. His face... was so swollen with purple and greenish bruises under his eyes and on one cheek. His lip had clearly had a significant gash that was doing its best to heal. Because of the location, though, the wound still looked fresh, likely from splitting back open with every small move. It all looked like it hurt like hell.

"Will you come home with me? We can talk there. I just need—or I guess I'd prefer to not be out in public with everyone staring at me like I got my ass kicked," he asked with palpable hope. "I didn't, for the record," he added with the hint of a smile but quickly thought better of it.

"Let me check in with Wren. I was supposed to do pickup today, but she's probably available."

"I'm sorry. I don't want to upend your schedule."

I just looked at him and then got up and went toward the door. "Can you check with Craig when we can meet again while I make a call home?" I asked with a bit of frustration. When I heard the tone of my own voice, I quickly added, "Please? He has access to my schedule, so he will know what works for me as well as Sebastian."

"Yes, of course. I'll wait for you by the elevator afterward," he said while packing up the stuff he had just gotten out two minutes before.

So many emotions were rioting inside my chest. That seemed to be where my emotional core was located. While some people felt all their emotions in their stomachs or in their necks, my emotional center was just beneath my sternum. Right inside the heart itself. When I was emotionally distraught, it could feel like I was moments from an actual cardiac incident.

It didn't cross my mind until we were descending in the elevator, I had no idea where Jacob lived. Last I'd heard, he was in an extended-stay hotel.

"Are you all right?" I couldn't help but ask. Every move he made seemed to take concentrated effort, and he maneuvered with such caution it was unnerving. "I mean, have you seen a doctor? Is something broken?"

"Yes, I was seen in the emergency room the night . . ."

He paused there, and I wondered if he was going to sugarcoat what happened or flat-out lie about it. But then, by the way he carefully sucked in a breath, I recognized he was truly in that much pain.

"Maybe I should take you back?" I asked. "Maybe they missed something."

"I'm fine, darling." He puffed out his cheeks with his exhale.

"You don't look fine. You're scaring me."

"I'm so sorry," Jake apologized with genuine intent. "I don't mean to. Yes, I'm uncomfortable at the moment. When the pain medication wears off, I definitely know it."

"Take something, then. Do you have it with you? I drove. I can give you a ride if you'd like. Why suffer like this?" My own aggravation and concern were on a mental seesaw, and the battle seeped out in my tone, sounding much more like anger than I intended.

Or maybe it was truly anger that was leaking through the cracks of my forced good nature and attempt at patience. This was the same guy who I allowed inside my body and then ghosted me for the better part of a week.

Yeah . . . there is still some unaddressed ire inside.

We got situated in my car, and he tapped his address into the navigation system.

"It's not far from here. I had an appointment with Grant Twombley's Realtor this week but had to cancel," he explained as I pulled out of the parking structure. "I still haven't called her back, but I need to."

Between sneaking glances at him while driving, I muttered, "That makes me feel marginally better."

"What do you mean? Do you want to find a place together? I found some things I think my girls would be happy with while searching online. I wanted to show them to you and see what you thought."

"Your girls, huh?" I laughed. "No, I hadn't even given consideration to buying a home together."

"Oh." He sounded defeated with that one word. "Well, I can't stay in this hotel much longer and remain sane. Plus, I can't even invite you and Vela over for dinner or anything, really, when I'm living in one room."

It all made sense—what he was saying about his housing situation, at least.

The part that didn't make sense was he still hadn't addressed the fact that he just blew me off for almost a week. How did he go from that to talking about purchasing a major investment together?

"Jacob." If he wouldn't tackle the issue, I would.

The man pointed out the windshield and instructed, "That's it right up there. Right where that blue car just turned in."

"You weren't kidding. This is super close to Shark Enterprises. Do you walk?"

"Usually, if I'm just going there. But I have an office on the other side of town as well, and if I'm meeting new clients or have drawings to work on, I go there. There's just nowhere to spread out in my room."

I nodded along while he filled the silence, and I concentrated on parking in a space marked for visitors.

"Stay put. I'll come around and help you," I offered. Of course, by the time I shuffled around the back of the car, he was already halfway out the door. "My God, you're so stubborn." I shook my head in disapproval and closed his door.

Once inside his room, he shifted to host mode. But most of the hospitality just seemed like a stall tactic.

Before I got downright pissed off, I asked, "Please explain to me what happened."

There was a small, clean-lined sofa squared off from a minimalistic coffee table. Jacob motioned with a sweep of his arm, inviting me to take a seat.

"Would you be more comfortable lying down? I can pull a chair over there by the bed. Why don't we get some ice on . . ." I drifted off there because it was hard to tell which injury was the worst.

"Actually, yes. I would love to lie down. This broken rib— well, ribs, I guess—feels much better when I'm horizontal."

"You have broken ribs? Jake!" I screeched with motherly worry. It couldn't be helped. Most mothers shifted to that same mien around an injured person. Somehow, with pregnancy, it gets hardwired into you.

"Cass, I'm fine," he said through gritted teeth while he arranged the pillows on the bed so he'd be inclined a bit.

"Jacob. You're turning as white as the bed sheets from moving pillows. You're not fine. Stop bullshitting me. It's insulting at this point."

I shifted between hovering, lecturing, and caregiving until he was settled on the bed. With a hand towel and some ice from the machine in the common area of the hotel, I crafted an icepack for him to hold on the worst of the facial bruises.

Jake studied me while I shuffled around his room, gathering things to set on the nightstand so he wouldn't have to get up every four minutes.

"Darling, please sit down. I have everything I need. Especially with you here."

I shot my hand up to signal stop at the same time I said, "Don't. Seriously, just save it."

"I am serious. What is this about?" he asked indignantly.

I glared at him with disbelief and asked, "Are you kidding me right now?" He didn't respond to the rhetorical question, so I went on. "Don't think I haven't noticed the way you've been expertly avoiding telling me what happened, even though I've asked you—in plain language—several times. Show me some respect and fill in the blanks here."

Jacob let out a heavy sigh, and I wanted to throat-punch him. If he knew what I'd put myself through the past week, wondering why he was ignoring me, maybe he'd have a little more patience for my demanding an explanation.

Finally, he spoke again. "The day after I was with you last, my sister's ex waited for her outside her house and got in her face. She was terrified and called me and one of our other brothers, Lawrence. We went and spent the night with her and Stella."

"What's his problem? Like, what did he want that he was so aggressive with her?" Immediately I regretted overstepping and grimaced. "I'm so sorry. That was so intrusive of me to ask that."

Jake chuckled, and I really couldn't understand why. So far, nothing that my brain came up with for possibilities of what might have transpired to result in a physical altercation was funny.

"I don't understand why you're laughing," I said.

"No, darling, I just chuckled a bit at the absurdity that you would be intruding on anything of mine. Ever. I want to be a completely open book with you. On all things. If you have questions, I want to give you the answers." He stared at me quietly for a moment. He almost looked like he was holding his breath.

"What?" I asked softly. "Are you in pain?" I reached out and put a hand atop his.

"No, I'm not in pain. Well, I am, but that's not what's wrong."

"What is it, then? Let me help you," I all but pleaded.

"I almost said something that I'm not sure you're ready to hear," he confessed. "I don't want to upset things between us when I just got a little hint of getting it back."

"You're confusing the hell out of me, Jacob. You're saying these lovely things right here, right now. The other night when we were together? It was as close to magical as I've ever had," I rushed out, trying to temper the accusatory tone.

He put his other hand on top of mine that was still resting on his. So now my one hand was sandwiched between both of his. "It was the same for me, Pia."

"Then why the hell would you ghost me like that? For so many days?" I pulled my hand away and stood up to pace around the room. "Do you have any idea how that made me feel?"

"I'm so sorry, baby. But I can explain . . ."

"I waited nine years to let a man touch me that way. Inside"—I lightly thumped my sternum—"I always felt like I belonged to you. I couldn't stand the thought of another man's hands on me. Let alone—"

He held up one hand to stop me from voicing the rest of the sentiment. "Please don't put that picture in my mind. I'm so moved by and cherish your devotion."

"If that's true, how do I not deserve to know what happened? Have I not earned the right to be by your side in difficult times? Instead of being shut out?"

"You do. You totally do. I know I fucked up with the way I handled what was going on, but I need you to hear me apologizing."

"I do hear you. But you also have to understand I'm a different woman now than the girl you knew in college. I became independent and capable of existing without being defined as someone's other half. I want to be someone's other half, but I don't need to be that to be happy or content."

And yes, that was a miniature lecture on my own liberation. But damn it felt good to put all those thoughts out into the room.

CHAPTER SIXTEEN

JACOB

Between the aches and pains from my beaten body, the medicine I took on the drive home, and Pia's twenty-minute lecture, I fought to keep my eyes focused and my attention on what she was saying. I'd been getting really shitty sleep all week, and I just wanted to close my eyes, feel her body in my arms, and drift off.

Finally, when my beautiful woman came up for air after her diatribe, I closed my eyes. Just for a second, I thought. Instead, it was her voice again stealing my hope of some shuteye.

"I'm going to leave you to get some rest, Jake," she said quietly, but I could tell she was standing beside the bed now.

My eyes fought to open while I said, "No, please don't go. Can you stay awhile longer?"

"Jacob, you can barely keep your eyes open. You need to rest so your body can heal. I'm being selfish going on and on about myself and my fragile self-worth, and you're the one who needs the TLC right now." As she finished talking, she leaned down to chastely kiss my forehead. She had her chestnut waves pulled back in a ponytail after work, and the thick mass of hair swung down and shrouded our faces.

Without considering the pain it would cause my ribs, I

shot my hand up and grabbed her tied-off mane and held her face inches from mine. Her breath caught in her throat and cut off her surprised protest. So I just kept her there for long moments and studied her features as her arousal built.

"Lie with me for a while, Star," I issued more than asked.

Her eyes searched my face as carefully as mine did hers. Just as she opened her mouth to speak, I dove in. Being so close to her stoked the fire in my heart and sent signals of unyielding lust over every inch of my body. Funny how the pain seemed to disappear completely with the possibility of getting inside her again.

The woman was the cure for everything that had ever been wrong. I believed in my core that she had the ability to make everything in my world right again. Pia Shark was the magic elixir I'd been searching for since we lost our way. Because I'd had so little relationship experience, I had to be extremely careful not to mess up what was right in front of me. In life, it seemed so rare that second chances came along.

My gorgeous, generous, giving woman relaxed on the mattress beside me. Eventually, she snuggled in closer and rested her cheek on my chest. The fragrance from her hair products added to the calming atmosphere. I sneaked greedy inhalations of the scent and focused on where our skin touched.

"Rewinding to the events of the past week," I said, breaking the silence. "I wanted to call you so many times, Star. I truly did. Once the police were involved, they told us to keep the details private so they didn't end up with a media circus disrupting their investigation and manhunt."

"Manhunt?" She tried to sit up, but I opposed her movement with my forearm, effectively banding her to my side.

But I owed her this explanation. "I told you about the

first night, what brought us to Cecile's. She was really shaken up because that bastard keeps threatening to take Stella from her."

Pia interrupted again. "But how? No court will allow a convicted child abuser custody of a minor. No way," she said with complete assuredness.

"See, you would think that, wouldn't you?" When she just stared at me in disbelief, I continued. "But Leo—that's her ex—has fabricated some bullshit story that Cecile was really the one hurting Stella and that he took the fall for it. That my family is powerful and privileged, and he was set up. Apparently, he hired some hotshot attorney with the money she's paying him for alimony, of course. The loser couldn't hold down a job if his family's well-being depended on it." I forced out a wry laugh and added, "Oh wait, they did."

"Oh, that son of a bitch. What makes people do these things? And dragging a child into a feud like this is wrong for so many reasons," Pia said, disgusted.

We were quiet for a few minutes again while I let her digest what I had said thus far. After the silence gained too much atmospheric pressure, she asked, "So how did you end up in a fight with him?"

"Law and I both went to work the next morning and came back to Calabasas to sleep. We promised we would stay until she felt safe again. So that second night, he came knocking again. The guy must have been on a bender or something, because he could barely hold himself up while he pleaded and begged my sister to take him back."

I shook my head, remembering what a pitiful state the man was in. "My sister ended up calling the police, and they hauled him away. And then they towed his car because he was so drunk."

"Where was poor Stella while all this was going on?" my concerned woman asked.

"She was at our family home with my mother and father from the first night. My sister didn't want to add to the kid's trauma, you know? The poor thing already has so many issues from this dumpster fire."

"Jake, I'm serious when I offer this. Anytime you or your sister need to take her somewhere safe, please know that my door is open. Vela would love someone to play with—anytime at all." Pia kept her set features fixed on me.

I leaned closer and softly kissed her. She was such a good woman—through and through. "Thank you for that, Star. I'll pass it on to Cecile. She's finally coming to grips with the fact that none of this is her fault and it's not a bad thing to ask for help when you need it."

Pia smiled. "That's a woman thing," she stated proudly. "Then it's compounded by being a single parent. I'm glad she's reaching out when she needs a hand, though."

"Well, she's definitely getting better at it. Let me put it that way." I was smiling too by the end of my comment. Even though my sister had what most would agree to being the shittiest year of her life, she'd remained completely devoted to Stella's well-being and happiness. My parents wouldn't tolerate anything else from their eldest daughter or for their only grandchild.

But now they had Vela too. It struck me in the strangest ways and at the worst times—I have a daughter.

"How's Vela doing? How was school this week?" I wasn't intentionally avoiding telling her how I got so banged up, but my guess was she'd accuse me of it.

"She's fine. Asking why you haven't come over. Or called. Or texted. I don't even know what I'm going to tell her about . . .

this," she said, waving her hand up and down.

"I'm sure I'll be right as rain in no time," I tried to assure her. But she wasn't buying it, based on the head tilt and single raised eyebrow look she gave me.

"You mean to tell me with those three men in her life, she's never seen a busted-up face?" I asked with a solid amount of disbelief.

"Three men?" she asked, confused at first, but then she realized I meant her brother and his two best friends. "Oh, well, no, I don't think she has. If they've ever had facial bruises or swelling or"—she looked me over for other injuries—"or cuts and scrapes. Jesus, Jake, what the hell happened?"

"My dear brother-in-law and a few of his lowlife friends jumped me when I came out of here the other night. I came back to swap out clothes and pick up a few things before heading back to my sister's, and the bastards were waiting for me when I walked out into the parking lot."

"Oh my God! How is it not worse with that many against you? You're probably lucky to be alive!" Pia worried at max volume. "Sorry, sorry. I know getting worked up isn't going to help anything at this point, but oh my God! I'm so thankful you're okay." She clutched at her throat like she was having trouble breathing.

I wrapped my arms around her and held her until she calmed down. There was a part of me that had to admit her over-the-top reaction was touching. She really cared about me, possibly more than she was still willing to admit to herself. That reaction was as pure and unguarded as they come.

"Ssshhh baby, I'm fine. I'm perfectly fine," I cooed to her quietly. I swept the short hair that had come free from her ponytail away from her face and just stared at her. I was so in love with this woman, it was difficult to articulate. There was no way she'd want to hear about emotions that serious right now. I wasn't that much of a clueless clown.

"Okay, you said there was a manhunt earlier. I'm assuming for this?" She pointed at my face again while asking.

"Yes, among a couple of other things they found at his bachelor pad. When I pressed charges, they went looking for him with a warrant and ended up busting the door down when he wasn't there. The rest is what I can't talk about. Sorry."

Pia narrowed her eyes at me, and I decided to wait for her to comment so I didn't misinterpret that particular look. It wasn't an expression of hers I was familiar with.

Finally, she said, "You can't possibly think I'd tell anyone."

Immediately, I agreed. "No, I don't think you would. I trust you, Cass. I trust you completely."

She faked a little smile in an attempt to be congenial, but she was a pretty shitty actress. I could tell she was still pissed—or something.

After taking a relatively pain-free deep breath, I continued to explain my motivation. "I don't want you anywhere near any of this. That's why I'm not going to fill in more details about that piece of shit. The man is a legitimate threat to those he thinks are standing in the way of what he wants. I won't have you put in danger because of your association with me."

Pia nodded. "There's a lot about all you just said that makes sense. I mean, the turmoil my own brother has been dealing with for the past two years makes him act similarly. But there's a heavy dose of reality you're ignoring here."

I tried to rationalize through her comment but felt a bit more confused instead. "I'm not sure what you mean," I admitted.

"The reality of a situation like this is that desperate people often behave in desperate ways." She fiddled with our entwined fingers while she explained. "A man like Leo will do what he wants, hurt who he wants, threaten who he wants, no matter what prior information the victim has or doesn't have." She waited a few beats, and I nodded to indicate I understood now. "I'm honored you want to protect me . . . or us, I should say. Thank you for thinking ahead like that."

"Let's close our eyes and rest now that all of that is out in the open. I really want to just relax with you in my arms."

"Just for a bit, though, because I can't sleep here, Jake."

"Of course you can. There's plenty of room in this bed." I knew what she meant, but I'd give my right thumb for her to agree to a sleepover. I'd missed her so much this past week. So, I refused to give credence to any excuse she came up with.

"You know what I mean. Vela will have the National Guard dispatched because I didn't come home. That girl is very set in her routine."

"Does that ever worry you?" I asked purely from curiosity, not questioning her parenting skills at all.

"I don't think I'd say it worries me—she's not showing signs that her rigidness gets in the way of living and enjoying life." Pia looked at me with an expression I couldn't read. I might have offended her without meaning to, so I took a brief moment to study her features.

"What is it?" I asked and stroked her cheek with the backs of my fingers.

This time her smile was genuine, and it warmed my heart instantly. "Nothing. Nothing at all."

"Don't bullshit me, woman. You had a look on your face that I don't quite know how to interpret, but then, just like that, it was gone," I said, with care to not sound accusatory. I truly wanted to learn all there was to know about this girl.

"I have a terrible habit of getting defensive when I think someone is questioning my parenting ability." Pia shrugged after her admission. "That girl became the sun in my solar system the moment she was born. Everything I do, every decision I make, is with her in mind."

I caressed her cheek with my thumb while cradling her face in my palm. "Darling, I can't imagine anyone saying you've been anything shy of incredible with and to our daughter."

The beautiful woman leaned into my touch and continued, "Like I said, it's a bad habit that was born from the insecure psyche of a very young mother. Seriously, Jake, I'm over it now. It just sneaks up on me sometimes."

There was no evidence that she was being dishonest. Being raised in the family I was, I could spot a liar a mile away. No, Ms. Shark was quite the opposite, actually. She was baring herself to me in a new way, and I was moved by the connection.

"Thank you," I said quietly and kissed her inviting lips. Just a gentle kiss, though, and when I pulled back, she chased for more. I watched her, still with her eyes closed and the pink feathers of arousal high on her cheeks. Until she let out a heavy sigh and popped her azure eyes open again.

"For what?" she asked with a lazy grin. "Letting you tease me like that?"

"No, for sharing with me. For allowing yourself to be vulnerable with me. It says a lot."

Her assessing gaze turned skeptical. "Really? Like what? What does my admitting I spent countless hours—days' worth, really—of precious time worrying about what other people thought of me?" She chuckled an almost bitter laugh.

"Don't be so hard on yourself. You were young, alone for the most part, no mother to turn to for advice—of course you were unsure of what you were doing." I couldn't help but kiss her again. We were lying with our faces just inches apart, and everything about this conversation beckoned to my need to protect and care for these two people I already loved.

While we lay together in the darkened room, I thought of the nights I'd lain alone, longing for her. For her touch, her lyrical voice when she was doting on me, even her strong-willed temper that could infuriate me in equal measure.

I had begged the universe to return her to me. There were times my need for her built to such a painful state, I'd head to the local cantina and drown in whatever someone would pour for me. Those nights were the worst because I'd only wake up the next day feeling worse physically, get no mercy from my mentor at work, and when all was said and done, still didn't have a clue where she was.

Not sure if I'd regret it or what her response would be, I was compelled to blurt, "I never stopped loving you, Pia Artemis Shark. Not for one single day."

She didn't say anything in return. Now I couldn't decide if that was worse than a negative response or better. Feeling that way made it obvious I was hoping she would have confessed the same thing.

Instead, she left me hanging on the edge of the unrequited love abyss. Well, there were only two directions things between us could go now. Fall down into a pit of depressed darkness and finally give up on the dreams we confessed to each other beneath the stars.

Or join forces and get through whatever life put in our path. Together as a family.

CHAPTER SEVENTEEN

PIA

Emotions were never my strong suit. Other than with Vela, I panicked whenever a moment became focused on feelings. My feelings, a friend's, my brother's, coworkers—anyone. I'd always thought this was the biggest piece of baggage I carried from the fucked-up childhood I'd endured. Countless hours of therapy later, I still didn't feel surefooted around the touchy-feely stuff.

It wasn't recognizing how I felt, or identifying what the emotions were, or even the catalyst for them. It was expressing myself to someone else. It made me uncomfortable for a host of reasons. The paramount one being my good-for-nothing father.

I knew he was devastated when our mother had died, but even before that. His response to one of us telling him we loved him would typically be to push us away physically, curse at us until he turned beet red in the face, and finish his rampage in a terrible coughing fit that rocked the entire shack of a house we lived in.

It was terrifying.

Every single time, it was terrifying. As Bas developed into a teen, he got vindictive pleasure from antagonizing the man. He had so many emotional scars by then, he didn't know how to feel anything other than anger and hostility toward most people.

I figured my response to emotional outpourings now was akin to PTSD. Well, my therapist said it was PTSD. I just had a hard time saying that when I considered myself mentally strong, healthy, and well-adjusted. But I had to routinely remind myself that the damage to my mental health was done *to* me. It was not a byproduct of a choice I made for myself.

The silence stretched between us while I had that internal stroll down memory lane. Jacob only knew the bare minimum when it came to the details of my childhood. How do you explain why you look like a deer in headlights every time someone tries to express their feelings to you? Especially knowing now that he grew up in the all-American family.

"Did you fall asleep?" he asked softly.

Popping my eyes open, I saw his concerned expression. I had to explain why I was silent for so long and decided to be completely honest with the man.

"No, I was deep in the gray matter. Sorry."

"No need to apologize. Do you want to talk about whatever it is that has you so pensive?" he asked caringly.

"Yes. Or we should, at least. This is definitely something I don't usually talk much about. But I told myself if we were going to be graced with a second chance, I would do my best to show up for it."

Jacob's grin appeared, but he winced when the bruises on his face pulled tighter with the expression. He said while wincing, "Thank you for that. For the commitment. You know I'm all-in here, too."

I nodded as much as I could while lying on a pillow. Our faces were so close together, if I wanted to distract him with something more enjoyable—like kissing—I was in striking distance.

Between tamping down that impulse and trying to gather the courage to say the things I needed to say, I was having trouble concentrating on one solid thought long enough to form a complete comment.

"I wish I were more like you," I started to say, and immediately Jake's face twisted with bewilderment. He knew how much I valued being a strong, independent, free-thinking woman. That was definitely an out-of-character comment for me to make.

He was patient through his initial confusion, and I forged on. "What I mean is I wish it were easier for me to tell you how I feel. I've been working on it a lot with my therapist, but it seems like the piece of the human puzzle that holds that skill is missing from my finished picture."

"Can I ask you something?"

"Of course," I said easily.

"Would you be willing to try an exercise I learned in therapy? Let's see if it works for you too. There's only one rule. You have to blurt out the first thing that pops into your head. Okay? It's a stream-of-consciousness thing."

Already, I felt nervous, but I had no reason to be. That was what made getting tongue-tied so frustrating. Eventually, I nodded and wordlessly agreed to give it a try.

What did I stand to lose, right?

"Remember, the first thing that you think, you say." He proceeded to ask me three or four questions that had basic answers. What was my full name, my age, did I enjoy interior design, all while tapping a steady rhythm on my hand. I started concentrating more on the spot where he touched me and tried to match the tempo of his taps in my mind. When he got to harder questions, I was nearly in a trance.

Tap … tap … tap …

"What negative consequences do you think will come about if you open up to me?" Jacob asked.

Without missing a tap in between his question and my answer, I said, "You'll reject me."

Tap … tap … tap …

"Who's done that to you before?"

Tap … tap … tap …

"My father."

"Oh, Star," he said, and I despised the pity in his voice. He stopped tapping my hand and said, "Look at me, please."

I finally lifted my eyes to meet his ever-patient ones. My God, how was one person so serene?

"I don't want pity, Jake. That's the last thing I want." I instantly regretted the bitterness in my voice. "I'm sorry. That sounded really shitty."

"First of all, this isn't pity you see on my face, darling. It's empathy. And as you know, the two are starkly different. Apology accepted for the attitude. I get where it's coming from and that it has nothing to do with me."

I looked at him with a side-eye for a moment but held my tongue about his smugness. The man was just trying to help me uncork some emotions. I needed to lighten up.

"Secondly, thank you for sharing those details with me. I don't know much about your family life before we met at school, and when I root around in my memory, I think that was intentional."

Sucking in lungsful of air, I got ready to accuse him, but he stopped me before a single sound came out.

"Just like I intentionally didn't talk about my family. We were escaping at that time, in a way, I guess. Or at least I was."

I nodded along while he spoke his truth because, yes, it was mine too. When I stepped out of my own funk for a moment, though, his words didn't add up.

"What were you escaping? You have the all-American family. The whole world knows that."

"You know better than to believe the hype you see in the media. Every single move my family makes is orchestrated by a team of PR people. A fucking *team,* Pia. The biggest gift my parents ever gave me wasn't a sports car when I learned to drive or company shares when I turned twenty-one. It was keeping me away from the spotlight."

I listened intently and took his hand in mind. I needed to feel closer to him. To let him know I was there to support him too. Like he was doing for me.

"I'm sorry. This isn't about me right now. All that just tumbled right out. Suffice it to say, you're not the only one with daddy issues." He squeezed my hand and then leaned in and softly kissed me.

Our lips moved gently against each other, but heat quickly built in the exchange. It always had, and I hoped it always would.

Danger signs flashed behind my closed lids while his tongue explored my mouth deeper. Already I knew I could come to rely on this man again. He understood me in ways most people didn't, and the things he couldn't make sense of, he inquired about until every piece snapped into place.

"I never stopped loving you either, Jack. Not for a second. I'm sorry for what I did to us." Tears started falling then, but I needed to finish this thought. "For robbing you of years with our daughter. I want to spend the next nine years making it up to you."

"Stay with me tonight," he beseeched.

"I don't think I can," I said, standing from the bed. "I don't know—"

"You haven't even called Wren to see if she can stay. You yourself said she's in your house more than her own. She really won't spend the night?" He was on his feet too then, stalking toward me. "Give me her number. I'll ask her."

I was shaking my head and chuckling before he got the last word out.

We stood toe to toe, and the man inquired in his deepest timbre, "Are you laughing at me, Star?" He seared holes through my already too-hot skin with his intense stare while waiting for my reply.

"Umm, yes?" I squeaked.

Was I in trouble now? Could a girl get so lucky?

"Do we need to see how many you can take from my belt these days?" he replied, backing me against the door. "You used to be pretty fond of that worn-in brown one—which I still have, by the way."

All it took was that one comment, and I was fighting the squirming sensation in my lower abdomen. It had been so long...

"I asked you a question, darling." Then he *tsk*ed. "You're so out of practice. Too many years apart. How long will it take, do you think, before you're crawling to me on your hands and knees with that strap between your teeth again?"

"Jack..." I said or possibly whimpered. "You're so cruel."

"The way you like me best. It's all right there, girl." He pointed inward to his chest. "Right under the mask I put on for the rest of the world day in and day out." He leaned into me, and I expected a passionate kiss. Instead, he brushed past my cheek with his stubble-covered one and said in a low, sexy growl right beside my ear, "I'm just waiting for your consent, and we're going to bring the roof down."

By the end of those few sentences, I was panting. My panties were so wet, when I shifted even slightly, I could feel the slickness between my legs. One more minute of this type of conversation, and I'd combust.

"You're in no physical condition to play right now, and you know it," I challenged.

"That doesn't stop me from telling you what to do, though, does it?" He grinned down at me, knowing damn well what he was doing to my body. This guy could play me like his favorite instrument from the moment we connected.

I put my hands against his defined chest and pushed a little. The heart beating beneath my palms pounded as erratically as mine. He didn't budge from my feeble effort, but I said, "Really, though, I'm going to go so you can rest."

Jacob kissed me again, holding my face in his palms while he mastered me. Just with a kiss, I was nearly convinced to stay.

Breath gone, I panted, "I'm leaving. I'll talk to you tomorrow, okay?"

He sighed heavily and finally caved after a moment or two. "I'll walk you out to your car."

"That's not necessary. Please, get in bed," I implored.

"No. With everything that's been going on with my sister, I'd feel much better knowing you got in your car and drove out of here safely. No more arguing."

"Fine," I muttered, and he scooped my hand up so fast and

yanked me back to his chest with a *thump* where we collided.

"I'm going to start counting, lady. So when you give me the word, I'll have a nice score to settle." He stared down at me with intense eyes, and that damn flip-flop feeling in my belly was back for an encore.

The night air had really cooled, and Jacob was just in shorts and a T-shirt. I didn't want him getting a chill on top of everything else he was dealing with physically.

We kept the farewell brief, and before he closed my car's door, he said, "Good night, Pia. I'll see you in my dreams."

"Night, Jacob."

One last wave—God, we were acting like teenagers again—and I drove the entire way home with a goofy grin on my lips.

CHAPTER EIGHTEEN

JACOB

On Friday morning, I rode the elevator up to the top floor of the Shark Enterprises building, blueprints tucked under one arm, computer bag on the opposite shoulder, and a bouquet of tulips for my favorite interior designer clutched in my hand. I really felt like the pack mule one of the guys in this very building teased me about being.

Pia would probably chew me out for mixing personal feelings with a business meeting, but I couldn't resist the stunning bouquet when I saw it on my way into the meeting. I had passed a street vendor camped out on one of the corners near my hotel and doubled back to bring my woman a treat. If she was pissed, too bad. She'd get over it.

Especially after the evening I had set up for us. Hell, if everything went according to plan tonight, she wouldn't be able to remember her name come sunup. Just thinking about it made my dick start to swell, so I had to mentally get on another topic—and fast. Men's dress slacks left nothing to the imagination when you had a hard-on. Even when you didn't, depending on the location of things, it was difficult to be modest.

Sebastian and Pia were already in his office when I arrived. We were all sticklers for punctuality, so I felt like a schmuck arriving last. Even though I was seven minutes early.

My woman's eyes lit up when she saw me, and even though she quickly schooled her features, I didn't miss her natural reaction. It just made me smile even wider as I greeted Sebastian with a hearty handshake.

"For me?" Shark asked, motioning to the flowers with a lift of his chin. "You shouldn't have, Jake."

The three of us gave cautious chuckles as I walked over to say hello to Cassiopeia. Her smile was warm and bright, and her eyes seemed to devour me as I approached.

"Hi." I leaned in and kissed her cheek. "These are for you," I said and handed her the lavender tulips.

"Hi," she said so softly it could have been called a whisper. Her voice gained volume and authority when she thanked me for the token of affection. "They're stunning. I don't think I've ever seen this color." She dipped her nose into the buds to enjoy their fragrance.

"Me neither. That's why I doubled back to get them."

"Okay, lovers," Shark said with a resounding clap of his hands. "Let's get down to business, yes?"

"I'm going to find a vase while Jake gets set up," Pia replied and darted into another room I'd never been in. I always thought it was a private restroom but didn't know for sure.

"Sorry about that," I said to Shark when Pia was out of the office.

"Sorry?" My apology confused the man, apparently. He followed with his trademarked, "Explain."

"I couldn't resist getting those for her. The color is magnificent and so unique." I gave a quick shrug, not knowing if I needed to say more.

"Dude. You can make my sister that happy any day of the

week. In fact, I insist on it. Do you know how amazing it's been to see her smiling? It's been a long time coming, Junior."

Sebastian Shark always gave it to you straight. I appreciated that trait in the guy. Especially regarding this topic.

"I endeavor to do just that," I said. "Hopefully for the rest of our lives, actually."

He raised a skeptical brow. "Moving a little fast, aren't you?"

"I know it seems like that to the outside world, but people don't realize we were together for the better part of four years in college. We both have found that those feelings never died," I explained with a small amount of annoyance that I had to.

Fortunately, Pia strolled back into the room with the tulips arranged in a clear glass vase. With her back in the room, I hoped her brother's inquisition would cease.

"Shall we?" I asked both my colleagues and motioned with a sweeping hand toward the blueprints I had laid out on the conference room table. "What we have here is the first look at the residential floor plan. I've taken your requirements and requests and a few liberties of my own and have come up with this." I tapped one of the prints.

"This looks great, Jake," Sebastian said, not lifting his gaze from my drawings.

"Thank you. It's always a pleasure to work on this project because you have such a clear vision of what you want. You give me so many details, it feels like I'm just a translator of sorts. I'm taking your desires and translating them into these drawings."

"As always, you've done an incredible job listening and paying attention to the little things. Look here at the transition from the lobby to the residential units. I know I was neurotically specific about these features and details, and on my first scan, it looks like everything I wanted was possible."

"There were some tricky issues between here"—I pointed to the spot I referred to with the end of my pencil—"to here. It just took some outside-the-box thinking, but I'm confident the solution meets your needs and wants."

I watched the guy's gaze dart around the print while I spoke. When I finished talking, the office was quiet.

Except for the busy scratching sound of Pia's pencil as she sketched something out on her pad.

"What are you thinking, Star?"

I heard the term of endearment cross my lips, and Pia's head popped up from her work so fast, I knew she didn't appreciate my slip-up either.

I mouthed a quick *Sorry*, and we both just pressed on rather than call more attention to my mistake. I'd likely get an ass chewing when we were alone.

"I think this lobby needs a showpiece of some sort. A sculpture or a fountain. I don't know…but something is missing here," the talented woman offered. "I'll sit with it for a few days and come up with something."

"I trust you," Sebastian told his sister.

Pia went on to comment, "We have that beautiful main lobby on the first floor. I think this secondary one, even though it only leads to the residences, maybe should echo that feel. I know you want everything to feel super high-end and glamorous, so a boring lobby just won't cut it. The residents will have to cross through that space every day. It should be something special."

We all agreed on her concept and also agreed she would

handle it from there with Sebastian's final approval. Just like every other decision on this project, he had final say.

"Okay, moving on to the blow-ups of the three residence options," I began. "This is the place I had a lot of fun. You should really look them over before signing off on them, though. I hit all your requirements and added some extra unique features and elements."

Pia studied one drawing longer than the others. Finally, she said, "I really like what you've done with this one. It's making me consider buying one."

But her controlling brother quickly weighed in on the subject. "You don't want to live in the city with Vela. It's a terrible environment for a kid. You know that as well as I do." Bas made the comment heavy with reminders of their young lives.

Pia nodded along while he spoke but then added, "Yes, that's all true. But for now, it would be a great investment. And as much as none of us likes it, she's not going to be little forever. This could be my place when I'm an empty nester."

I wanted to interject and correct her, *when* we *would be empty nesters*, but I stopped myself in an effort to remain professional. But as the siblings discussed the option for my woman to buy one of the spaces, I could feel my frustration grow. She was talking about her future and didn't mention me or *us* once. Had she changed her mind? Or was this just a show for her big brother?

But why pretend? He was going to have to warm up to the idea eventually. I had a feeling Sebastian was going to have a hard time dealing with the fact that he wasn't in charge of his sister's life anymore. Or his niece's. They belonged to me now, and we would be a family whether he approved or not.

As I felt my irritation grow, I figured I better wrap the meeting up before I said something I'd regret. "So these are yours to keep and look over. Make notes, mark them up, whatever works for you. I can schedule with Craig on my way out to meet for first-round changes." I knew the drill by now, and announcing my plans rather than waiting for Shark to tell me what to do would at least give me the illusion I had control of what was going on here.

Pia's phone rang, and she excused herself after looking at the caller identification on the display.

"Hey, Wren, how's it going?" Pia made eye contact with me and held up her index finger, signaling me to wait for a moment.

Thankfully, Sebastian went over to his desk and immediately got busy behind the three massive monitors.

"Oh, no! Are you okay? Where are you?" My woman's posture straightened one anxious inch at a time while she listened to whatever her assistant was telling her. Then she said, "Okay. Are you sure? I don't mind. I just finished the meeting I was in." A few long moments passed when she was quietly listening to details from her aide, nodding along while the young girl spoke.

I approached and captured Pia's worried look. "What's going on? Is it our daughter?" I was scared to hear the answer.

Pia quickly shook her head to alleviate my worst fear, and I let out a tense breath. Something was definitely wrong, though.

"Good. Thank you. I'm glad you're not going to be stubborn. Let me grab something to write on."

I quickly grabbed a notepad from the conference room table and handed it to her.

She got off the phone a minute later and filled me in on what was happening. Wren was in a car accident but was okay for the most part. Pia said the girl was really upset because her car appeared to be totaled and she was stranded at the intersection where the accident took place. All of these details were given to me as we shuffled her belongings together and hustled to the elevator.

"Oh, shit!" she said while we waited for the lift to make it to the top floor.

"What is it?" I asked. "And please calm down. I don't want you driving this agitated and ending up in the same situation."

"I know. You're right." She took an exaggerated deep breath and then another.

"Now what did you just think of, and please let me help. I'm clear for the rest of the afternoon."

She stared at me for a few beats as if she were contemplating something. The elevator signaled its arrival with a loud *ding* and shook her from her thoughts. The doors slid open, and Grant Twombley and Elijah Banks stepped off, deep in conversation.

"Hey, lady, how's it . . . Whoa, what's wrong?" Banks said, immediately noticing Pia's demeanor was off-kilter.

Both men gave her quick hugs and then noticed I was standing there.

"Is he bothering you?" Grant asked.

"No, he's not bothering me," Pia said with a gentle smile.

"No, I'm not bothering her," I said at the exact same time, but mine was bitten out and laced with irritation. These three men were so protective of my woman, it was as aggravating as it was endearing. They all needed to find a way to back the hell off.

"Guys, I have to go. Wren was in a car accident, and I need to get down there to help her."

"Was Vela with her?" Elijah quickly asked as we stepped in the waiting elevator. "Are they okay?"

I spoke up this time before Pia could answer. "Our daughter is in school at the moment and Wren says she's fine, but she's very upset. We'll know more when we get there."

Both men stared at me with their brows lifted to their hairlines.

"What?" I barked, fully sick of their bit at this point.

"Nothing, man. Get going, then. Hope she's okay," Grant said as a wide grin spread across his face.

Elijah, on the other hand, stood beside his best friend and glared at me.

Pia waved while saying, "Thank you, boys. I'll let you know how she is later."

The door slid shut, and it was just Pia and me inside. I pulled her into my arms and gave her a comforting hug. After telling those two Vela was in class, I wondered about after-school pickup. Depending on where Wren's accident occurred, Pia wouldn't be able to get to the school in time to pick her up.

I walked with Pia to her car and waited while she got situated and put the window down. "Do you want me to pick Vela up at school? I think you'll be cutting it too close." Every Southern Californian knew that Friday-afternoon traffic was always worse than the other days of the week.

"You're not on her list. I'll figure something out if it comes to that." She tried to minimize the conflict.

"Let me take this off your plate, please. I have all the clearance paperwork on file at the school because of Stella. If you call them and let them know, I'm sure it would be fine."

"I'll text you after I see what I'm dealing with regarding Wren. She has a tendency to downplay things, so I don't worry. Fair enough?" Pia said. "I can't think straight."

"Okay. I'll wait to hear from you. I may head up that way just to be on the safe side. It won't do us any good if we're both stuck in traffic."

She just nodded to that comment. Before she put her window up, I leaned in and kissed her softly. "Please be careful. Are you sure you're okay to drive? I can hop in and take you."

"No, Jake, I'm fine. Honestly. I'm just a little wound up. Let me go, though. I promise I'll text you." She put her car in reverse to back out of the parking space, and I stood away from the car. I couldn't help but watch her until she was long gone from the lot.

Seeing her so upset had me stressed out in equal measure. I sent out a quick plea to the universe to keep her safe. I'd just gotten her back. I didn't want to endure another moment of my life without her in it.

CHAPTER NINETEEN

PIA

The accident scene was chaos. It took circling the block three times before I found a place to park. Glass and car pieces littered the intersection, and police were directing traffic around the debris. Just like I suspected, Wren had totally downplayed what was going on here.

I asked the first official-looking person if they knew where the drivers were on the scene and identified myself as family. He pointed to a throng of people on one of the sidewalks, and I hustled over and pushed my way through the crowd. Lots of grumbling and comments about my assertiveness, but I didn't care. The longer it took to find Wren, the more frantic I became.

Finally, I saw her up ahead, reclined with an EMT hovering over her, taking her vitals.

"Wren!" I shouted, and she looked around.

She seemed dazed but definitely heard me calling to her. As I got closer, I called her name again, and she looked in my direction. For some reason, it gave me comfort that she was coherent enough to put those pieces together.

Blood was splattered across her forehead and cheeks. Bloody rivulets ran from the obvious source at her hairline down her face and neck and stained a red splotch on her T-shirt.

The first responder was tending to the wound, but Wren tried to sit up to see who was calling her name. I reached her quickly and dropped to my knees beside her.

"Ma'am, please lie back," the young man asked. "We can get this gash to stop bleeding if you cooperate."

"Hey, hey you." I grabbed Wren's hand, careful not to disturb the IV already established, and gave it a tight squeeze. "You're in so much trouble, do you know that?"

She gave me a hazy grin, already knowing what I was about to say.

"This looks a bit more intense than you admitted on the phone, young lady."

She tried to sit up again, and this time I stopped her.

The EMT gave me a grateful look and let out a sigh. "Please be still."

"Cooperate with this nice young man, please. Maybe he has a nice big shot to give you if you don't listen."

She tried to waggle her brows at me, but it must have hurt because instead of the giggle I expected from her, she let out a low groan. Automatically, her hand shot up to the source of the pain, but the guy stopped her from touching the bandage he'd just placed there.

"Don't mess with it. I know it hurts. You've got a good-sized cut there. Were you wearing your seat belt?" His question had us both listening then instead of trying to be playful.

"Yes, of course," Wren mumbled. "I always wear it. I don't even know what cut me."

I didn't understand why she seemed so groggy. I worried there was more wrong than what was visible to the naked eye.

"It looks like it's from the airbag, if I had to guess. Those things save lives but not without a few bumps and bruises. How fast do you think that guy was going when he smacked into you? Can you estimate that?"

"Shit, I don't know," Wren said, now seeming to be having trouble staying awake.

"What's wrong? Why is she falling asleep?" I asked, on the verge of panic. "Wren, don't go to sleep. What if she has a concussion? She shouldn't be sleeping, right? Right?"

"Ma'am, either calm down or step back with the other bystanders. You're not helping me or your friend acting like that," the EMT said with a new tone of authority.

"Sorry. I'm worried. I've never dealt with anything like this. This woman is my family. I want her to be taken to the best hospital you contract with. I'm Pia Shark, and I will assume financial responsibility for her care. But I want it to be the best. Are we clear?" I attempted to hand him a business card, but he held up his hand to stop me.

"That's not necessary, Ms. Shark. You can address your demands with the hospital when we arrive. We're going to St. Thomas on Willshire. You can meet us in the emergency department."

From that point, I was pushed back while they loaded my young friend into the ambulance. No one wanted to give me any more information other than where they were taking her. I asked about her injuries several times and was ignored.

Fury was burning hot in my veins when I got back in my car.

I really wished Jacob had come with me now. Maybe he could've gotten more answers from the EMTs. I thought by telling them I would pay for whatever care she needed, they would treat her better, but that really seemed to piss the guy off.

Jake picked up after the first ring. "Hey! How is she? What's going on?"

"Hi," I said flatly, and he must have been able to tell from my tone that I was not a happy camper.

"What's going on? You sound angry."

"Livid, more accurately. They pushed me out of the way and would only tell me where they were taking her. I kept asking what her injuries were, and you would have thought I was speaking a foreign language," I rushed out.

"Please don't drive, darling, until you calm down," Jake implored. "We don't need a second accident."

I didn't respond because I was already driving toward the hospital.

"Cassiopeia? Did you hear me?" he asked, and I could hear the way his tone was shifting to the commanding version.

"I heard you just fine, but you're too late. I'm already on the street heading toward the hospital."

"What hospital are they taking her to?" Jake inquired.

"St. Thomas. At least it's a decent facility." I took a deep breath and blew it out through tight lips. "God, Jake, I'm not good at this stuff."

"You're doing a great job. I'm sure of it," he said in the most soothing voice. "And baby, there's only so much you can do. You have to be patient while the medical professionals take care of her. Did you talk to her? Was she conscious?"

"Yes, we even joked for a moment, but then she got really lethargic and couldn't keep her eyes open. I kept asking what was happening, and they just shuffled me out of the way." I ramped up again as I recounted the scene.

"Settle down. Try to stay calm, please. Do you have your supplies with you? I know what this level of stress can do to your body."

"Yes, in my purse. I'll check my number when I get to the hospital. Before I go inside," I promised. How amazing was this man? Still putting my welfare above everyone and everything that was concurrently happening.

"Good girl. Thank you," he said, and his comment flowed over me like thick honey. There was magic in that particular tone, because I could feel my grip on the steering wheel loosen by degrees while his caring baritone filled my car's interior.

"If you're going to the hospital to advocate for Wren, I need you to call the school and tell them I have permission to pick up our daughter."

"I can just call Bas or one of the guys," I said. "Then we don't have to worry about the school getting nosy about our business."

All three of the men were on Vela's pick-up list, and it would be so much less controversial.

"I'm her father, Pia. There's no reason to take one of those men away from their job when I'm only ten minutes from the school."

I could hear that I'd wounded him.

"I'm sorry, Jacob. I didn't mean to offend you. Or shut you out, or whatever I just did. My head isn't on straight."

Internally, I was battling a new freak-out, though. Was he equipped to handle her on his own? I had no proof of that. Would she be okay going with him in the first place? Throughout the short number of years of her life, we'd tried to teach her a reasonable amount of awareness and suspicion when it came to strangers. And really, in the grand scheme of things, that was what Jacob Cole still was to my daughter.

Our daughter, I heard his voice correcting in my head.

Sighing, I said, "Okay, I'll call them when we hang up. I

think this is the ambulance with Wren pulling into the lot right now. Let me call the school quick, and I'll text you if there is a problem," I said, battling every alarm bell in my mother brain not to do this. I was just being pulled in too many directions at the same time and couldn't focus on any of the things that needed my attention.

But my daughter shouldn't be the one to pay the price for that.

Before Jacob disconnected, I stopped him. "Jake!"

"Yeah, baby?"

"Does the school know you as Cole or Masterson?" It was a legitimate question, and there didn't seem to be a rhyme or reason which name he used.

"They know me as Masterson. It made the most sense because, previously, I only picked up Stella," he explained. I didn't detect any frustration in his tone, so likely I was the only one uncomfortable having to ask that question.

"Okay, I'll talk with you soon. And Jacob?"

"Yes, darling?"

"Thank you," I answered on a heavy sigh. "I can't say it enough."

"Cassiopeia, I'm honored to have this privilege to pick up my daughter at school. You have no idea."

I could hear the genuine happiness in his voice, and it gave me a moment of peace in this stressful afternoon.

"Bye," I nearly whispered because I was feeling oddly choked up. My life—the same life I controlled down to the letter—felt like it was spinning out of control. And they were all circumstances beyond my power. I didn't like the feeling one bit.

Inside the hospital, I found someone who would help

after trying three others not interested in doing so. A nurse personally walked me to the admissions desk in the emergency room when I broke down into tears of frustration.

"Oh, honey, it's okay. We'll find your friend, and you can see her just as soon as possible," the kind, gray-haired woman cooed. "Don't cry, okay?"

"Sorry. It's been a stressful few hours," I admitted.

I felt like if given a few more minutes with the woman, I would've fully word vomited on her about all the things kick-boxing my chest at the moment. There was a dull ache right behind my sternum signaling I was really dealing with a lot of upheaval.

On top of everything else, I thought I had my type 1 supplies in my purse and only now remembered I transferred them to my briefcase to lighten the load in my pocketbook the day before when we went to the mall. I promised myself as soon as I set eyes on Wren and knew she was okay, I'd run out to the car where I left my briefcase and test my blood sugar.

The woman at the admissions desk chatted with my new nurse friend for a few minutes before she even noticed I was standing there growing intensely impatient. No, I didn't care that her daughter was starting her first year at Baylor. I just wanted to know where they were treating my assistant.

"I'm sorry, miss, can you spell that?" she asked, fingers poised over her worn-out keyboard.

"Yes, it's W-r-e-n. Last name Whitesides. Do you need me to spell that?" I didn't intend to sound condescending, but based on the look she gave me over the top of her reading glasses, it must have come out that way.

I was not about to apologize to one more person in this goddamned place, though.

"Okay, it looks like your friend is in bed three, but I'm sorry, only next of kin at the bedside in the emergency department. If that's not you, you can wait in the waiting room at the end of the hall, through the double doors and to the right. Can't miss it."

I just stood there with my mouth hanging open. I started to say something, then closed it again.

"You don't understand. She doesn't have family. None at all. She lives in my home, and I'm the closest thing to family she has." I tried appealing to whatever shred of kindness might be lurking deep within her.

"I'm sure, dear," the woman said, and then she actually walked away from the window through which we were speaking.

If I had to call Sebastian to get involved, heads would roll. My brother was a generous donator to many hospitals around the city, this one included. If I had to start leveling threats or, worse, get him on the phone to raise hell, the entire staff on duty this evening would regret it.

But I didn't want to have to be that person. I was always mortified when Bas acted so high-handed. Suddenly it seemed completely reasonable.

I paced in the waiting room for a while, and family after family was called in by their loved one's doctor while I sat there fuming. I needed to give in and call my brother and just get it over with.

Digging around in my purse for my phone, the thing began ringing with the ringtone I'd set for Jacob. Shit... I'd completely forgotten to call him and tell him that I spoke with the school and everything was good to go.

I fished the device out from the bottom of my bag and

stepped outside the automatic doors to take the call. Vela probably wanted to check on Wren when Jacob explained why he was there to pick her up.

"Hello?" I said, suddenly hearing the exhaustion in my voice. All the emotions from Wren's accident had worn me down. Before Jacob said a word, I said tearfully, "You have no idea how glad I am you called."

"Star..." Jacob croaked. Yes, croaked, and I instantly went back to red alert.

"Jake? What is it? What's wrong?" My voice ticked up an octave every two words. By the end of the second question, I was screeching.

"Where are you right now?" he asked.

"I'm outside the emergency department at St. Thomas hospital on Willshire. Why? Jake, what's going on? Is Vela there? Is she okay?"

I could hear him relaying my location to someone else—a man, by the deep vibrations I could make out rather than the person's voice.

"I need you to listen to me. Take a deep breath, please," he commanded, and my body instinctually followed his instruction. "Good girl. Thank you. Star, listen to me, okay?"

"Jacob, you're scaring the shit out of me. What's going on?" My voice quavered as I spoke.

"Elijah and Grant should be pulling up in front of you any moment. Luckily, they were still downtown and we could get a hold of them. Please get in the car with them." Jake waited for me to agree.

"But Jake, Wren is here alone. She needs someone to advocate for her," I insisted, not having a clue what the hell was happening.

"I know, baby. Rio and Abbigail are coming there to do that. You trust them, right? You know they will take care of Wren?" he asked, and this whole situation was unnerving me. "Just answer me, darling."

"Yes, of course. Jacob, tell me what's going on this instant or I'm hanging up the phone."

"Don't you dare."

The seriousness and dominance in my man's tone with that one sentence made me freeze in place. I gripped my phone so tightly I was shocked the device didn't crack.

"You're scaring me..."

"Have the guys pulled up yet?" he asked in place of the explanation I was desperate for.

"No, not yet," I replied but then saw a familiar vehicle turning in to the hospital's lot. "I see Elijah's car turning in to the hospital property right now."

"Good. Very good. Now listen very closely, baby..." He paused, and I could actually feel the gravity of whatever was about to tear up my world.

"When I got to Vela's school about twenty minutes ago, her teacher told me she'd already been picked up."

Although we had a perfectly clear connection, a low buzzing started in my ears. I'd heard what he'd said, and my mind went to the worst fear in every mother's heart.

Somehow, I still asked, "Who? Who did she go home with? Your sister?" I had to hold on to hope.

"No, they said it was a man claiming to be her uncle. Sebastian is on his way here now, and they are pulling the security camera footage so we can review it."

"Jacob, what are you saying? Who took Vela home?" I was yelling into the phone when Grant threw open the passenger-side door and was to me in seconds. He wrapped his arms around me and held me against his tall, strong frame.

"The man said he was her Uncle Caleb."

"That can't be ... no ... Jake, no. They must have made a mistake! My brother Caleb died at birth with our mother. What the hell is going on? Where is our daughter?"

"She's missing, Cass."

ALSO BY VICTORIA BLUE

Shark's Edge Series:
(with Angel Payne)
Shark's Edge
Shark's Pride
Shark's Rise
Grant's Heat
Grant's Flame
Grant's Blaze

★

Elijah's Whim
Elijah's Want
Elijah's Need
Jacob's Star
Jacob's Eclipse

Misadventures:
Misadventures with a Book Boyfriend
Misadventures at City Hall

Secrets of Stone Series:
(with Angel Payne)
No Prince Charming
No More Masquerade
No Perfect Princess
No Magic Moment
No Lucky Number
No Simple Sacrifice
No Broken Bond
No White Knight
No Longer Lost

**For a full list of Victoria's other titles,
visit her at VictoriaBlue.com**

ACKNOWLEDGMENTS

Thank you to the team at Waterhouse Press for continuing to support this series and providing the professional guidance to make each and every book I write the very best it can be. Thank you, Scott Saunders, for your keen eye, careful devotion to every word, and sense of humor that always makes the process a joyful one.

Personal gratitude for Megan Ashley, Amy Bourne, and Faith Moreno for keeping my social media life active and interesting. I'd be lost without each one of you.

And a very special thank you to Angel Payne. Not only do you keep my focus where it needs to be, but also you listen to me bellyache about the trivial stuff along the way.

Also, my dear friend, Helen Hardt. I appreciate you more than you know—both professionally and personally. I'm so grateful you're in my life.

ABOUT VICTORIA BLUE

International bestselling author Victoria Blue lives in her own portion of the galaxy known as Southern California. There, she finds the love and life-sustaining power of one amazing sun, two unique and awe-inspiring planets, and four indifferent yet comforting moons. Life is fantastic and challenging and every day brings new adventures to be discovered. She looks forward to seeing what's next!

Visit her at VictoriaBlue.com